Tom Derringer
in the
Tunnels
of Terror

OTHER NOVELS BY LAWRENCE WATT-EVANS

Vika's Avenger
One-Eyed Jack
The Chromosomal Code
Touched by the Gods
The Rebirth of Wonder
The Nightmare People
Among the Powers
Shining Steel
(with Esther M. Friesner) *Split Heirs*
(with Carl Parlagreco) *The Spartacus File*

THE ADVENTURES OF TOM DERRINGER
Tom Derringer and the Aluminum Airship

THE FILES OF CARLISLE HSING
Nightside City
Realms of Light

THE FALL OF THE SORCERERS
A Young Man Without Magic
Above His Proper Station

THE ANNALS OF THE CHOSEN
The Wizard Lord
The Ninth Talisman
The Summer Palace

THE OBSIDIAN CHRONICLES
Dragon Weather
The Dragon Society
Dragon Venom

THE LORDS OF DÛS
The Lure of the Basilisk
The Seven Altars of Dûsarra
The Sword of Bheleu
The Book of Silence

LEGENDS OF ETHSHAR
The Misenchanted Sword
With A Single Spell
The Unwilling Warlord
Taking Flight
The Blood of a Dragon
The Spell of the Black Dagger
Night of Madness
Ithanalin's Restoration
The Spriggan Mirror
The Vondish Ambassador
The Unwelcome Warlock
The Sorcerer's Widow
Relics of War
Stone Unturned (forthcoming)

Tom Derringer
in the
Tunnels of Terror

Lawrence Watt-Evans

Misenchanted Press

Takoma Park

Tom Derringer in the Tunnels of Terror

Published by Misenchanted Press
www.misenchantedpress.com

Cover design by Lawrence Watt-Evans & Connie Hirsch

Frontispieces by Kyrith Evans

Dedicated to
Kenneth Estes
for his help in
researching the history
of California

"*I risked a quick look around the corner and got my very first look at one of the Skyless.*"

"The artificial caves where the glowing fungi grew were strange and beautiful..."

TOM DERRINGER

Chapter One

I Learn the Nature of My Quest

I first heard the name Gabriel Trask from a self–proclaimed emperor in the skies above southern Mexico, in the year 1882. I was sixteen, almost seventeen, at the time, and newly commenced upon a career as an adventurer – an occupation which, curious as it may seem, is my family trade.

That conversation took place aboard a gigantic airship, where I had confronted a would-be conqueror by the name of Reverend Hezekiah McKee. I was there entirely of my own initiative, but Reverend McKee did not believe that; he was quite certain that I was in the pay of one of his old enemies and named this Gabriel Trask as the most likely candidate.

I had, as I said, never heard of Mr. Trask before that moment. Had McKee survived those events I would have liked to have questioned him about this person, but I regret to say that Hezekiah McKee did *not* survive. My curiosity remained utterly unsatisfied until some weeks later, immediately after my safe return to New York City.

I had business to conduct there with Dr. John Pierce, proprietor of the Pierce Archives, concerning certain details of my Mexican adventure, and when I had concluded that more or less to my satisfaction I asked him, "What can you tell me about Gabriel Trask?"

"Trask?" he replied. "The name does not immediately bring anything to mind. Where did you encounter it?"

"When I confronted Reverend McKee, he supposed that I was working for this Trask," I explained. "He said that Gabriel Trask employed a cabal of spies and assassins and was not to be trusted, but that was all I learned. The circumstances were such that I could not inquire for more details."

Dr. Pierce nodded. "I see," he said. "Let me see what I can turn up." He rose and crossed to a wooden cabinet.

We were, I should explain, in his private office, at the rear of the Pierce Archives. This unique establishment occupied the entire second floor of a very large building on Lafayette Street in New York City, perhaps other space, as well, and housed the most complete records anywhere of the doings of adventurers past and present. Here were copies of virtually every treasure map ever to come to light, along with notes on whether the treasure in question had been recovered or yet remained to be found. Here, also, were reports on every villain apprehended, every monster slain, by any of Dr. Pierce's clients – or those catered to by his father, or his grandfather, or *their* fathers, for the Pierce Archives had been in operation for some three hundred years. Here was gathered the accumulated knowledge of scientists and mystics of every stripe. If knowledge that would be of use to an adventurer was to be found anywhere in the civilized world, it was most probably here in the Pierce Archives.

I had traded the right to copy my late father's journals for a full membership and free use of the archives, and that included the services of the archivist himself, Dr. Pierce, and his employees. If I wanted information on Gabriel Trask, then any information there might be about such a man in the archives I would have.

Thus I sat and watched as Dr. Pierce pulled out a drawer and shuffled through the folders therein. After a moment's search he slid the drawer closed and said, "He has never been a client here – at least, not under that name. Come, let us check the cross references."

I rose and followed as he led the way out into the main room, where what seemed like miles of shelving held hundreds, perhaps thousands, of books, ledgers, journals, and file boxes of various sizes, as well as innumerable stacks of loose documents.

I would have had no idea where to begin, but Dr. Pierce was the master of this vast domain of paper and ink; he led me directly to a high shelf where dozens of leather-bound volumes stood.

I am not a short man; I stand only a little below six feet in height. Even so, this shelf was above my head, and I am not certain I could have reached those books. Dr. Pierce, however, was a man of extraordinary stature; by lifting up on his toes he could read the spines, and he had no trouble in selecting the tome he wanted.

A white label on the cover read TRAB – TREA, and I glanced up at its companions. If this fat book covered so small a portion of the alphabet, that explained why the complete set ran fifty feet or more along that shelf.

I watched as Dr. Pierce set the book on a reading stand and flipped it open. He made no attempt to conceal the pages, so I took the liberty of reading over his shoulder – figuratively, for in fact he was tall enough that I instead leaned around his side.

The content was hand-written and unevenly spaced; I realized that these records were still being kept, and that space had been allowed for future entries. I watched Dr. Pierce as he turned pages until he finally found the entry he sought.

"Trask, Gabriel A.," he read aloud. "See Norton, Joshua, Emperor." He glanced at me. "Are you familiar with the late Emperor Norton?"

"I have heard of him," I said. "But he's been dead for some time, hasn't he?"

Dr. Pierce nodded. "More than two years now."

"Was he Gabriel Trask? I don't understand. McKee must have known he was dead."

"Oh, I wouldn't be too certain of that," Dr. Pierce replied. "After all, McKee spent most of that time since the emperor's death out in the Arizona desert, building that monstrous airship. But no, Gabriel Trask and Emperor Norton are not one and the same. Let us see what the connection was." With that he restored the volume to its place on the top shelf, then led the way to another part of his establishment. Here he readily located, presumably from memory because he did not bother to read any of the labels pasted on the leather spines, another set of journals – perhaps a dozen fat volumes, on a shelf at waist height. He drew out the last of these, opened it seemingly at random, and began thumbing through the pages.

I waited patiently until at last he found what he sought. He nodded to himself, then peered over the book at me.

"It appears that Mr. Trask was in His Imperial Majesty's employ. According to this, Mr. Trask was rumored to be the head of the late emperor's secret service."

"Emperor Norton had a secret service?" I exclaimed. "But I thought his claim to be emperor was a joke, the ravings of a lunatic that the people of San Francisco found it amusing to humor!"

Dr. Pierce smiled a dry and humorless smile. "In time I think you may find, Mr. Derringer, that the distinction between a madman's fantasy and the real world is not always as clear-cut as one might expect. Emperor Norton was indeed mad, or at least so everyone believes, but his delusional reign endured for more than twenty years, and in that time it acquired some of the characteristics of a real government. He had the respect of many important men; Dom Pedro, the Emperor of Brazil, met with him as an equal. The legitimate authorities in San Francisco treated him with some deference. And this man Trask, it seems, attended His Majesty intermittently for over a decade, and the circumstances surrounding these meetings led more than one observer to conclude that Mr. Trask was the emperor's spymaster."

"But then..." I struggled to make sense of this. "Then had McKee run afoul of our self-proclaimed emperor? He gave no indication of this."

Dr. Pierce slid the book back into its place on the shelf. "I have no idea," he said. "I cannot even say with certainty that the man associated with Emperor Norton is the same Gabriel Trask to whom McKee referred. I can only report that I have no other records of anyone by that name." He tapped the spine of the journal. "This tells me that there were more than a dozen reports of a man calling himself Gabriel Trask keeping company with His Majesty, and that two of my correspondents – a woman named Felicity Samuels, and a young man who goes by John Beckwith – independently surmised that Mr. Trask was in charge of at least some of the emperor's confidential agents."

"I still find it astonishing that the emperor *had* any confidential agents!"

Dr. Pierce smiled again. "Perhaps he did not. Perhaps Miss Samuels and Mr. Beckwith were mistaken, or embroidered the truth for some reason. I am amused, though, that you find it so unlikely, given your own recent experiences."

I did not see any very great correlation with my own adventures, but did not care to argue. Instead I asked, "And you have no other references to a Gabriel Trask?"

"If I do, they have not yet been indexed, and I cannot hope

to find them for you any time soon."

I nodded thoughtfully, then thanked Dr. Pierce and took my leave.

It did make a certain amount of sense. McKee had said that Trask commanded spies and assassins; perhaps those spies and assassins had been working for Emperor Norton. Perhaps that gentleman's government had indeed been a little more real than I had been led to believe. Oh, certainly he was never really the Emperor of the United States or Protector of Mexico, and his edicts ordering Congress to disband had all been ignored, but could it be there had been more to his position than pure fantasy?

If so, did any of his organization still exist? If it did, what was it doing now that Joshua Norton was dead?

Was he truly dead?

I found these questions fascinating. I had no real business with Mr. Trask or any of the late emperor's other acquaintances, but my curiosity was piqued.

Perhaps, I thought, I should investigate the matter. If Gabriel Trask really commanded a cabal of spies and assassins, then wasn't that a criminal matter? Shouldn't he be brought to justice?

There was no great urgency to it, though. I had only just returned from Central America and had not seen my mother or sister in months. More immediately, I was to be guest of honor at a dinner party that evening, celebrating the completion of my first adventure. Following that, it was my intention to spend the night at the Robertson Hotel, and in the morning to take the first train north to my home town. Other concerns could wait; I wanted to see my family, if only to reassure my mother that I had indeed survived my journey intact. I did not intend to *stay* home, but a visit of moderate duration really seemed the minimum of filial duty. At the very least, the Christmas holiday was approaching, and I wanted to spend it in the bosom of my family.

Accordingly I took my leave of Dr. Pierce and carried on with my plans. The celebratory dinner was held at a downtown restaurant and was rather overwhelming, but certainly enjoyable; I told and retold the tale of my journey from Flagstaff to Belize Town, and was introduced to individuals who had been, up to that point, only legends to me. There was much discussion of whether I should join the Order of Theseus immediately, or further establish my credentials as a serious adventurer first.

The evening was well advanced when I finally took a hansom cab to my hotel and took to my bed.

And in the morning I made my way to the Grand Central Depot and boarded my train.

That brought certain wistful memories. It had been on a train on that route, albeit one bound in the opposite direction, that I had first met Miss Elspeth Vanderhart, the brave and brilliant young woman who had accompanied me on my adventures, and who had in fact been instrumental in the success of that expedition. It would probably not be an exaggeration to credit her with saving my life more than once.

In that first encounter she had called herself Betsy Jones and had been amused by my naïveté. There had been times in our subsequent experiences when she found it not so much amusing as infuriating, and indeed, in retrospect, I had sometimes been foolishly innocent.

I had very much enjoyed her company, though, and I very much hoped I would see her again. Perhaps, after spending a few days assuring my mother and sister that I had not forgotten them, I might make a little trip to New Brunswick to bring that meeting about. Or perhaps I might write and invite her to join us for the New Year festivities.

That would certainly be more sensible than heading out to San Francisco in the depths of winter in pursuit of the mysterious Mr. Trask...

Well, I told myself as the train rolled northward past snow-covered hills, I did not need to decide my entire future immediately.

Chapter Two

An Unexpected Visit

There is no need to describe in detail my arrival at the family homestead. Rest assured that I was greeted enthusiastically by not just my family, but the neighbors, as well. My throat tightened at the sight of our house, the familiar bare trees overhanging the snow–covered lawn, the white–painted swing on the broad front porch pulled up for the season, the sunlight glittering through the beveled glass in the parlor windows. I was treated as a conquering hero – I had been slightly concerned that there might be some lingering displeasure that I had gone off on an extended journey on little more than a whim, spending a significant amount of our money in the process, but there was no sign of any such cloud shading the glorious sunlight of my mother's welcome. Even my sister Mary Ann treated me with respect.

Sleeping in my own bed was a delight; eating my mother's cooking another. There were times I thought I must have been mad to leave.

But once I had been home for a few days there were other times when I felt a certain unease, and those pleasant surroundings seemed confining, even stifling. Retelling my adventures, which had been great fun at first, grew tiresome. When these moods struck me I would consider how I might best investigate Mr. Gabriel Trask. Obviously San Francisco would be the place to start – but San Francisco was more than three thousand miles away.

Of course, modern express trains could make the journey from New York to the San Francisco Bay in less than a week, and I had just returned from an expedition that had covered well over three thousand miles in all, so the distance was not so very daunting, really. It was, however, enough to keep me from heading out west immediately; the prospect of at least four days aboard a train was not very appealing, especially at a time of year when the mountain passes of the far west might be blocked by snow. I had recently made the trip from New Brunswick in New Jersey to Flagstaff in the Arizona Territory by train, and it had been rather tedious.

This was an aspect of the adventurer's life that I had not fully understood until I experienced it firsthand – adventuring required of long stretches of boredom between the moments of excitement. Now that I knew this, I was a little reluctant to undertake any such open-ended enterprise. During my visit to the Pierce Archives I had thought of heading west within a day or two, but why should I fling myself into an extended period of discomfort and inconvenience? If I was to be bored, I might as well do it in the comfort of my own home, rather than aboard a cramped and noisy train.

There was also the question of what I would *do*, if and when I found Mr. Trask. I had no evidence that he had committed any crimes beyond the allegations of a would-be conqueror who most definitely *had* violated more than a few laws. Was there a *point* to going in search of this reputed spymaster?

In quite another way, I also thought about going to New Brunswick to pay my respects to Betsy Vanderhart – a much shorter journey – or at least writing her a letter to broach the subject of a visit, but somehow my nerve failed me. What would I say to her, either in person or by pen? We had shared a remarkable adventure, but what else did we truly have in common? And the longer I hesitated, the more difficult it seemed – how would I explain this delay?

Christmas came and went, a properly joyous celebration where I was jokingly chastised for having gone all the way to Mexico without bringing back any gifts for my mother and sister. The New Year of 1883 arrived, and the snows of winter deepened significantly. The season had already seen some severe coastal storms, as well. Any attempt to travel before spring would be challenging.

During these winter days, when leaving the house required an effort, I did finally gather the courage to write to Miss Vanderhart. I had hoped that she might open a correspondence first, sparing my nerves, but no letters arrived, and of course I knew that no proper young lady would be expected to begin such an exchange unprompted. At last, in mid–January, I overcame my own reserve and sent her a brief missive, thanking her for her services and inquiring after the health of her family.

There was no reply. I waited for a fortnight, and then ventured another note, and this time included an apology for any hardships my actions had visited upon her.

Three more letters followed as the snows melted and buds appeared and then opened on the trees, until finally, in my last letter, sent in early May, I wrote that it was now clear that she did not wish to hear from me, and I would trouble her no further, but that I would welcome a change of heart, or a brief explanation. Even a card merely stating that I was correct in my assumption that she wanted no further contact would relieve my concerns for her well–being.

And with that, I resolved to move on. No great inspirations for adventures I might pursue had presented themselves over the course of the winter; the idea of a journey to California to find Mr. Trask had not been abandoned, but there were, as I saw it, three reasons to not undertake such an expedition as yet.

Firstly, I had gone over our accounts with my mother and was dismayed by how much damage I had inflicted upon our finances in my pursuit of the Reverend McKee's airship. While a trip to California would not cost as much as had purchasing, shipping, and supplying the Vanderhart Aeronavigator, it might well prove expensive. I thought I should allow more time for the exchequer's recovery, or perhaps even seek an adventure that would be remunerative.

Secondly, my mother was not eager to see me leave. She professed to enjoy my company, and I was, now that I was nearly a grown man, useful around the house when sheer physical size and strength were wanted. She had managed by herself for years, of course, but was in no hurry to return to doing so.

Thirdly, and most importantly, I still hoped, quite irrationally, that I might hear from Miss Vanderhart, that I might even receive an invitation to visit her, in either the family home in New Brunswick or her father's *pied-à-terre* in Manhattan.

But by the end of June I had tired of domesticity and decided that I really ought to do *something*. I resolved to take a trip to New England, to visit Boston and Lowell. This would be a holiday, and one that I could cut short on a moment's notice should I receive word that my mother or Miss Vanderhart wanted me elsewhere, or should I come across any circumstances I thought deserving of investigation.

As it happened I had a few noteworthy experiences, in Lowell and elsewhere, but I will leave those stories for another time.

I returned home in mid–August to find that nothing had changed in my absence, and I once again settled into the bosom of my loving family.

I was in a curiously unsettled mental state, though, constantly wavering between staying where I was, and heading out to seek new excitement, either in California or elsewhere. I kept an eye on the newspapers, watching for oddities that might provide a springboard to adventure, often reading and re-reading them while sitting in the porch swing, while my mother sewed in the parlor and my sister was out with her friends.

August of 1883 ended without any resolution of this uncertainty. The weather began to cool suddenly in the month's final days, sometimes driving me from the porch and lawn to indoor activities. The skies seemed to have dimmed prematurely, as if summer had ended early – though the sunsets around that time were spectacular.

I was in the upstairs study one afternoon, going over the volume of my father's journals describing his visit to California in 1855 and studiously ignoring the railroad timetables I had acquired a few days before, when I heard the distinctive sound of the heavy brass knocker on our front door.

I was not expecting any callers, nor had my mother mentioned any, so I guessed it was most likely someone come to see my sister, either one of her girlfriends or a would–be suitor braver than most – despite her tender age, she was beginning to attract the interest of some of the local lads. I heard footsteps, and thus reassured that someone would be answering the knock, I resumed my reading.

I was rather startled a moment later when my mother

called, "Tom? You have a visitor."

I put down the journal, found an old envelope to mark my place, and then arose, setting the book aside. I did not care to show any unseemly haste, but I was quite curious about who it might be; from the tone of my mother's voice I did not think it was merely one of the neighbors. Perhaps Tobias Arbuthnot, who handled our family's business affairs? Or "Mad Bill" Snedeker, once my father's fellow adventurer? To the best of my knowledge Mr. Snedeker did not know our address, but he certainly had friends who did. I trotted across the upstairs hallway and started down the stairs.

And I very nearly lost my balance and tumbled down those stairs when I saw who was waiting for me at the bottom. "Miss Vanderhart!" I exclaimed. "What an unexpected pleasure!"

Indeed, it was Elspeth Vanderhart who stood beside my mother at the foot of the stair. She was staring up at me with the most remarkable expression; I thought I saw anger and unhappiness and defiance under the polite smile she cast my way.

"Tom," she said. "I thought we had agreed you would call me Betsy."

"We had," I admitted, as I managed to untangle my feet and make my way down the steps. "But I did not want to presume upon that invitation when we have not maintained any sort of communication." I reached the floor and took her hand, brushing my lips against her fingers.

The chivalrous thing to say at this juncture would be call those fingers dainty, or delicate, or soft, but in fact hers were none of those things. Hers, though small, were strong and hard, roughened by her work on a variety of machines. This did not make them any less appealing to me; if anything, it added to their charm.

Her smile wavered as her eyes met mine, and then she abruptly flung herself against me, crying, "Oh, Tom!"

My arms wrapped about her quite without any conscious act on my part, and I found myself, for the first time in my life, embracing a beautiful young woman. Under other circumstances this might have been delightful, but I was standing not three feet from my mother, and I had no idea what Betsy was doing there, or why she had thrust herself upon me. It was most thoroughly unlike her. I managed an awkward pat on her back, but then stood in helpless confusion, with no idea what I should do next.

"Well, I see you two do know each other," my mother said.

"Yes," I said, lowering my hands. I could think of nothing else to say. I could not move away without falling over the bottom stair, but Betsy had collected herself sufficiently to step back, breaking our embrace.

She threw my mother a glance. "I'm so sorry, Tom, Mrs. Derringer," she said. "I just... it was so good to see Tom again."

"The pleasure is mine, I assure you," I said. "But I confess you have caught me off guard."

"I'm sure I did!" She managed to restore a weak smile to her features, but it was plain to me she was desperately unhappy about something, in a way I had never seen before. I had seen her faced with deprivation and danger, but slogging through jungles, or facing tropical storms, or plummeting from great heights, or being shot at, had only made her angry. Whatever had befallen her now was clearly something very different.

"What's happened?" I asked.

"I..." she began. But then she stopped, looking silently up at me. She turned to look at my mother for a moment, then back to me. She swallowed. "I will tell you, Tom, but not just yet," she answered.

"As you please, then," I said. I would not press her. "Will you be staying for supper?"

She threw my mother another glance. "If I may," she said. "In fact, Mrs. Derringer, I'll stay for as long as you'll have me."

"Oh," my mother said, startled.

"I left my bags at the station," Betsy said.

Mother blinked. "Well, we'll send Tom for them later, shall we? And I'll have Mary Ann make up the guest room."

"Thank you," I said.

"That's very kind, Mrs. Derringer," Betsy said. "I'm so sorry to impose on you, but I just didn't know where else to go."

This time my mother looked at me, as if seeking a signal that would tell her what was going on, but I knew nothing more than she did, and could only raise a shoulder slightly, in an intimation of a shrug. "Well, you're certainly welcome to stay here for a few days," she said.

"I'm sorry," I said, hoping to restore some normality to this extraordinary situation. "Have you two been properly introduced? Good heavens, where are my manners? Mother, this is Miss Elspeth Vanderhart, who accompanied me from Flagstaff to Belize Town as my engineer. Betsy, allow me to present my mother, the former Arabella Whitaker, one of my late father's companions in adventure as well as his wife."

"It's a pleasure to meet you, Miss Vanderhart," Mother said, taking her hand. "Tom's told us so much about you!"

"Thank you, Mrs. Derringer," Betsy replied, with just a slight dip, well short of a real curtsey. "Tom certainly spoke highly of you during our travels." She threw me a glance. "But you know, I don't think he ever told me *both* his parents were adventurers."

"Oh, I was never very serious about it," Mother said. "I just went along to keep Jack company."

That was followed by a brief but awkward silence, and it occurred to me that I had never heard my mother refer to herself as an adventurer, though I knew from my father's journals that she had been an active participant in several of his expeditions. I had never really talked to her about it; she was my *mother*, and that was not really the sort of thing we discussed.

"Well," I said, "why don't we settle in the parlor, rather than standing about like this? We can talk more comfortably there. Would anyone like a cup of tea, perhaps? I can put the kettle on."

"Oh, I'll do that," Mother said. "I'm sure you two have much to catch up on." With that, she headed for the kitchen.

I led Betsy into the parlor and guided her to the big armchair by the hearth, then seated myself on the horsehair sofa. "I can't tell you how glad I am to see you," I said. "I feared, when you did not answer my letters, that I had somehow offended you. If I did, perhaps now I'll have a chance to apologize."

She stared at me. "You wrote letters?"

"About half a dozen, last winter and into the spring," I said. "You did not get them?"

"Oh," she said. "I thought..." Her voice trailed off, leaving the sentence unfinished.

That was not at all like the Betsy I knew. I had promised myself I would not press for an explanation of her actions, but I could not help myself. "You thought what?" I asked, while silently berating myself for my impatience.

"I thought perhaps you *might* have written, but I never received any of your letters. They must have been intercepted."

"Intercepted by *whom*?" The question left my lips with no conscious volition on my part; I could no more have held it back than I could have suppressed an unexpected sneeze.

"My parents," she said.

I could hear my mother moving around the kitchen, two rooms away, and wondered whether she could overhear us – but I had no secrets from her. "Do you think they would do that?" I asked. "Have I offended *them* somehow?" It occurred to me that it was very possible that they had thought I was courting their daughter and that they considered me unsuitable for her – adventurers made notoriously unreliable husbands, prone to wandering off on long journeys on short notice, and with a very short life expectancy. Discouraging my attentions, while somewhat underhanded, was understandable.

"Ha!" Betsy's tone was bitter. "*You* didn't offend them; *I* did."

"What?" I was baffled and made no attempt to hide it.

"They were, as they told me at great length more times than I could count, absolutely *appalled* at my behavior in Mexico – beginning with the fact that I ever *was* in Mexico; they seem to think that I should have refused to fly across the border with you."

"But I...but it was your father who insisted you accompany me!"

"A detail that my mother has used to berate my father endlessly these past few months."

"I don't understand," I admitted.

"Neither do I, despite their attempts to explain it to me," she said. "When I first returned to the bosom of my family I was greeted with all the warmth one might expect, embraced and showered with words of welcome."

"Of course," I said.

"That lasted perhaps half an hour, possibly as much as forty-five minutes, and then my mother started telling me I should be ashamed that I worried her so. I should have left you to your own devices, she said, the instant I realized that you were taking me into danger."

"A mother's natural concern..." I began.

"And she told me that I should have realized you were being reckless," she continued, interrupting me, "by the time we crossed the border into Mexico, because everyone knows all of Mexico is a savage wilderness inhabited by heart-eating Aztecs and degenerate Spaniards and gigantic snakes and vicious bandits and man-eating jaguars."

I blinked. The Mexico we had seen was nothing like that.

"I protested that Father had sent me to help you fly the Aeronavigator and had never said anything about abandoning you if you crossed the border, and I had wired them at every opportunity to reassure them that I was safe, but they were having none of it. By this time they were both reprimanding me – my mother for risking myself, and my father for risking his airship. In truth, he seemed more upset that I had allowed the Aeronavigator to be destroyed than anything else."

"But that was entirely *my* doing!" I exclaimed.

"And I said as much! Ungenerous of me, perhaps..."

"Merely truthful," I assured her.

"Thank you. It's nice to know *someone* agrees with my version of events."

"Still, while I can understand that they were upset, surely after a few days..."

She shook her head violently, and I did not finish my sentence. "They might have gotten over it," she said, "were it not for one thing. They found out it was *I* who shot and killed Hezekiah McKee."

"But..." I frowned. "That was self-defense."

"That doesn't matter – at least, not to my mother. As far as she was concerned, I was no longer her eldest daughter, but a depraved murderess who must seek redemption at once. She immediately called our minister and began a relentless campaign to save my soul, whether I wanted it saved or not."

"That seems..." I could not find the right words.

"Ridiculous!" Betsy exclaimed, with the first flash of her old fire that I had seen since her arrival. "It's just *ridiculous!*"

"I..."

"And she won't *stop!*" Betsy continued. "Every day, morning and night, nagging me to devote my time to prayers for forgiveness. The minister is at our home more than he is at his own church, though in truth I think it is as much for my mother's cooking as for any concern for my immortal soul. I am allowed no privacy, nor the company of anyone my own age, lest I be lured into the more common follies of youth – the murder of the Reverend McKee, it would seem, has so warped my judgment that I am now considered susceptible to the temptations of liquor, gambling, and harlotry, where a year and a half ago my father would blithely send me roaming about the country unescorted, running his errands."

"It's absurd," I said.

"It is! And I had no idea it was coming. While my mother has always attended church regularly, she was never so devout as this must imply. Apparently during my long absence her worries about me drove her to the comforts of religion, provoking this sudden obsession with my salvation."

"And your father agrees with her?"

"No, he does not," Betsy said. "And that lack of support seems to have driven her to redouble her efforts. Thank heavens, my father realized this was happening months ago, and while he did not dare openly defend me, or send me on any errands of the sort he so often employed me for in times past, he did provide some comfort and sympathy – until a few days ago."

"What happened a few days ago?"

"Oh, some volcanic island in the Dutch East Indies exploded – Krakatoa, I believe was the name."

"I believe I saw a report to that effect; whatever does that have to do with your father?"

"It seemed he absolutely *must* go to visit the site, as soon as he could put together an expedition. The scientific knowledge to be gained is, so he said, incalculable. He and Mother fought furiously over it, but he would not yield – he is off to Sumatra. His ship sailed from New York this past Saturday morning, leaving me at home with my mother and siblings."

"I am surprised you did not arrange to accompany him."

"Oh, I tried, but Mother would not hear of it. She said... Oh, she said terrible things, Tom! She accused us both of horrid betrayals and abominable behavior, and said, in no uncertain terms, that if he allowed me to go with him that when we returned she would not be there – she would sell the house and take the rest of the children and begin a new life somewhere else."

"Do you think she really would?"

"I don't know. She might. But we will never know, because my father gave in. I don't know that he really *wanted* me along – what would he need with a messenger and engineer on such a voyage? Not to mention the costs and inconveniences of bringing a girl along. So he yielded the point and left without me.

"Since he did, Tom, my life has been absolute Hell, as my mother has nothing restraining her any longer, and I have no refuge, no one to whom I can speak who is not fully on her side, no one who might sympathize with me. My siblings dare not say a word in my defense, not even little Nicholas; indeed, they dare not come near me, for fear our mother might think some of my depravity has contaminated them. I think she has them spying on me – I have twice caught Cornelia going through my belongings. It has been a constant nightmare since Father left, and I could see no prospect of any improvement. When I could stand it no longer, I packed my bags and came here."

"Oh, I..." And then a realization burst upon me. "They don't know you're here, do they?"

"No." She shook her head and smiled. "I've run away from home, Tom, and I've come to you, as the one person I still dare trust."

Chapter Three

A Request for Sanctuary

I had no idea what to say to this request. While I was quite happy to see her and would welcome her company for as long as she chose to stay, I recognized the unacceptable impropriety of allowing an unmarried girl to remain in our home without her parents' knowledge and consent. Adventurers are allowed a certain leeway in the social niceties, as a recognized element inherent in the nature of the profession, but it did not extend that far, not without some very serious mitigating circumstances! Had I just rescued Miss Vanderhart from a Turkish harem, or retrieved her from the clutches of some monster, then she could spend a few days recovering from her ordeal before anything need be done, but when she had, by her own admission, simply run away from home? That was inexcusable.

Of course, the two of us had spent months unchaperoned during our travels through the Arizona Territory, Mexico, and British Honduras, and back, but that had been in the course of an adventure and was therefore pardonable. Here in my home, though, was another matter.

It could certainly be argued that there was a certain hypocrisy in this, but nonetheless, appearances mattered. We both knew that – but Betsy was sufficiently distraught just then to not care about appearances, and I did not know how to put it into words the conflicting emotions that beset me.

Fortunately, before the silence grew unbearable and prompted me to say something regrettable, my mother returned, tray in hand. No tea was visible, but she had brought the sugar bowl and a plate of butter cookies.

She saw our faces, observed the silence, and I am sure she formed some idea of what was going on, but what she did was to set the tray on a table and say cheerfully, "The tea will be ready in a moment. Tom, could you give me a hand?"

"Of course!" I said, leaping to my feet. While I like to think of myself as a generous and helpful person, I will readily admit that my primary and more selfish motivation for acting so promptly was the opportunity to remove myself from the conversation with Betsy. Recognizing this, and ashamed of that recognition, I assured her, "I'll be right back." Then I followed my mother to the kitchen, where the kettle was steaming vigorously.

I collected the cups on a second tray, along with the little cream pitcher, while Mother filled the teapot, and as we worked she remarked, in the most casual way imaginable, "She isn't supposed to be here, is she?"

"What?" Again, I was at a loss for words. Despite eight years of training in the adventurer's arts, I did not yet have the quickness of thought that can be so essential in the trade.

"If her parents knew she was coming, they would have wired us, would they not?"

"Not everyone cares to spend the price of a telegram on such a thing," I said, making entirely unnecessary adjustments to the positioning of the cups and saucers.

"But they *don't* know she's here, do they?"

"Probably not," I admitted. "I think it fairly certain her father does not; he is traveling."

"But her mother is at home?"

I nodded. "With the other three children."

"How serious is it? Do you know yet?"

"She seems to have...disagreements with her mother regarding our experiences in Mexico."

"Does Mrs. Vanderhart think you have debauched her daughter?"

"Oh, I certainly *hope* not!" I exclaimed. "I assure you, I never...I did no such thing."

"I never thought you did," she replied. "I know you better than that. But Mrs. Vanderhart scarcely knows you at all, and any young man may be suspected."

"Betsy has not mentioned any such suspicion," I assured her. "But it seems her mother thought she was reckless in accompanying me into Mexico, and that her..." I hesitated, looking for an appropriate euphemism, then decided on bluntness – after all, my mother knew what had happened. "That shooting Reverend McKee was a mortal sin, requiring repentance and penance that Betsy has refused to display to her mother's satisfaction."

Mother plopped the lid on the teapot and set it on the tray. "I see," she said. I stepped aside as she lifted the tray. "Will you allow me to discuss the situation frankly with our guest?"

"I am hardly one to tell you what to do in your own home, Mother!"

She nodded, and lifted the tray. I followed her back to the parlor, where we went through the customary polite little ceremonies of serving tea. Betsy did not take cream or sugar.

When we were all seated, with teacups in hand and cookies nearby, Mother said, without any preliminaries, "Am I to understand, Miss Vanderhart, that you are here without your family's knowledge or consent?"

Betsy threw me a look, but I widened my eyes and gave my head a small shake; I had not revealed the situation to my mother, but had only confirmed what she had already guessed.

"I am afraid that is correct, Mrs. Derringer," Betsy replied, setting down her cup. "I'll go, if you want..."

"Oh, I didn't say *that*," Mother exclaimed. "Drink your tea."

Betsy picked up the cup, eyeing my mother warily.

"Tom tells me that your parents were upset by some of your actions in Mexico," Mother continued. "Having heard Tom's account, I can see how someone unfamiliar with the life of an adventurer might be. Having been in such situations myself, though, I am *entirely* on your side – there are situations where the niceties of civilized life, or even common human decency, will get you killed; you need to be able to respond quickly and decisively and hope for the best."

Betsy blinked at her. "Yes," she said.

"Well, you did what you had to do, and because you did we are all here, safe and sound, and Reverend McKee is not waging some monstrous aerial war against the Mexican government. *I* am not going to fault you for that!"

"Thank you, Mrs. Derringer," Betsy said, and she appeared to relax a little.

"That said, I am afraid that we cannot allow you to stay here for long – certainly not without informing your family. You are not yet twenty-one, are you?"

"No. I'll be eighteen next month."

"You are very mature for your age, my dear; I'd have taken you for a year or two older. But it is twenty-one that matters; until your twenty-first birthday the law views you as a child, and your parents' responsibility, and keeping you hidden from them is a crime – perhaps not by statute, I have never investigated the matter, but certainly in practice. Quite aside from the law, allowing you to stay here with Tom – and no matter how we might disguise it, the world will certainly see you as staying with him, rather than with me or Mary Ann – would be a scandal."

"I suppose it would," Betsy acknowledged. "But you said you didn't want me to leave – what *are* you proposing?"

I had no more idea than Betsy what my mother had in mind, so I listened closely and said nothing.

"It is a curious feature of the adventurer's profession," my mother said, "that behavior that would be completely intolerable in other circumstances becomes acceptable if it occurs in the course of a successful adventure – assuming, of course, that the adventure is undertaken with a good purpose in mind. No one will consider it unforgivably scandalous that you spent weeks traveling with Tom by wagon and airship without benefit of chaperone – oh, it may cause a few tongues to wag, but there is a general understanding that you are *adventurers*, and certain rules can be bent..."

"*I'm* not an adventurer!" Betsy interrupted. "I'm an engineer!"

Mother sat back in her chair and smiled indulgently. "Miss Vanderhart," she said, "you piloted an airship across the length of Mexico, infiltrated a would–be conqueror's flying fortress, shot and killed him, improvised an escape from his doomed airship, and then made your way to safety through a hundred miles of jungle; how can you possibly *not* be an adventurer?"

"I never intended to be one!"

"Neither did I, really, but if you mention the name Arabella Whitaker to anyone who knew me before I married, the response will almost certainly be, 'Oh, the adventurer?'"

Actually, I thought the response was more likely to be, "Oh, Jack Derringer's girl?" but I was not foolish enough to say so; I continued to hold my peace.

"But I'm an engineer!"

"One can be both, you know."

"No, I *don't* know! Adventuring is a stupid and dangerous thing to do, and I have better sense than that."

I suppressed a smile at this blunt opinion of my own career choice.

"Yet you did not turn back when Tom offered you the opportunity," my mother said. "You constructed that breathing device and helped him destroy McKee's airship."

"I just..." She stopped, took a deep breath, then started again, more calmly. "I do not consider myself an adventurer, Mrs. Derringer, however my actions in Mexico might appear."

"That's fine, my dear; you can see yourself however you choose. But how do *others* perceive you?"

"What does it matter?"

Mother smiled again, and shook her head. "Miss Vanderhart, you are not as quick as I hoped; I must assume that you are rattled by your present stressful situation. Cannot you see that I am offering you a respectable choice that does not involve either staying here and causing a scandal, or returning home to suffer your parents' disapproval?"

"No, I do *not* see that! What are you talking about?"

I was tempted to speak up, since I thought I finally did see where my mother's thoughts led, but I restrained myself.

"You can stay here and become the target of gossip and opprobrium, or you can return home to domestic tyranny, or you can go adventuring with Tom. Unless you have other friends who will take you in and not deliver you back to your parents, I see no viable fourth choice."

"Go...adventuring?"

"Yes." She turned to me. "I believe you had something in mind?"

This was an occasion that called for something more than another trip to New England. "Well, it may turn out to be of no significance," I said, "but there is something I want to investigate in California – a possible remnant of Emperor Norton's retinue."

"Emperor Norton?" Betsy looked utterly baffled. "Who is Emperor Norton?"

"The late Joshua Norton was a madman who declared himself Emperor of the United States and Protector of Mexico," I explained. "It amused the people of San Francisco to treat him in some regards as if he were an actual monarch."

"I don't understand."

"Well, I can explain it, if you like, but I think we should first decide whether it matters. I think my mother has hit upon rather a clever solution, actually. If you accompany me to California as a fellow adventurer, it will give you a sound reason to stay away from your parents, and a way to do so without any great impropriety."

"Does your investigation require the services of an engineer?"

I shrugged. "Who knows? It might. A clever and resourceful companion is bound to be of use even if I do not, in fact, require your skill with machinery. I would be very pleased to have your company. In fact, the major reason I had not already departed on such an errand was that I had hoped to hear from you and could not reasonably expect that to happen while I was on the far side of the continent. Should you agree to join me, there will be nothing to prevent me from heading for California at the first opportunity."

I thought I saw a hint of a blush in her cheeks.

"You don't need to answer immediately," Mother told her. "I can wire your mother and tell her that Tom has offered you a position, and you have come here to discuss it in detail before deciding whether to accept."

"I don't..." She stopped, thinking.

"I can assure you," I said, "I have no plans for any travel by airship this time, nor for any expeditions beyond the borders of the United States."

"Though one can never be certain of what might happen, when one goes adventuring," my mother added, in perhaps her least-helpful contribution to the conversation.

"My parents don't want me to be an adventurer," Betsy said.

"No sane parent would," Mother replied. She did not look at me as she said this, and I admired her self-control.

"Your parents are *already* unhappy with you," I said. "Could accompanying me make matters any worse? Indeed, the separation may serve to ameliorate matters – tempers will have time to cool, and the natural familial bond may thereby reassert itself. You will not have your mother's constant attentions troubling you, and she may find herself more concerned with your physical safety than with the well-being of your soul – not that I think either to be at any great risk – to salutary effect on your future interactions."

"Staying here, on the other hand, she will most likely see as a terrible threat to your virtue and reputation," Mother said.

"As if there won't be plenty of opportunities while traveling!"

"There is far less privacy on a train," Mother said. "And many people overestimate how much care hoteliers take to protect their female clientele, and assume their daughters will be kept safe."

"We won't be camping out in a wagon, then?"

"I don't have any plans to do so," I replied. "At present, I am unaware of anything that would take me out of the city of San Francisco, once we have reached it."

"You were unaware we would cross the Mexican border last time."

"That's true, and it's possible we'll wind up in Siberia or Timbuktoo, but *at present* I am unaware of anything that would cause that to happen. And you can always leave me to my own devices and return home by yourself."

She managed a smile. "You are such a charmer, Tom Derringer, offering to abandon me on the Barbary Coast!"

I smiled back. "I will do what I can to please a lady."

"You don't need to decide this very minute, dear," my mother said, rising and reaching for the teapot. "Think it over. Would you like more tea?"

Chapter Four

Our Journey Begins

I will say that Miss Vanderhart did not rush into anything; she had me explain at great length everything I knew of Gabriel Trask, Emperor Norton, and the Pierce Archives. She demanded to see my father's journals, and I allowed it. She did not read through them all, but skimmed several volumes, stopping now and then to read a passage more carefully. She studied maps of California, railroad timetables, and what few other relevant sources of information we had in the house.

"And you have no particular reason to suspect this Mr. Trask of nefarious deeds or evil intentions?" she asked me, looking up from a page of notes.

"None," I admitted, "save that his name was on the mind and lips of Hezekiah McKee, who spoke of him as a master of spies and assassins."

"But you're going to California in search of him, all the same?"

"So it would seem, yes."

"Idle curiosity hardly seems sufficient justification for crossing the continent!"

"Yet I had nothing more than idle curiosity driving me when I bought your father's airship and shipped it to Flagstaff to pursue reports of a mysterious flying object."

She could scarcely argue with that. "Let us hope that this time your investigations are a little less hazardous," she said.

"*Our* investigations," I corrected her.

"If I agree to go."

"If you do not, I may well leave Mr. Trask untroubled."

She frowned at that, and returned to her studies.

And finally, at suppertime on her second full day with us, she announced that she would accompany me to San Francisco if we could agree upon a suitable wage for her services as my assistant.

The negotiations did not take long; my mother had not yet served out the pumpkin pie for our dessert when we settled our terms. I had the impression that Betsy had thought her demands extravagant, but I found them reasonable enough, and I wondered what her father had paid for her services in the past, when she had acted as his messenger – or whether he had paid her at all!

After that we needed another two days to prepare, including sending a telegram to her mother to inform her of our plans and gathering the supplies I thought appropriate. On the third morning after her acceptance we were aboard a train bound for New York, the first step in our journey.

Upon reaching the city I brought Miss Vanderhart to meet our banker Tobias Arbuthnot, and my father's old friend, Mad Bill Senedeker. I showed her the Pierce Archives, and introduced her to Dr. Pierce. If she was to play the part of an adventurer, it seemed only fitting to make her acquainted with a little of the professional community – and of course, I wanted to call on Messrs. Arbuthnot, Snedeker, and Pierce myself.

At the archives I reviewed some of the known facts about the late Joshua Norton, but there was so little about his connections with Gabriel Trask that I saw no point in studying excessively. I made polite conversation with some of the other adventurers, introducing them to Miss Vanderhart, but made no effort to deepen my acquaintance with any of them.

I had turned down a dinner invitation from Mad Bill Snedeker, but Tobias Arbuthnot was harder to refuse, so we dined with him at a finer restaurant than any I had ever before visited.

And then at last we boarded our train for Chicago. There we would change trains, and continue westward. There would be further transfers in Omaha, where we would pick up the Union Pacific's famous No. 3, and in Ogden, in the Utah Territory, where we would switch to the Central Pacific for the final leg. In all, the journey would be slightly over a week; perhaps more research might have found a better route, but I was satisfied. For every portion of the trip I had booked us adjoining sleeping compartments.

"I seem to have spent half my life on trains," Betsy remarked, as we settled in and stowed our luggage.

I could not think of an appropriate response, so I smiled silently.

And then we were on our way.

She joined me in my compartment so that we could chat. I reviewed with her what I knew of Joshua Norton and Gabriel Trask, told her a little about my recent visit to New England, and regaled her with some of what I had read in my father's journals about my parents' adventures. She, in turn, explained how she had become her father's assistant as a very young girl, as he was tired of training a new student as his aide every few years, only to see that youth graduate and leave. She had learned the engineering necessary to build and maintain his various inventions; he did not want to waste his time on mere mechanics and devoted his own efforts to theory and design.

She had also been sent everywhere from Boston to St. Louis to carry his messages and to deliver the assorted devices he had created; he hated to travel, since he could not very well tinker while riding in a Pullman car or driving a buggy.

Her mother had always been the mistress of the household, seeing to the everyday business of keeping her husband and children fed and clothed and their house clean and in good repair. She had never put on any great display of religious devotion and had tolerated a fair amount of irreverence and anti–social behavior from the professor, but apparently learning that her daughter had killed a man had brought about a sudden revulsion against her earlier tolerance and a zealous determination to drag her family back to the path of righteousness.

Betsy did not care to be dragged anywhere.

She was able to discuss her mother more calmly now; the few days away from her, and the promise of a good many more, had had a salutary effect on her emotions. Simply having someone to talk to about the matter seemed to help immensely, so I let her talk as much as she cared to, even when her outraged protestations grew repetitious and ultimately tedious.

She was still talking about how unreasonable it was for her father to have sided so often with her mother when it was he who had been responsible for her unorthodox upbringing when we made our way to the dining car for a late supper. We were, I believe, somewhere in eastern Pennsylvania at this point, and many of the trees rushing past the windows were already showing their fall colors, making a splendid display.

I made some remark about the scenery and how it was quite different from what we would see on the train west from Chicago. Then the steward showed us to our table, and we had just taken our seats when a man in a battered bowler hat tapped my shoulder.

Startled, I turned. His face looked vaguely familiar, but I could not place it.

"You're Tom Derringer, aren't you?" he asked.

"I am," I acknowledged. "And who might *you* be?" I asked in return.

"Edward Hancock," he said, extending a hand. "Call me Teddy."

I recognized the name. I took his hand and shook it. His grip was firm, but not excessively so, and his gaze was friendly and open.

"Steady Teddy" Hancock was an adventurer, one of fairly modest accomplishments, but with a reputation for honesty and for being a good man to have at your back in a tight spot. I had no reason to doubt that this man was he.

"Tom," I said. "And this is Miss Elspeth Vanderhart."

"I recognized you from the Pierce Archives," he said.

"You must join us for dinner," Betsy said, gesturing at one of the unclaimed seats.

"No, no; I've already eaten, and I would not want to put you to any trouble. I did wonder, though, what your destination might be. I thought I overheard something about a westbound train from Chicago. If we have the same goal, perhaps we could join forces."

"We are bound for San Francisco," I said. "And you?"

"Ah. I'll be disembarking at Ogden, Utah. Then you are not...well, we are clearly not pursuing the same matter."

"Apparently not," I said. "Might I ask..."

"Oh, I'm sure it's nothing," he said hastily, before I could complete my inquiry. "Just a rumor."

"One I had not heard, it would seem."

"So it would seem. And what takes you to San Francisco?"

"A name," I said. "A name I heard from a man who is no longer with us."

"And what would that name be?"

"Gabriel Trask."

I waited to see his reaction; did the name mean any more to him than it had to me?

He cocked his head to one side for a moment, considering, then shook his head. "I don't recall ever hearing it before. Why are you looking for him?"

"Hezekiah McKee was convinced I was in Trask's employ. I'm curious as to why he thought so."

"And McKee is dead, so you're planning to ask this Trask fellow about it?"

"Exactly."

"Doesn't sound very lucrative."

"I don't expect to earn a cent."

"Ah! Well, I have hopes of coming home with something I can sell to a museum. I'll wish you well in your search, then. It's been a pleasure, Mr. Derringer, Miss Vanderhart." He tipped his hat and turned away.

I might have followed him to ask for more details of his own quest, but just then the steward arrived with our menu cards.

When we had ordered our meal, Betsy asked me, "Does that happen often, one adventurer encountering another on an unrelated mission?"

"I don't really know," I admitted. "It has never happened to *me* before, but I'm still just a beginner in the trade. I don't recall many such meetings mentioned in my father's journals."

"He seemed wary of telling you what he was after."

"I noticed that."

"Perhaps you should not have been so quick to tell him your own intentions."

I dismissed her concern with a gesture. "He's after a treasure of some sort, I suppose, and doesn't want competition. You heard what he said about a museum. I, on the other hand, am merely seeking knowledge, and I don't see how that would concern him."

While Betsy was considering this, I added, "And I don't see what harm it could do if he knew everything I do about Mr. Trask and our intentions. Even if he should decide to join us, what would that do to interfere with my own interests?"

"He might not believe your intentions are as benign as you claim."

"And what if he does not?"

"He might warn Trask that you are looking for him."

"Again, what harm would there be in it?"

She waved the question away. "Oh, don't mind me. I am full of dire imaginings of late – I suppose from listening to my mother. I see assassins on every side."

"There are very few active assassins in the United States these days; these are the Appalachians around us, not the Balkans."

"Pay me no mind."

I shrugged, and put the matter aside.

After that, though, we spoke much less; I was not sure just why, but she seemed much quieter, almost withdrawn, through our supper and into the remainder of the evening. We were preparing to retire to our separate compartments when she asked me, "You do remember, don't you, that Reverend McKee said that Trask employed spies and assassins? We may not be in the Balkans, but this Trask might still be dangerous."

I did not answer immediately. In truth, I had let the image of Mr. Trask as spymaster to a prancing comic–opera buffoon sway me and had assumed he would turn out to be harmless, but *McKee* had certainly not thought him to be harmless. He had thought Trask might be a serious obstacle to his plans to build an empire. And McKee had clearly had direct dealings with him, whereas everything I read at the Pierce Archives was at best second–hand reporting. I might indeed be underestimating Trask.

But why should I worry Betsy, who by her own admission had been of late prone to unpleasant fancies?

"He might be," I said. "But I doubt it. Still, I shall be careful, I promise you. I shall be more circumspect in the future than I was with Mr. Hancock, as well."

She did not seem entirely reassured, but she turned to her compartment door without further protest. "Good night, Tom," she said.

"Good night, Betsy."

I retreated to my own compartment, where I removed my coat and boots, but I sat in thought for a moment before undressing further.

I remembered how often Toby Arbuthnot and Mad Bill had warned me about the dangers of an adventurer's career and how they had both listed many sad and gruesome deaths that had befallen my compatriots. I remembered my mother's warnings and how much effort she had put into seeing that I was properly trained. I remembered how many of my father's adventures, as described in his journal, had involved treachery and other unexpected hazards. Not all of his companions in Darien Lord's band had survived.

Betsy was right. I needed to be more careful, in word and deed. Hezekiah McKee had thought of Gabriel Trask as a formidable adversary; Trask's association with Emperor Norton might have been a ruse, some sort of protective coloration to conceal real and dangerous schemes.

Henceforth, I promised myself, I would tell no one any more about my quest than absolutely necessary. From the first moment we arrived in San Francisco I would strap on my Colt and travel armed at all times. My Winchester rifle was in the baggage car, but the revolver was in a case by my feet; I debated opening it, but then dismissed the idea. I thought it was more likely that I would accidentally shoot a steward than that I would actually need it to fend off a real foe.

With that resolve fresh in my mind I extinguished the lamp and settled in my berth.

Chapter Five

We Arrive in San Francisco

No untoward incidents or irregularities troubled us on the way to Omaha, which was a bustling little city on the western banks of the Missouri. I admit to some excitement upon seeing the Union Pacific name on our next train; we were crossing the entire continent! Messrs. Lewis and Clark had needed a year and a half to accomplish the feat we would complete in scarcely more than a week.

We found our compartment and settled in. To avoid any risk of missing the train's 12:15 departure we had foregone taking our luncheon in any of Omaha's dining establishments, and had instead packed a few sandwiches, which we now unwrapped and ate. By the time we brushed away the last crumbs we were well under way, rolling westward across the plains of Nebraska.

I cannot say the scenery that streamed past our windows was of any great interest, and in short order we resorted to reading two of the books we had brought, and rode on in companionable silence.

Our conversation was more sparse on this leg of the trip; I think we were both running out of things to say to one another. We had spent a great deal of time traveling in each other's company on our previous adventure, after all, and were already a few days into this new journey.

The scenery improved on the second and third days out of Omaha, as we climbed into the hills and mountains. I glimpsed Teddy Hancock in the passage once or twice, but did not speak to him.

We were almost an hour late pulling into Ogden, the transfer point between the Union Pacific's Number Three train and the Central Pacific's Number Two, as well as the junction with the Utah & Northern's narrow-gauge line. The various agents and salesmen on the platform seemed to have been wearied and annoyed by the unaccustomed wait, but we were able to fend them off and make our way to the boardwalk that led from the station to the heart of town without making any purchases.

The station itself was rather disappointing – a two-story wooden structure that seemed to be surrounded by mud anywhere that was not actual rail bed – and our late arrival meant that we had missed a chance to see the magnificent mountains east of the city as anything more than pale shapes in the distance, their stony peaks gleaming faintly in the light of a crescent moon. That boardwalk, though, kept our feet out of the worst of the mire and led us to a thriving town that offered a choice of several small hotels and boarding houses. We chose one called the Reed Hotel, which proved to be entirely comfortable and reasonably priced.

As we were registering for the night, Teddy Hancock and two companions walked in. He gave me a curious look, as if wondering whether our presence was mere coincidence or something more sinister, and I interrupted my discussion with the desk clerk to call a greeting.

"Mr. Derringer," he replied. "A pleasure to see you again – but I thought you were not stopping in Ogden."

"We are not staying long, Mr. Hancock; we will be taking the Central Pacific tomorrow afternoon."

"You cannot stay on the train tonight?"

"Not that I am aware of, nor would I want to remain in such cramped quarters when I have this fine establishment available to me!" I waved an arm to take in the Reed's lobby, a lobby that would be a shabby embarrassment back in New York, but which I was fairly certain was the best one could expect in this part of the country.

"Ah. Perhaps I will see you at supper, then."

"Or at breakfast."

But in fact, we did not see him again during our stay in Ogden; indeed, when we had our keys and were being shown to our rooms, I glanced back and saw Mr. Hancock arguing with the other two men; then all three turned to go, having apparently reconsidered their choice of the Reed.

The following day we took in such sights as there were, admiring the grand mountain vistas to the east and the lakes to the west, and we strolled the streets with some caution – I did not take Ogden to be an entirely safe place and was careful to keep Betsy in sight so far as I reasonably could. The locals at the hotel had told us proudly that just a month before a company had been formed to build and operate mule–drawn streetcars, but we saw no sign of their efforts.

By mid–afternoon we made our way back to the depot, and we were comfortably ensconced on our train when its whistle sounded and the wheels began to turn.

As the train pulled out of the station I leaned out the window and glanced back and saw a group of half a dozen men watching our departure. I thought one of them wore a familiar bowler.

It seemed to me that there was something curious about all this, and I wondered what to make of it. Had I done something to antagonize Mr. Hancock? What *was* his business in Ogden? I had certainly seen no sign of anything that would interest a professional adventurer.

Whatever it might be I was leaving it behind and was on my way to San Francisco to find Gabriel Trask. I drew my head back into the carriage and closed the window.

The remainder of the journey was uneventful, and after two nights on the train we arrived in Oakland and transferred to the railroad's ferry, which landed us safely in San Francisco around midday.

We were well out of the mountain snows here, but a chill wind blew off the water and we wasted no time in consulting the locals regarding a suitable hotel to serve as the home base for our search. I had learned from the Pierce Archives that in 1876 the late Emperor Norton had met with Dom Pedro II, the actual Emperor of Brazil, at the famous Palace Hotel, so that establishment was my preferred choice, and I was assured that it was indeed convenient and despite its fine reputation, not excessively expensive.

We might, I suppose, have taken the new Market Street cable cars from the ferry port, but I felt more comfortable riding a more familiar and private conveyance, so we engaged a hansom cab.

A short ride brought us to the Palace Hotel, at the corner of Market and New Montgomery Streets, where we took adjoining rooms on the fourth floor, looking across at the topmost levels of the smaller, but still splendid, Grand Hotel on the other side of New Montgomery Street.

I have previously referred to the shortcomings of our hotel in Ogden; the Palace had no such lacks. It was easily the equal of the finest I had seen in New York. Its proprietors claimed it to be the largest hotel in the world; I have no reason doubt the claim. Its splendors were many and obvious, and it was not surprising that the Brazilian monarch had chosen it for his residence when visiting the city.

Having completed our transcontinental journey we felt no great desire to do anything but recuperate, and we therefore spent much of the next two days simply enjoying the hotel's myriad comforts. The search for Mr. Trask could wait until we were rested and until the aches that had accumulated in a week of bone-rattling travel and sleep in inadequate and over-active bunks had subsided.

We did venture to the local telegraph office, though, where I wired my mother to let her know we had arrived safely.

Betsy then wired her mother to the same effect, but concluded her message with, "Tom has been a perfect gentleman."

I thought this final sentence was a mistake and announced, "I have another message to send."

The telegrapher readied his pen.

"To Mrs. Aloysius Vanderhart, same address," I said. "Dear Mrs. Vanderhart – I have not debauched your daughter. Stop. Sincerely, T. Derringe..."

I had not completed the final syllable of my name when Betsy hit me on the arm, with more power than one might expect from so small a frame.

"That's not funny, Tom."

"No? I thought it was, but if you're sure..."

"Don't send that message," she ordered the telegrapher.

He pulled the page from his pad and tore it in half. "Just as well," he said. "I don't believe I know how to spell 'debauched.'"

After that we returned to the hotel and took tea in the conservatory on the top floor.

At last, though, I felt sufficiently rested to pursue our purpose in being there. I had chatted with some of the staff and the other guests in the Gentlemen's Grill and had learned a little more about the late Emperor's habits. He had lived a few blocks away, on Commercial Street, on the top floor of a place called the Eureka Lodgings, but had largely held court elsewhere, as his meager home did not provide sufficient space for any sort of gathering.

I was told that his room had been ransacked after his death, in response to rumors that he had concealed various treasures there, but nothing unexpected, and nothing of significance, had been found; for that reason I decided I did not need to explore it myself. I did not exclude the possibility that secrets might have been gone undetected, but I did not think I had any special aptitude for seeing what others had missed.

He had spent much of his time walking the streets and, when the weather permitted, chatting with his friends and subjects on the city's sidewalks or in Portsmouth Square. It was in this square that he had most often met with the officers of his court, such as they were. Accordingly, on our third morning in the city Betsy and I set out for that little park. The weather being above reproach, particularly for the final week of September, we walked the dozen or so blocks up Kearny Street rather than employing any sort of wheeled transportation.

I confess to being somewhat startled to see, on the west side of the street as we neared our destination, shop signs not in English, but in Chinese. I knew of course, of San Francisco's famed "Chinatown," but I had not realized we would be traversing its boundaries for much of our stroll.

But then, I should not have been surprised; the late Emperor Norton had been famous for his advocacy of fair and liberal treatment for the city's Chinese inhabitants, and indeed his so-called Grand Chamberlain was a Chinaman, so it was perfectly reasonable for his court and residence to be located near the Chinese community.

Portsmouth Square was a pleasant enough place, a rectangle of trees and grass in the midst of the city. We strolled across it, then settled on a convenient bench.

For several minutes we watched the people of San Francisco come and go. Many were simply traversing the park on their way from one place to another, while others spent a few minutes reinvigorating themselves before moving on.

I was most interested, however, in those who did not move on, but settled on a bench, as we had, and stayed. I thought these were the people most likely to have known His Imperial Majesty. Most were a little shabby, of course; their mere presence indicated they had no job demanding their attention elsewhere.

After perhaps half an hour I selected one of these lingerers, a short man of advancing years, with long unkempt black hair and sunken cheeks, who looked to me as if he was very much at home in the square, as if he had been coming there for years. I got to my feet, crossed the walk, and sat down beside him. Betsy followed, and took a seat on his other side.

"Good morning," I said.

He looked at me warily. "S'pose it is," he said.

"Do you sit here often?"

He cocked his head to one side. "Weather permittin'," he said.

"Been doing it for some time?" Something of his manner was rubbing off on me.

"Long enough."

"Back when Emperor Norton held court here?"

His attitude, already wary, grew downright hostile. "You a reporter?"

"Good heavens, no!" I said. "Ask my companion. I'm an adventurer."

"Look young for that trade."

"I'm just starting out."

"If you're lookin' for poor old Norton's treasure, you can forget it. He never had none."

"I know that. You knew him, then?"

"I talked to him once or twice. Can't say I knew him well." He coughed. "And if you're hopin' to find out what he and Dom Pedro talked about, ain't nobody knows now but Dom Pedro. Emperor stuff, I s'pose."

"No, I...well, I won't say I wouldn't like to know, but that's not what I'm after. I'm looking for a man who might have worked for Emperor Norton."

"*Worked* for him? Ain't nobody *worked* for him; he didn't have no money to pay anyone."

That was almost certainly true and brought up a number of questions I realized I had not given sufficient thought, but I put it aside for the moment. "All right, then, a man who did favors for the emperor."

"Plenty o' them around; which one did you want?"

"A man named Gabriel Trask."

He scratched his head and gazed thoughtfully at me, then said, "Can't say I know the name."

That was disappointing. "Do you know anyone who might?"

"Could be. What's in it for me?"

I fished a half-dollar from my vest pocket, secreted there earlier for this very purpose, and pressed it into his palm. "There's another of these for you if I find Mr. Trask."

The half-dollar disappeared. "Don't know if I can find *him*, but I can find you someone who knew the emperor better 'n almost anyone."

"That would be sufficient."

"Then be here tomorrow 'round noon, with that fifty-cent piece o' your'n, and I'll introduce you."

"Thank you."

"I'll see you then, in that case," he said, and got to his feet. He ambled off toward the west side of the square.

I was tempted to follow him, but Betsy, who had not said a word since we left the Palace, put a hand on my arm to stop me. "Tomorrow," she said. "We'll see if he keeps his word."

I nodded.

We ambled about the park after that and spoke to a few of its other denizens, but found no one else who would admit to having known Emperor Norton. Around noon we betook ourselves to Martin & Horton's, an establishment said to be patronized by a variety of colorful characters, and where the late emperor had often eaten lunch. Several of the saloon's habitues had known Emperor Norton, but no one admitted to any knowledge of Gabriel Trask. Two or three gentlemen acknowledged having heard the name before, but none had any notion of where he might be found, or just what his connection to the late emperor might have been. It seemed Mr. Trask had not been any part of Martin & Horton's regular crowd; his interactions with Mr. Norton had all taken place elsewhere.

From there we wandered back to Portsmouth Square, but a brisk wind was blowing in off the Pacific and the skies were threatening, driving away the park's usual clientele. I suggested that we might proceed back to the Palace, but Betsy had an alternative to propose: shopping.

I protested, but Betsy was insistent. "I did not pack for a journey of this duration," she said.

I could hardly deny *that*. I mentioned seeing a dry goods emporium nearby, but she shook her head. "I can't sew," she said. "I was always too busy running errands for my father to learn; my mother made my clothes while I was away. I can't cook, either, beyond the campfire cooking I picked up on our previous travels." She gave me a look I can only describe as defiant. "We'll need a dressmaker."

"Of course," I said, and we set out to find one.

Chapter Six

The Grand Chamberlain

The next morning we visited another dressmaker and a milliner, then frittered away the remainder of the morning in casual exploration of the city and in conversation with some of its inhabitants – pleasant enough, but in no way advancing our search for Mr. Trask.

Shortly before noon we found our way to Portsmouth Square again and quickly spotted our informant; he was standing near the bench where we had spoken, deep in conversation with an elderly Oriental gentleman in a faded black frock coat. We approached deliberately, and our man spotted us.

"Here's the feller," he said to his companion.

They both turned to face us, and the Chinaman bowed, in the fashion of his homeland. I essayed a small bow in return, then held out my hand.

"Tom Derringer," I said. "I don't think I thought to introduce myself yesterday."

The Chinaman took my hand and bowed again. "I am called Ah How," he said, in slightly accented English. I recognized the name as that of Emperor Norton's so-called Grand Chamberlain. Before I could respond, he continued, "Derringer? Have I heard that name before?"

"It's possible," I admitted.

"I have, but it was not in reference to yourself," he said, raising a hand. "Do you know a Jackie Derringer? An adventurer?"

"He was my father," I said, startled.

"You say 'was'?"

"He has been dead these thirteen years."

"I am sorry to hear it. You are pursuing the same trade as he?"

"I am." I realized that we had by this time exchanged several sentences, and he had asked me several questions, while I, who had come seeking information, had asked none. I started to open my mouth to inquire about Mr. Trask, but the other man spoke before I could.

"Satisfied, Mr. Derringer?"

"Absolutely, sir," I said, as I drew forth the promised half-dollar. He closed his hand around it, tipped his hat, wished us a good day, and strolled away.

Ah How, Betsy, and I watched him go. When he was perhaps twenty feet away I turned back to Ah How, but before I had gathered my thoughts he asked, "Are you aware you are being followed?"

I opened my mouth, then closed it again. I blinked, astonished. Then I said, "I am?"

"Yes. There are two of them – a man behind you to your right, in a string tie and flat–brimmed hat, and another to your left, in a red vest and dented bowler hat. I do not believe they can hear us, so if you do not look at them they will not realize they have been spotted."

I kept my eyes focused on Ah How's face while I considered his words and realized that I had seen individuals matching those descriptions more than once since arriving in the city, but had paid them no particular attention.

"Interesting," I said. "Have you any idea who they are, or why they might be watching me?"

"I have seen them before. The man in the string tie calls himself Smith, but I do not believe that is his real name. He can be hired for a variety of services, not all of them legal, and often works with adventurers. The man in the bowler is Andrew Bowlby, and he worked for the Pinkerton Agency until his drinking interfered with his employment. When he is sober enough, he takes odd jobs."

"You seem remarkably well informed," I replied.

"I have found it advisable to pay attention to what goes on around me."

"Do you have any idea why they are following me?"

"No, Mr. Derringer, I do not."

I glanced at Betsy, who had not said a word. She shook her head, which I took to mean she did not want to be involved any more than necessary. I turned back to Ah How. "I understand you were a good friend of the late Joshua Norton."

His expression saddened. "I was."

"I am looking for a man said to be associated with the emperor," I explained. "A man named Gabriel Trask."

Ah How's eyes narrowed. "Where did you hear that name?"

I considered giving some vague or incomplete answer, but this man had demonstrated remarkable perspicacity and, it would seem, done me a favor in pointing out that I was under observation.

"From the lips of the Reverend Hezekiah McKee," I said. "He accused me of being in Mr. Trask's pay."

"Did he say who Mr. Trask was?"

"No, he did not, but he said that Mr. Trask employed spies and assassins. That made me curious, so I did some research, and found that some people believed this Trask to have been the emperor's spymaster."

He nodded. "And what is your interest in this matter?"

"I am an adventurer, sir, and follow my whims. Further, I would prefer not to let assassins roam the world unhindered. Accordingly, I have come to San Francisco to see whether there is any truth in McKee's accusations."

"And if there is?"

I had reached the limit of my tolerance for his endless questions. "Is there?"

He sighed, his breath fluttering the tips of his mustache. "Mr. Trask was not the emperor's spymaster," he said.

"Oh?" He seemed reluctant to say more, so I pressed him, "Who *was* Gabriel Trask, then? What was his connection with Joshua Norton?"

"You must understand, Mr. Norton was a poor man in worldly wealth, but rich in friends, and despite his claim to a foolish and unreal title, rich in wisdom. He could not pay for anyone's services, nor demand them, but there were those who offered their services nonetheless, and those who accepted my friend's advice and counsel. Mr. Trask was one such."

"And what services did he offer? Spies and assassins?"

He sighed again. "You let your imagination run away with you. There are wonders in this world, young man, but assassins who serve an emperor who cannot pay them? *That* is not something I have ever encountered."

"What, then?"

"Mr. Trask was not the emperor's spymaster. He was the emperor's ambassador to the hidden people of the world."

It seemed that we had reversed roles, and now I was the one asking endless questions. "Hidden people?"

"Those who choose not to walk openly among us," he said. "Those who live in secret places in the far mountains, or in caverns beneath the earth, or in the waters of the sea."

Comprehension burst upon me. "Places like El Dorado, or Shamballah."

He nodded. "Exactly. Mr. Trask served as their advocate to the emperor and his friends."

"And his encounters with Hezekiah McKee?"

"Ah, that I cannot say. I do not know anything about them – or about Mr. McKee. I had not heard the name until you mentioned him a moment ago. Could it be, though, that this McKee attempted to rob or exploit some lost tribe, and Mr. Trask objected?"

"That is *exactly* the sort of thing McKee might have done," I acknowledged. "Exactly." This suggestion fit the available facts so perfectly that it seemed almost a certainty.

"Then is your curiosity satisfied?"

I had no immediate answer for that, as I did not know myself. If Gabriel Trask was neither the mastermind of a cabal of assassins, nor the mysterious companion of a harmless and beloved madman, was there any real justification for seeking him out?

"I think we will need to consider this further," Betsy said, startling the two of us.

Ah How nodded, in a peculiar movement that was almost like a small bow, and I realized how rude I had been in my focus on getting answers. "Where are my manners?" I said. "Ah How, this is my companion – my assistant – Miss Elspeth Vanderhart."

"I am honored, Miss," he said, and this time there was nothing small or indefinite about his bow.

Betsy curtseyed, a trifle awkwardly.

Ah How asked, "Could it be, Mr. Derringer, that it is *she* who is being followed?"

Betsy threw me a glance.

"I don't know," I said. "I don't know why anyone would be following *either* of us."

"Could they be in Mr. Trask's employ?" Betsy asked. "Perhaps word reached him that we were looking for him, and he was concerned about our intentions."

"That seems quite unlikely," Ah How replied. "As of my most recent information, Mr. Trask is in Los Angeles, hundreds of miles from here."

"Then it's a mystery to us both," I said. "And a rather troubling one."

"Do you have enemies?"

"None I am aware of – at least, none who are still alive." As I finished that sentence I realized it sounded rather more belligerent than I had intended; I had meant it as a simple statement of fact, but it came out as a threat.

"Could it be that these people are looking for Mr. Trask and hope that you will lead them to him?"

"Perhaps," I said, "but until a moment ago I had no idea where he might be."

"They may not know that."

"Would they not have asked *you*?"

"That would depend what they already know."

I nodded. "You said, sir, that you thought Mr. Trask to be in Los Angeles."

"Before we discuss this any further, Mr. Derringer, there is another matter I think we must address."

"Oh?"

"I think I have been of some service to you?"

"Indeed, very much so!"

"I mentioned that Joshua Norton was not blessed with earthly goods and was in fact quite poor by most reckoning. I am perhaps better off than he was, but I am not wealthy."

"Oh, of course!" But then I stopped. While he clearly wanted payment, I had no idea at all of what sum would be appropriate. Obviously, more than the dollar I had given the man who introduced us, but how much more? I fumbled a half-eagle from my pocket and glanced at it. "And what would you say your time is worth, sir?"

A finger flickered toward the coin. "That would be sufficient."

"I hope you will find me to be generous, rather than merely sufficient." I added a second half–eagle and presented them both.

He accepted the coins, then bowed. When he straightened up, he said, "I understand that after the emperor's death Mr. Trask decided to abandon our world entirely and went to live among the tunnel dwellers beneath Los Angeles."

I blinked. "Tunnel dwellers?" I reviewed what I knew of the deserts of southern California, and said, "You mean the lizard people? I had not realized their tunnels extended under the town of Los Angeles."

"I have heard them called that; I do not think they like that name. They are humans, not lizards, and they call themselves the Skyless."

"Do they? I had not known that. And Mr. Trask has gone to live with them?"

"That was his intent when last we spoke."

"Then am I to take it that they are not hostile to outsiders?"

Ah How shook his head. "Mr. Trask served well as the emperor's ambassador to their nation. I do not think others would be treated as kindly as he. If they wanted to conduct commerce with the rest of us, they are free to do so, yet they remain in their tunnels and are thought by many to be extinct, if indeed they are acknowledged to have ever existed at all."

That was an excellent point.

"Thank you," I said. "Is there anything else you think I should know?"

"Oh, many things, I am sure, Mr. Derringer. But if you mean is there anything else I think I should *tell* you, I cannot say there is."

"Then again, Mr. How, I thank you, and I wish you a good day." I tipped my hat to him.

He bowed one last time in return, then turned and ambled away to the west.

Betsy and I watched him go. Then I asked, "Shall we return to the hotel, or take luncheon at Martin & Horton's?"

"I would say return to the Palace," she said. "I think we have things to discuss that do not need an audience."

"I cannot disagree," I said. I offered her my arm, and we headed across the park to Kearny Street.

Chapter Seven

Our Mysterious Pursuers

W e were dining in the American Room at the Palace when a bellboy approached our table. "Mr. Derringer?" he asked.

I acknowledged my identity.

"A messenger brought this for you just now."

I accepted the paper and tipped him a dime; he hurried away.

The letter I held was sealed with red wax stamped in Chinese and was addressed in an unfamiliar hand. I looked at Betsy.

"Open it," she said. "I'm as curious as you are."

I did, and read this:

My dear Mr. Derringer,

After our conversation today I returned to my offices on Grant Avenue, and no more than an hour later I was accosted there by Mr. Smith – you will recall I pointed him out to you in Portsmouth Square. He questioned me at length about our discussion, relying on a mixture of threats and paltry payments to coax answers from me.

I am afraid the answers I gave him were not entirely truthful, and they were certainly not complete. I thought you would be interested to know that only a single mention was made of Mr. Trask's name; when I denied knowing any such person my answer was accepted without argument.

Most of his questions that were not about your own plans – about which I professed complete ignorance – were directed toward the history of Joshua Norton. Mr. Smith seemed to believe your visit to San Francisco was in pursuit of my late friend's imaginary treasure, or some other secret involving him that might yield a sufficient fortune to interest a professional adventurer such as yourself. I did nothing to dissuade him, for two reasons: First, because I did not believe he *could* be dissuaded, and second, because I thought it best to let him pursue what your people call a wild goose chase.

And a third reason, I confess, would be that I simply do not like the man.

I told him that you had asked me many of the same questions he did. I assured him I knew nothing of any treasure, and convinced him of my veracity in this matter by pointing out that had I known of any treasure I have had more than two years to claim it for myself and have not done so. However, I said nothing that I thought likely to persuade him that no treasure exists. Let him chase that goose.

Incidentally, he made no mention of your lovely companion at all.

In hopes that I have acted in a way you would find satisfactory, I remain,

                                                Your friend,

The signature was two Chinese characters, and I can only assume that they represented the name Ah How; a quick inspection showed me that they matched the characters on the sealing wax. Other than that the handwriting, while slightly out of the ordinary in its style, was beautiful and quite clear.

I passed the message to Betsy, who read it carefully.

"He writes better English than any of my father's students," she remarked. "Probably better than my own."

"He is an educated man and has been in this country a long time," I said.

"What do you suppose is going on? Who has hired this Mr. Smith, and why is he so interested in you?"

"I can only conjecture," I said. "I would guess that someone noticed my arrival in San Francisco, recognized me as an adventurer, observed my inquiries about Emperor Norton, and concluded that I must be seeking his supposed treasure."

"How could anyone think that poor man had some hidden treasure?"

"I cannot say. Perhaps they assume his madness extended to playing the miser, as well as the monarch?"

She shook her head. "Poor Emperor Norton."

I looked at the letter again, and frowned. "One thing strikes me here," I said. "It would seem that Mr. Smith *did* ask about Gabriel Trask, though he did not pursue the matter. But I have been cautious in mentioning Mr. Trask's name. I cannot recall speaking it to anyone in San Francisco except Ah How and the man who introduced us to him." I suddenly regretted never learning that man's name. "Have you heard me say it to anyone else?"

She thought for a moment, then said, "I have no knowledge of what you might have said in the Gentlemen's Grill, of course, nor to hotel staff when I wasn't there. You might have been overheard in Portsmouth Square; I'm not familiar with the acoustics there."

I was momentarily puzzled by what the term "acoustics" might mean in reference to a public park; every so often Betsy's background in science and engineering would crop up in ways that baffled me. In this case, though, I concluded she meant the ease with which one might be overheard from various locations, as in the assorted famous "whispering galleries" around the world.

Before I could comment, though, she continued, "Other than that, the last place I heard you tell someone you were looking for Gabriel Trask was when you spoke to Teddy Hancock on the train."

"Oh," I said. "*Oh*." I remembered Teddy Hancock's behavior in Ogden, and the other men I had seen him talking with. Perhaps he had not believed me when I said there was no money to be had in my current quest and had hired Messrs. Smith and Bowlby to investigate.

But I had not mentioned Emperor Norton to him, so far as I could recall. Someone had clearly been observing me in San Francisco, as well. Had Smith himself learned I was asking about Emperor Norton, and assumed that was my real target, and Trask's name a mere smokescreen?

That would be rather amusing, if so, since the only reason I had sought out the emperor's acquaintances was to find out what they knew about Mr. Trask. My pursuers, whoever they were, had apparently gotten everything precisely backward. Let them search for the emperor's new clothes if they wished!

"You think he's involved?" Betsy asked.

"I think he must be," I replied. Then I reconsidered. "Either that, or our nameless friend from the square saw an irresistible opportunity." I shrugged. "I don't suppose it really matters. What matters is that someone thinks I know something about an imaginary treasure. I can't very well lead them to something that doesn't exist, can I?"

"Then what *are* you going to do?"

"I don't know," I admitted. "It seems I may have already accomplished my goal. If Ah How is to be trusted, and I have no reason to think he is not, then Gabriel Trask is an ally of the lizard people who live in tunnels beneath the southwestern deserts, and his conflicts with Reverend McKee were presumably the result of some attempt McKee made to interfere with them. The mystery is solved. But I do not think I am ready, as yet, to simply go home. To come so far and stay for so brief a time seems...foolish? Inefficient?"

"Both," she agreed. "I'm not ready, either."

"You don't think your parents are ready to be reasonable?"

She shook her head. "I don't," she said. "Particularly if I come home and tell my mother that I did nothing on this adventure except buy clothes."

I smiled at that.

"Do you think...are you absolutely *sure* Emperor Norton had no hidden wealth?"

"Quite sure," I said. "Need you even ask? Half of San Francisco has been looking for some sign of it for three years now and has turned up exactly nothing. The man who was perhaps his best friend in the world says there is nothing to find."

"We could go back to Ogden to see what Teddy Hancock is up to."

"He has quite a significant head start on us, while we have no idea what he's after."

"All right, then, if we eliminate *those* ideas, and you don't have something better, that just leaves a trip to Los Angeles to see what Gabriel Trask is really up to, and whether Ah How was right."

I had wondered when she would state the obvious. "Would you be willing to attempt it?"

"I wouldn't mind giving it a try."

I nodded, then folded up the letter and slipped it inside my jacket. "That has the advantage of making it harder for our friend Smith to keep watch on us."

"Mr. Smith, and Mr. Bowlby, and whoever they're working for."

I picked up my knife and fork. "Indeed," I said, as I cut myself a bite of steak.

Alas, the letter and subsequent conversation had let it grow cold, but we made a meal of it anyway.

We spent the remainder of the evening making rather half-hearted plans. We agreed that we were in no hurry and had had enough of railroads for the present and would therefore take a steamer to San Pedro, that being the closest port to Los Angeles. Beyond that we had little to go on. We had come to San Francisco because I had been told Mr. Trask had worked for Emperor Norton, but I had no names to use in seeking him out in Los Angeles. I had a general idea of where some of the entrances to the hidden realm of the lizard people might be found, from my studies in the adventurers' geography, but none of the *exact* locations, and none of the entrances I recalled were in Los Angeles itself. The information could probably be found in the Pierce Archives, but those were in New York, with no branch office or equivalent operation known to me in either San Francisco or Los Angeles. I did not know anyone in Los Angeles personally and did not feel myself in a position to further impose on anyone in San Francisco. I thought I had heard that the Order of Theseus had a small office here, but I was not sure, and I had never gotten around to actually *joining* the Order in New York, so I did not think I would be in a position to exploit the Order's resources should I find it.

The evening was well advanced, and I was considering suggesting that we retire, when Betsy asked, "Couldn't you wire Mr. Snedeker and ask him to consult the archives for you?"

I blinked, and may even have gaped at her, before gathering my wits and saying, "Of course I could! I'm a fool not to have thought of it sooner. Thank you, my dear. I shall do precisely that in the morning."

"Sometimes, Tom, I think I may be better at this adventuring business than you are!"

"I rather think that if you chose to pursue it seriously you would rapidly leave me in the dust."

"Lucky for you, then, that I have no intention of pursuing it seriously." She laughed, and I smiled in return, even as I realized it was the first time I had heard her laugh since she first appeared on my mother's doorstep weeks before.

In the morning we made our way to the telegraph office once again, where I wired my questions to Mad Bill Snedeker. Since we were there, I also sent a message to my mother, assuring her that we were well, and were making good progress, and would be leaving for Los Angeles shortly.

Betsy's wire to her mother was surprisingly brief, and I quote it here in its entirety:

STILL FINE – STOP. LOS ANGELES NEXT – STOP.

Apparently she either did not wish to speak to her at length, or did not want to waste my money.

From there we headed down to the pier, where we discovered the next steamer bound for Los Angeles would not depart for another three days; this time of year they sailed only twice a month. Most people preferred the train, it seemed. We booked passage, then returned to the hotel.

We were now free to do as we pleased until our ship was ready to board, so we spent the following days in exploring the city and seeing the sights. We did stop in for a cup of tea with Ah How – we did not have an address, but knowing he was located on Grant Street, a few polite questions brought us to his door, and we were able to thank him for his letter and his other kindnesses.

We saw Mr. Bowlby once or twice, and I thought I caught a glimpse of Mr. Smith once as he vanished into a doorway, but we gave them no heed. Let them observe us, if they chose; we were doing nothing of consequence and had nothing to hide.

Betsy continued with her shopping. She was not at all extravagant, but I noticed the bills were beginning to add up.

The day before our scheduled departure, as we returned to the Palace, the desk clerk called to me.

"A telegram, Mr. Derringer."

I accepted it eagerly, and saw that it was from New York, as I had hoped. I unfolded and read it.

It was quite long; Mad Bill Snedeker must have spent a small fortune sending it. It answered all my questions, though.

As I had remembered, there were six known tunnel entrances scattered across California and the Arizona and New Mexico territories. I had not been certain of this, but the telegram confirmed that none of them were in Los Angeles itself. The nearest was in the San Gabriel Mountains, well east of town; the telegram provided the exact location in surprising detail, explaining that the information came from the Gabrieleno Indians, who had once traded with the lizard people there. I found the tribal name's similarity to Mr. Trask's Christian name an interesting coincidence.

That the precise location was known was fortunate, since four of the six entrances could only be narrowed to a general area rather than an exact spot, but that it was so far from the town was a disappointment. Still, it would give us a starting point. I showed the telegram to Betsy.

"Ah How said Mr. Trask was living beneath Los Angeles," she said.

"But there aren't any tunnel entrances in Los Angeles. At least, not any that are listed in the Pierce Archives."

She frowned.

"We'll just have to hope the tunnels all connect up," I said. "Or that the lizard people at this location can direct us to an entrance to tunnels under Los Angeles.

"I suppose so. And really, if we don't find Mr. Trask, it's no great catastrophe – *he* isn't trying to conquer the world."

"Well, not so far as we know."

She laughed. Her mood definitely seemed to have improved of late; I think the knowledge that we had learned Mr. Trask's whereabouts without hardship or violence and that we would not be returning her to New Jersey for a while yet was responsible.

The next morning we sent our luggage to the pier and checked out of the Palace. I doubted we would find so fine a hostelry in Los Angeles and said as much to the clerk.

He surprised me by saying, "Oh, you'll find nothing like the Palace, but the United States on North Main Street isn't bad, nor is the St. Elmo. The Pico House has the reputation, but good luck getting a room there!"

I had not expected anyone in San Francisco to be so knowledgeable about lodgings practically at the far end of the State of California, but the clerk saw my surprise, and said, "I talk to a good many travelers, sir, and I listen to what they tell me, so I can pass it on to others like yourself."

"Of course," I said. "Thank you!"

And with that we left our temporary residence and made our way to the pier, where we boarded our ship and were shown to our cabin – which, due to the limited accommodations aboard, we would share, a fact I hoped that Professor and Mrs. Vanderhart would never learn. We inspected the room and our baggage and found them both satisfactory, then went back out on deck to watch our departure.

As the ship pulled away from the dock I saw a familiar flat-brimmed hat. Mr. Smith was standing on the pier, watching us go. I could not resist; I waved to him, then formed a trumpet of my hands and called, "Farewell, Mr. Smith! Best of luck in your treasure hunt!"

To my surprise, he called back, "Goodbye, Mr. Derringer – for now!" Then he turned and shouldered his way through the crowd.

We watched him go, and then watched the city itself fall away and dwindle behind us as the steamer turned west and sailed out through the Golden Gate.

Chapter Eight

We Reach the San Gabriel Mountains

The cruise from San Francisco to San Pedro was not without excitement; we were caught in a storm – just a squall, really – off the coast just south of a village called San Simeon, and while the captain assured the passengers that we were never in any real danger, he altered course to keep us well away from all known hazards to navigation and slowed the engines to further reduce the chance of mishap, adding significantly to the duration of the journey. We were at sea almost four days in all, where the norm was somewhere between two days and three, but we arrived in San Pedro unharmed.

With the recommendations from the desk clerk at the Palace in mind, once we had made our way ashore and taken the train from San Pedro into Los Angeles itself, we took rooms at the United States Hotel on North Main Street. It was not particularly large or modern, being built in the style of two decades past and rising a mere three stories behind a fairly narrow facade, but the rooms were comfortable and well appointed.

I knew that ten years before Los Angeles had been a notoriously rough town, but that was said to be largely in the past; still, I thought it advisable to wear my revolver on my belt, rather than keeping it packed away, and I made a point of stopping in at a local shop and buying Betsy a double-barreled derringer and a box of cartridges for it.

I hated to do it; the similarity of my name to Henry Deringer's had always been a source of irritation, and the use of my family's name to designate the products of his imitators (with the double R, as distinguished from the single R and capital initial of the genuine article) was downright annoying. Nonetheless, it was the most practical weapon to provide for Betsy's self-defense, as it could be easily concealed on her rather diminutive person and would not weigh her down.

She accepted it without argument and reviewed the device's operation with the salesman before tucking it away out of sight.

When we had secured lodging and provided for our defense, we found a telegraph office and once again reassured our mothers. That done, we set about acquainting ourselves with the city.

It was larger and more populous than I had realized, sprawling over an extensive stretch of flat plain, and up into surprisingly steep brush-covered hills and canyons to the north. It struck me as entirely possible that an entrance to the tunnels of the lizard people – or rather, the Skyless – could be somewhere in those hills, completely undetected.

Or perhaps Ah How was mistaken, and Mr. Trask's new home lay beneath empty desert somewhere east of the city, rather than under the city itself.

We did not learn much that first day. On the next I continued to study Los Angeles itself, but also discussed matters with the gentlemen at the hotel's front desk, both staff and casual visitors. I asked if anyone knew a Gabriel Trask – I described him as an adventurer like myself, one who was thought to be seeking a lost treasure.

The men I spoke with were fascinated to learn I was a professional adventurer. In San Francisco it made me just another of the city's numerous eccentrics, but here I was a rarity to be admired. I was able to trade tales of adventure for the information I wanted – what there was of it; no one knew anything of Mr. Trask.

Of course, even for the little I learned, my own adventures were not yet extensive enough to fill the demand, so I drew on some of my father's, as well.

I discovered that the location Mad Bill Snedeker had given me was almost forty miles away, more than halfway to the inland town of San Bernardino; it would take two days just to get to the general vicinity, and we could not expect to find any sort of lodging there. A tent and camping gear would be required.

My funds were becoming depleted by this point, and I found it necessary to wire Tobias Arbuthnot for more money so that we could purchase camp supplies and a pair of horses. The money arrived that same afternoon, and I begin compiling a list of what we would need.

This was when I discovered that Betsy did not want to ride horseback. While I had thought a certain minimum level of horsemanship was necessary for any civilized member of our society, male or female, Betsy insisted that this, like cooking and sewing, was a basic skill she had never acquired. She had always traveled in carts, wagons, buggies, boats, and trains when her own two feet were not adequate – oh, or airships. I remembered her in Mexico, bounding across the jungle canopy, supported by hydrogen balloons, and wondered that a woman who would dare such a thing balked at climbing onto a horse's back, but balk she did. She insisted we should buy a wagon, pointing out that this would allow us to bring more equipment than we could load on two riding horses, even if we added a pack mule.

"If you intend to be an adventurer, you'll eventually need to learn to ride," I chided her.

"Yet another reason I don't want to be an adventurer," she retorted.

I had no reply to that.

In truth, once I looked at the complete list of what I thought we might need, buying a wagon seemed to be the more sensible option, so I acquiesced. Acquiring the wagon and everything else we needed took another two days. I also arranged storage at the hotel for those portions of our baggage that would be of no use on the journey; there was no point in overloading the wagon.

We were well into October, but the weather remained warm and for the most part sunny; it seemed unnatural to those of us more acquainted with northerly climes, but made for easier travel. We encountered no difficulties in setting out to the east.

As we rode the terrain, never lush, grew more barren; this was dry country, and we were heading out into desert, not unlike what we had flown over between Flagstaff and Phoenix the previous year. There were scattered ranches and even small villages wherever water could be found, but for the most part the land seemed empty and desolate, with greenish-brown brush covering the hills to our left, and bare flat earth to our right.

There were other people on the road, in both directions; we greeted the westbound travelers politely, and also acknowledged the horsemen who overtook us going east – some of whom we saw more than once, when they stopped to rest and we passed them. Despite the area's reputation for violence, no one seemed hostile or even unfriendly.

Betsy kept glancing behind us, but did not say anything of what she saw there.

Late on the first day of travel, as the sun was setting behind us, we came across a vineyard nestled against the base of the San Gabriel Mountains; from my conversations in Los Angeles I guessed this was a property a man named Joe Phillips had bought the previous year, in hopes of establishing a town. It seemed as good a place to make camp as any, so we found a sheltered area and pitched our tent for Betsy, while I slept in the wagon – by her choice, as I would have thought the reverse a safer arrangement.

In the morning we gathered ourselves up and continued to the east. I began looking for landmarks and checking my compass, which slowed us a little.

It was as I checked a particular outcropping against a written description I had received that Betsy remarked, "I think we're being followed."

I looked up, startled. "What?"

"That man back there – he was behind us most of yesterday, too."

I glanced back in the direction she indicated and saw that there was indeed a horseman riding behind us, perhaps as much as half a mile back. He was wearing a broad-brimmed hat that shaded his face, and his clothes were dark and undistinguished. His mount was a bay horse, but I could not make out any further details.

"He's been matching our speed," Betsy said. "Everyone else has fallen back or caught up and passed us, but he's always there, about the same distance away."

I started to ask if she was certain, then thought better of it; Betsy was not given to foolish imaginings. I frowned, and checked that my Colt was loaded and secure in its holster.

"If he is, he's wasting his time," I said.

"Are you going to do anything about it?"

"I don't see what there is to do."

Betsy did not seem particularly satisfied with this response, but apparently could not think of a better one.

We rode on, and around mid–afternoon I recognized one of the landmarks I had been watching for. I had been afraid I might miss it, but when at last I spotted it, just where I thought it should be, it was unmistakable. I hope my readers will forgive me if I am not more specific than that, but I do not wish to encourage anyone to seek out the ancient tunnels we hoped to find.

"There," I said, pointing. Betsy looked, and nodded. I pulled the left rein and swung our team off the road.

In a surprisingly short time we reached a slope too steep for the wagon; we stopped, got out, chocked the wheels, and unhitched the horses. I was about to head on up toward where the tunnel opening should be when Betsy tugged at my sleeve. I turned to see what she wanted.

She said simply, "Look," and pointed to the west.

The sun was on the horizon. Despite the deceptive warmth, it was late October and the days were growing shorter. If we wanted to have daylight to pitch the tent, we needed to make camp immediately.

"Right," I said. I paused and scanned the area, looking for any hazards that might endanger a camp in that particular spot, and for a water source other than the keg in the wagon.

I saw neither hazards nor water, but I did see a tethered horse at the foot of the slope, and a man in a broad–brimmed black hat standing beside it and looking up at us.

"Do you suppose that's Mr. Smith?" I asked, pointing. "He could have come by train and found us."

"I think it must be," Betsy replied. "Who *else* would be following us?" She glanced up the slope. "He probably thinks we're after the emperor's treasure here."

"Joshua Norton never visited Los Angeles, let alone this wasteland," I said.

"Does *he* know that?" she retorted. "And maybe he thinks someone else hid the emperor's treasure for him."

"He's a fool," I said, then stepped to the wagon to lift out our tent.

The sunset was fading fast by the time we had our campsite properly set up; I lit a cookfire while Betsy rummaged through our supplies, looking for something that would serve as our supper. I had hoped to shoot a jackrabbit or some other small game, but had not seen anything suitable, leaving us to rely on salt beef and canned beans.

Once I had the fire lit I looked down the hillside. Our unwanted companion's horse was still there, but I saw nothing of its master, nor anything that could be a tent. Worried that he might be creeping up on us, I retrieved my Porro prism binoculars from our luggage. With their aid I spotted an occupied bedroll near the horse; apparently our pursuer had not brought a real shelter, but was not completely unprepared.

It struck me as slightly odd that he should already be tucked in for the night; had he eaten? Perhaps he wanted to rest while he could, in case we tried to slip away under cover of darkness.

That might, I thought, not be a bad idea. I did not like being followed.

I adjusted the binoculars and tried to get a look at our pursuer's head, and succeeded better than I had anticipated, getting a fairly clear view of his face, catching the last of the fading sunlight. It was unquestionably Mr. Smith.

He might be in his bedroll but he was awake, and staring up the slope at our own camp. It was entirely possible he could see my binoculars; I half expected him to wave to me.

He did not, and I lowered the glasses. I realized the fire was behind me, so he had probably not had as good a look at me as I had at him. "Betsy," I said quietly.

She put down the can opener and looked at me.

"That's Mr. Smith down there, all right," I said, holding up the binoculars to explain how I knew.

"I thought it must be," she murmured.

"He's settling in for the night. Probably intends to wake up before we can break camp."

"Yes."

"If I'm right, the opening into the lizard people's tunnels is less than a hundred yards up the slope. I could take a lantern and look for it while he's asleep, and maybe we could get down into the tunnels and slip away in the middle of the night. Underground it won't matter whether it's daylight or pitch black out here. Come morning, he wouldn't know where we'd gone."

"What about the horses?"

I opened my mouth to say that we could leave them, then closed it again. That wouldn't be right, leaving them. Even if someone found them...

And there was the wagon, and all our supplies.

"We could take a look, anyway," I said. "See whether the lizard people have guards or gates – assuming there really are lizard people; most of the stories I'd heard back east say they're extinct. If they really are there, maybe we could send a message with them to Mr. Trask."

She considered that for a moment; I couldn't see her face very clearly by firelight, but I could see how she held herself, and she was plainly thinking about it. Then she shrugged – I could see *that*.

"I won't stop you, if you want to try," she said. "But *I'm* not about to go gallivanting about in the dark on a hillside where you *know* there are holes we could fall through, with no idea how deep they are."

"I'll be careful!" I said – and was careful to keep my voice down, even now.

"Then please yourself."

I glanced down the slope again; Mr. Smith was scarcely visible in the gathering gloom. "Whatever we do," I said, "I think we had better keep watch, so that our friend down there can't get the drop on us."

"I won't argue with *that*," she said.

"I'll take the first watch, then."

"Fine – but let's eat some supper before anyone stands watch or goes to sleep, shall we?"

"Right," I said, and set about stirring beef and beans into a pot, while Betsy set up our folding tripod over the flames.

Chapter Nine

We Find the Entrance

The sky was beautifully clear, the stars sharp and bright, and I was able to keep time by them without pulling my watch from my vest pocket – practical astronomy had been one of the subjects I studied in my eight years of training to be an adventurer. I knew it to be a little after midnight when I decided to move around a little. Betsy had been asleep for hours, and there had been no sign of activity from Mr. Smith since we finished our supper; I had the night to myself.

I could have awakened Betsy to take her turn on watch, but I preferred to let her sleep; besides, now that we were so close to the next step in our search I was full of nervous energy and did not think I needed to rest. Moving as quietly as I could – and stealth was another area I had been trained in – I rose from my post, made my way to the wagon, and found one of our two lanterns. After making sure the oil reservoir was full I took a splint from the campfire and set it to the wick, then adjusted the flame to my liking before restoring the chimney. Moving cautiously, I set out up the slope, looking for the tunnel opening.

I thought I saw signs of an old trail, probably long abandoned, and I followed that, in hopes that it was one that had been used by those long–ago Gabrieleno traders. It was definitely heading the right direction.

I moved very slowly, not setting foot anywhere until I had shone the lantern on each spot and determined it to be solid ground. Thus, step by step, triangulating from the landmarks visible by starlight, I proceeded toward the location Mad Bill's telegram had described.

I thought I still had another dozen yards to go when the lantern's glow fell on a shadow under a stone outcropping, a shadow that did not disappear when the light struck it. I stopped abruptly and set the lantern down carefully. I broke a branch off a nearby bush – not a variety I recognized, but one that was common in the area – and lay down beside the boulder, then thrust the stick gently into that patch of darkness.

It penetrated without difficulty and did not touch bottom.

Moving cautiously, I slid forward a few inches and continued to probe that darkness until the hand holding the stick was elbow-deep into a hole beneath the stone. Moving the stick from side to side, I determined the opening to be wide enough for a big man's shoulders.

This was undoubtedly the tunnel entrance. I had been imagining something like the mouth of a mine, where a man could walk in upright, but that, I realized, had been foolish; if there were so obvious an entrance as that, the lizard people would not have remained as little known and mysterious as they were.

I drew my arm back, rearranged myself, and pushed the lantern into the opening. The light showed me the shape of the tunnel – a space beneath the boulder just large enough for a man to squeeze through that widened somewhat, into an oval perhaps three feet high and four feet wide, before slanting down into the hillside farther than I could see. The walls of this tube were smooth brownish stone – and obviously artificial, though I could see no seams nor chisel marks.

That was not a wide passage, to say the least. The idea of crawling down into it was not appealing in the least – but to turn back now, after coming so far, seemed cowardly.

Of course, I was not ready to venture into the depths; Betsy and the horses were sleeping perhaps two hundred feet down the hillside, and I could not simply vanish and leave them there. I withdrew, pulling the lantern out of the hole, then got to my feet and brushed myself off. Then I picked up the lantern and started back down toward the camp.

It was even slower going down than it had been coming up, because the risk of falling and tumbling down the slope was greater, but in a few moments I was back at our campsite, gently shaking Betsy's shoulder. I had taken a look with the binoculars and concluded that Mr. Smith was still in his bedroll, apparently asleep, and to ensure that did not change I held a finger to my lips where Betsy could not help but see me as soon as she opened her eyes.

"My turn?" she whispered, sitting up.

I had almost forgotten about standing watch, and it took a second or two before I realized what she meant. "I suppose it is," I said, as quietly as I could, "but I want to show you something."

"What is it?" she asked.

"I found the tunnel entrance," I said, pointing uphill.

"Tom!" she said. "You were just supposed to stand watch!"

"I got bored. Come on, I'll show you."

"It's the middle of the night!"

"So Mr. Smith won't see us, and honestly, I think it makes it easier to see inside the tunnel."

As I had hoped, that piqued her interest. Realizing she was not going to get any more sleep in any case, she sighed and followed me out of the tent. I had left the lantern burning by the flap; now I picked it up and said, "This way."

"Let me put my boots back on."

I could hardly argue with that, so I waited impatiently while she donned her footwear and retrieved a shawl from the wagon. Wrapping the shawl around her shoulders, she said, "Lead the way."

I did, and held the lantern so that it illuminated the shaft leading down into the mountainside. She stared for a moment, then said, "You intend to climb down *that?*"

"Well...yes," I said. "An adventurer's career does require getting dirty now and then."

"Yes, of course, but *that?* Sometimes, Tom Derringer, I think it's *you* who should be called mad and not Mr. Snedeker!"

"Is it really so terrible as all that?"

"*I* think so! Look how slick those sides are! And what if it turns downward further in? You'll slide right down and never get back out!"

I realized she had a point, but I was not about to give up. "I'll climb down a rope," I said. "You can anchor it to something up here and pull me out if I signal that I'm in trouble."

"Pull you out? Tom, I'm scarcely half your size!"

"Betsy, I've *seen* how strong you are, despite your sex and your size, and of course I'll be helping, pushing against whatever surface I can reach, or simply climbing the rope."

"What is there around here to anchor it to?" she demanded.

That, I had to admit, was a valid point. There were no trees, and the bushes and shrubs that abounded did not look strong enough to support my weight; if we tried to use one of those and I fell, the rope would most likely yank it out by the roots.

"We'll have to bring the wagon up here," I said.

Betsy looked around at the dark hillside – or really, to be fair, the dark mountainside – and demanded, "How?"

"I don't know!" I replied, rather more loudly than I had intended.

Betsy glanced warningly down the slope toward Mr. Smith's encampment.

"I'm sorry," I said, my voice lowered again. I looked up at the stone above the opening, then down into the darkness, where I could barely make out the shape of our wagon and the fading embers of our campfire. "How much rope do we have?" I asked.

"You bought it; you should know."

I had, in fact, bought a large coil of good hempen rope without paying much attention to just how much I was getting. I knew it was considerably more than a hundred feet. I had been thinking more in terms of leaving a trail, rather than lowering myself with it, but I knew that rope was a good thing to have for any number of reasons.

"It might be enough," I said, "to run up here and into the hole without moving the wagon at all."

"Tom," she said, "can't you just come back to camp and get some sleep? We can deal with this in the morning, and you'll be clearer headed after you've had some rest."

I was reluctant to acknowledge it, but she was right. There was no need to dive into the hole right away; for one thing, what if Mr. Smith were to wake up while I was down in the tunnel, and Betsy was up on the surface alone?

I realized I had not really planned this expedition very well at all. I had focused entirely on locating the entrance to the realm of the Skyless. I had expected to find a tunnel where we could simply walk in and find lizard people to talk to, rather than a narrow, sloping shaft, and I had *not* expected to be followed out here into the wilderness.

I did not think my father would be very impressed with me.

I came up with three or four possible approaches, but did not say anything about any of them; instead I agreed, "I'll get some sleep. We'll talk in the morning."

Together, we walked back down the slope to our camp, where I climbed into the wagon, pulled a blanket over me, and went to sleep.

When I awoke the sun was high in the east, and I found Betsy asleep by the ashes of our campfire – she had obviously dozed off while on watch.

There was no harm done, though; the wagon was undisturbed, the horses still tethered where we had left them. I looked down the hill and saw Mr. Smith sitting by his horse, holding a spoon and a bowl of something. His bedding was not visible; he had presumably rolled it up and put it away.

This, I decided, was ridiculous. There was no reason to go on pretending we didn't know he was there, and I didn't see any reason I couldn't have a few words with him. I left Betsy where she was while I fetched my Winchester from the wagon, straightened my clothes, and started down the slope.

Mr. Smith saw me, of course. He set down his bowl and got to his feet. He made no move toward the gun on his belt.

"Good morning," I called, when I was close enough to be sure he could hear me.

He tipped his hat, but did not speak.

"I've heard your name is Smith," I said, as I drew nearer. "Is that right?"

"That's what some folks call me," he replied.

"Would you care to tell me what brings you out here?"

He let out a bit of a laugh. "I could ask you the same."

"You could," I acknowledged. "But I don't see that it's any of your business. It looks to me as if you've been following me, though, and I'm curious as to why." I was no more than twenty feet away now, which seemed close enough; I stopped walking. I kept the rifle in my right hand pointed at the ground.

"Fact is, Mr. Derringer, I had more than one reason. Rather a collection of them, in fact."

"Would you care to tell me a few? You and that fellow Bowlby were following me back in San Francisco; what for?"

He smiled and shook his head. "Someone asked us to, of course."

"Teddy Hancock?"

"Teddy? No. I won't say he wasn't involved, but he wasn't the one who hired us; he's off chasing fairy stories in the Utah Territory somewhere."

"Then Hezekiah McKee? Did he survive somehow?"

He seemed genuinely startled. "Good Lord, I hope not! That man was a snake, and we're all better off if he's gone. I'd heard you shot him dead; are you telling me you didn't?"

"I wasn't the one who shot him," I said, "but I saw him die. Or at least I thought I did."

"Well, I haven't heard a word to the contrary."

"Who was it, then?" I shifted the rifle a little – I didn't mean it as a threat, exactly, but a reminder that this was not just polite conversation. "One of McKee's men?"

"Mr. Derringer, it's nothing to do with McKee. You were closer to the truth when you asked about Teddy Hancock."

"I'd appreciate it, Mr. Smith, if you'd get to the point."

He shrugged, keeping his hands well away from his gun belt. "If you insist. It seems that you spoke to Teddy at some point on your way west and told him you were bound for San Francisco on some mysterious errand involving Gabriel Trask.

Teddy mentioned this to some gentlemen of his acquaintance, and they became curious as to just what this errand might be. One of them wired me from Ogden and asked me to keep an eye on you, in case there was money to be made that you might be persuaded to share."

"I *told* Teddy there wasn't any money in it."

"I'm sure you did, but not everyone believed you. I can't speak for Mr. Hancock, but the gentleman who sent me that telegram thought you were merely disinclined to share. That's hardly unusual among adventurers, after all; your own father contrived to wind up richer than any of Darien Lord's other companions."

"He was more careful with his investments," I said, annoyed at his implication. "He never took more than his share; ask Bill Snedeker."

"Oh, I didn't mean to impugn his honesty! I never met the man, and his reputation is about as good as any adventurer could ask. But he did wind up with a goodly sum to his name."

"And your mysterious employer thought this might be a case of like father, like son? That I might be on the trail of some great treasure?"

"Exactly! And really, is that so very unlikely?" He smiled, but it was not an endearing expression.

"I can see how a fellow might think it's not, but the fact is I'm not in this for the money; as you said, my father did very well. I don't *need* money."

"It's a rare man who wouldn't like a little more, though."

I couldn't very well argue with that. "That's as may be," I said. "But in this particular case, I'm not after money."

"You're after this man Gabriel Trask."

"Yes."

"Seems to me, Mr. Derringer, that the two aren't mutually exclusive."

"And what would you know about Mr. Trask?"

"Well, I met him a few times."

That caught me by surprise, and I almost dropped my rifle. "You did?"

He nodded.

For a moment neither of us spoke; then he said, "I'm guessing, Mr. Derringer, that you did some research at the Pierce Archives."

"I did," I admitted "But I don't see what that has to do with it."

"You said you'd heard my name was Smith; well, that's what I call myself when I'm looking for work where I think it might be unwise to use my real name. Most folks assume it's not the name I was born with, and they're right. But I use other names at other times, and when I'm selling my reports to Dr. Pierce, I go by John Beckwith. Does that strike a chord, by any chance?"

It sounded familiar, but I could not place it immediately. "I can't say it does. But you say you sell reports to Dr. Pierce?"

"Indeed I do. Perhaps I have over-estimated the value he places on them, though, or perhaps Gabriel Trask is better known than I thought..."

"Oh!" I exclaimed, as my memory finally made the connection. "You were one of his sources! You and a woman..." I stopped, even though I now, after a few seconds' thought, remembered the name Felicity Samuels. There was no reason to reveal to Smith – or Beckwith, if that name was any more authentic – everything I knew.

"There was another? Someone else reporting to him about Trask?" Smith looked genuinely surprised, then smiled again, more broadly this time. "Well, who would have thought it?"

"You said that Trask was Emperor Norton's spymaster."

"I did," Smith agreed. "To the best of my knowledge, that's exactly what he was. And one reason I followed you was the hope that you would lead me to him, so that I might see just what's become of Emperor Norton's secret service. Even if you have not, in fact, learned the whereabouts of the late emperor's legendary treasure, unemployed spies can be valuable."

It was my turn to smile. "It's a shame, Mr. Beckwith, that you never earned Ah How's trust. You could have saved yourself a trip. There are no spies, and there is no treasure."

"You trust the old Chinaman?"

"I do."

"*I* never did."

"Indeed, that was my impression."

"If there is no treasure, and there are no spies, then what, Mr. Derringer, are you and your pretty assistant doing out here in the desert? I had assumed you either knew the location of some hidden valuables, or had arranged to meet someone here – perhaps Mr. Trask himself. When you came down here to speak to me, I thought perhaps you wanted to chase me away so that whoever you've come to see could approach you privately."

"We aren't meeting anyone out here," I said.

He shrugged.

"So let me see if I have this straight," I said. "You have spent the last two weeks following me all over San Francisco and halfway across the entire state of California because some acquaintance of Teddy Hancock suggested I *might* – I say, *might* – have information about some lost treasure."

"Well, that's a part of it. That's certainly what got me started. But you knew the name Gabriel Trask, which to the best of my knowledge not very many people do, and that got my own curiosity up. Mr. Trask met with the emperor several times and insisted on complete privacy for these meetings, and he would generally disappear for months at a time immediately after their little discussions, only to eventually turn up and do it all over again. Is it any wonder I assumed he was carrying out secret missions for His Imperial Majesty?"

"I suppose not," I acknowledged. "But I'm still trying to wrap my mind around this. You followed me out to the middle of nowhere because you thought I was meeting with Mr. Trask, or one of his theoretical underlings?"

"Or retrieving a treasure, or some clue to a mystery of some sort. Yes."

"You have the funds to waste this way?"

"Oh, I'm not spending my own money; Teddy Hancock's friends are still paying my expenses. They even gave me the train fare to Los Angeles. They don't know what you're doing, but they're convinced it's worth paying me to find out."

I considered this. It sounded foolish, but plausible. There was more than one case in my father's records of Darien Lord racing some other adventurer to a particular treasure.

And was it really any more foolish than traveling across the continent just to find out what a dead man's words had meant?

But if this was all true, what should I tell this Mr. Beckwith? Would he believe the truth? Should I tell him what Ah How had told me about Gabriel Trask? Should I explain that we were within a few hundred feet of an entrance to the tunnels of the lizard people?

I was turning this over in my mind, trying to decide what to say, when Betsy called from behind me, "Mr. Smith, would you care to join us for breakfast?"

Chapter Ten

An Addition to Our Party

"I will be blunt with you, Mr. Smith," I said, as I passed him a bowl of warmed-over beans. "I cannot decide what to do about you."

He smiled. "Well, I can't make the decision for you, but I'm relieved you don't seem inclined to shoot me."

Nettled, I said, "I haven't ruled it out."

Betsy gave a most unladylike snort. "You were never quick enough shooting *anyone*, Tom Derringer," she said.

"I'd forgotten the gun wasn't loaded!" I exclaimed. Which was not literally true; I had remembered, but had hoped I was wrong. "It's not a mistake I intend to repeat."

Of course, I was assuming she was referring to one specific instance; there might well have been other occasions when she thought I was too slow in resorting to violence.

Our guest clearly had no idea what we were talking about, but I saw the smile vanish from his face. "Now, wait a minute..." he began, as he set the bowl aside.

"Oh, don't worry," I said. "I'm not going to shoot you unless I must. It would upset Betsy's mother."

"I don't know whether she'd care if *you* shot him," Betsy said, "as long as *I* didn't."

"I think she would not consider me appropriate company for her daughter to keep if I were to shoot Mr. Smith here. At least, not unless he gave me far better reasons than he has to date."

Smith eyed us warily, clearly unsure whether we were joking – which in fact we were not. "I'd just as soon not get shot, no matter what Mrs. Vanderhart thinks," he said. He tried a smile. "And wouldn't *your* mother have something to say about it, Mr. Derringer?"

"*My* mother has no problem with such things," I said. "You forget who she married."

His smile disappeared completely.

"All right, then," he said. "What do you want of me?"

"Well, first," I said, "I'd like you to stop moving your hand toward your own gun. I don't think anyone would take it well if *you* shot either of *us*. Your employer would be disappointed if you killed the man who might have led you to a treasure."

His hand drew back.

"Next, I think we have talked quite enough about shooting one another. Following us might be rude, but it's not a capital crime, and you want us alive to lead you to whatever brought us here."

"Fine, then. What do you propose?"

"Can't we just tell him to go back to San Francisco and leave us alone?" Betsy demanded.

"And what makes you think he'd do it?" I asked her.

"Well, if he's being paid to follow us, can't we pay him to stop?"

Smith was smiling again. "First," I said, "I don't intend to start a bidding war. My family isn't so rich that I can throw money around without thinking about it. Second, what makes you think he wouldn't turn around and come after us again the moment he's out of sight, only being more careful not to be spotted?"

"I wasn't *trying* to not be spotted," Smith interrupted. Apparently I had stung his professional pride."

"You were at first. You stopped once you knew we'd seen you."

He started to argue, then caught himself. I was speaking the truth, and we all knew it.

"What do we do with him, then?" Betsy asked.

"We could just call it off and go home," I said.

"Back home? Oh, no. Not yet."

"We could go looking for some other adventure," I said. "Maybe go see what Teddy Hancock is up to in the Utah Territory."

"But we've come this far!"

"Yes, but to what end? We were just here to satisfy my curiosity, we don't actually have any *business* with Mr. Trask."

"Really?" Smith asked.

I glanced at him, mostly to be sure his hand was still well away from his gun. "Really," I said. "Hezekiah McKee thought I was working for Mr. Trask, so I wanted to see where he could have gotten such a notion."

"Honestly? That's it?"

"Is it so *very* unlikely, Mr. Smith?" Betsy asked coldly.

"Well, yes, ma'am, it is," he replied.

"We also had reason to stay clear of Betsy's parents," I said. "This venture gave us an excuse to put thousands of miles between them and ourselves."

"Tom! That's none of his business!" Betsy sounded genuinely shocked.

Smith considered that for a moment, looking at us with his head cocked a little to one side. Then he said, "That telegrapher really *couldn't* spell 'debauched.' Took me ten minutes to figure out what he meant. Cost me five dollars to get him to show me the telegrams you'd sent. Or decided not to."

"*That*, sir, is not why we are avoiding her parents." My voice was at least as cold as Betsy's. "I may have cause to shoot you after all, should you continue to imply anything of the sort."

He thought that over, carefully keeping his right hand up against his chest, nowhere near the pistol on his belt. "So there's really no treasure? You were just looking for an excuse to go west?"

"That's right."

"And you are not...doing anything inappropriate?"

I could see Betsy blushing. "We are not," I said firmly.

"Then why don't I join you? Another pair of hands might be useful, and if anyone questions Miss Vanderhart's presence, I can act as your chaperone."

This proposition startled me, but I could see a certain logic to it. Still, I did not like it. "Why should we trust you?" I asked.

"Why not?"

"Because you are...your reputation..."

"I'm an unsavory character," he said. "I won't deny it. But so what? If there's no treasure, you don't have anything worth stealing. I could kidnap you, I suppose, and try to get a ransom from your parents, but that's always a risky business, and you outnumber me."

"If you believe we aren't after a treasure," Betsy asked, "then why don't you just go back to San Francisco and leave us alone?"

"Because as long as I stay with you, those fools back north will keep paying me. Besides, I'm curious what's become of Trask now that old Norton's dead and gone; if you really know how to find him, I'd like to see him again."

Betsy and I exchanged glances. Then I beckoned her aside and told him, "Give us a moment."

He waved, and picked up his bowl of beans.

Our whispered discussion lasted long enough for our own breakfast to get cold, but kept circling back around to the same few arguments. If we were going to continue, there was no reasonable way to keep him from following us, and if he was coming, we might as well keep him close at hand. Neither of us really *liked* the idea, but we could see no better alternatives. Shooting him, while a possibility, did not seem better.

Finally we returned to camp, where I extended a hand to him. "Welcome to our company," I said. "Should I call you Smith, or Beckwith?"

"I'd prefer Beckwith, I think," he said, as he took my hand. "I use Smith for business, but it doesn't seem as if what we're doing together really qualifies. Now, what are we doing out here, halfway to San Bernardino?"

"I'll show you," I said.

We left Betsy in the camp while I led Mr. Beckwith up to the tunnel entrance. I knelt by the rock face and pointed it out to him.

He stared at it for a long moment, then asked, "What the devil *is* it?"

"Ever hear of the lizard people?" I said.

"The old stories the Hopi Indians tell? I've heard something."

"Well," I said, "that's an entrance to their tunnels. And according to Ah How, Mr. Trask went to live in the tunnels the lizard people built under Los Angeles."

"Under *Los Angeles*?" he said, astonished. "I thought their tunnels were out in Arizona, around Springerville."

"Well, they are," I said, a little startled by the extent of his knowledge, "but they're here, too. According to the Pierce

Archives there are six likely entrances to the tunnels, and two of those six are confirmed – this one, and one in Springerville."

"This isn't exactly Los Angeles, all the way out here."

"We're still in Los Angeles County," I said.

He straightened up and looked down the slope. "I wouldn't be too sure of that," he said. He shaded his eyes and scanned the horizon. "I'd put the county line over that way a couple of hundred yards." He pointed west. "And if I said they were under Los Angeles, I'd mean the city, forty miles from here."

"Well, none of the six entrances are in the city," I said. "This is the closest I could find. And I don't suppose Ah How knows much about the geography out here."

"So you think Trask is somewhere down this hole?"

"I do."

He stared at me for a moment.

"You don't need to come," I said. "You can go back to San Francisco and tell your employers you lost me."

"I probably should," he said, looking back at the tunnel. "But you've got my interest. No telling what's down there, is there? For all we know it's not the lizard people's tunnel at all, but Pegleg Smith's lost mine."

"Pegleg Smith? I thought that was on a butte in the Colorado Desert."

"It's supposed to be on a butte in the Colorado Desert, yes, and the Colorado Desert starts just a few miles over that way." He pointed to the southeast. "Old Smith told so many different versions of the story that it could have been anywhere within a hundred miles, though, and the butte might have just been a mountain. Like the one we're on."

"The Pierce Archives say this is the lizard people's tunnel."

"Well, maybe it is. And if so, there might be some interesting artifacts down there."

"I'm just looking for Mr. Trask."

"So you're planning to climb down there?"

I nodded.

"How?"

"With a rope and a lantern," I said.

He considered that. Then he nodded. "Let's see what's down there, then." He turned and headed back toward camp. I rose and followed.

It took most of the morning to get everything ready. We emptied the wagon, and with Mr. Beckwith adding some extra muscle we were able to shove it farther up the mountainside. We then secured the rope – which, according to the receipt, was a coil of 600 feet of five-strand hemp – to the wagon's frame. I looped the other end around my waist, lit the lantern, and after some consideration of my options I turned and let my legs down into the hole; I had decided that I was not going to be able to see much either way, and if I slipped and fell, I would rather land on my feet than on my head.

Then I looked up at Betsy and Mr. Beckwith, and it struck me that I was leaving her at this stranger's mercy.

She must have read my expression. She knelt down and whispered, "Don't worry about me; I can take care of myself."

I could scarcely argue with that. I began lowering myself into the shaft with one hand, holding the lantern in the other.

The initial opening was a tight squeeze, but it opened out quickly – though not very far. As I had seen before, the hole was only about three feet high and four feet wide. The passage was steep enough that I had no trouble pushing myself along, but not so steep that I ever slipped out of control; the stone sides were smooth, but not slick. I scraped over traces of sand every so often, but it was otherwise bare stone.

The oval of daylight at the top shrank as I slid down into the darkness. At first I could see Beckwith's hands paying out the rope, but before long I was too far down to make out such details.

There were small ridges in the stone under me, one every five or six feet, that I thought might have been intended as handholds and that caught some of the sand that had drifted in. I began to wish I had been counting them; the shaft seemed to go on endlessly, down into the darkness, and a count would have given me some sense of how far I had come. After the first several minutes I started to wonder whether six hundred feet of rope would be enough, especially since the connection to the wagon had used a portion of it.

I was on the verge of calling to be pulled back up when the shaft abruptly ended; instead of more of the sloping passage my feet suddenly emerged into empty air. I lost my grip on the latest of those inadequate handholds and slid down, out of control – for about three feet, whereupon my feet slammed into a hard horizontal surface, and the walls that had been so uncomfortably close around me vanished as the tunnel widened out around me. Rather than sliding down a diagonal shaft, I was standing upright.

I pulled the lantern down out of the mouth of the shaft and held it up, then looked around.

I was in a much larger tunnel now, a horizontal one. I was standing against one golden-brown stone wall, where the shaft I had just descended emerged about four feet above the floor – or rather, four feet above the step on which I stood. Four more sand-strewn steps led down to the tunnel floor.

In the light of my lantern I could see that where the entrance shaft had been frighteningly narrow, this new tunnel was comfortably broad. The walls and floor were all the same golden-brown stone, all fairly smooth. The ceiling was rounded, a barrel vault that extended for as far as I could see in either direction. The entrance shaft had run almost due north, as best I could judge, which meant this larger passage ran east and west, and in either direction it extended absolutely straight for as far as I could see; the lantern's light revealed no end, no curve, no features to mark one part from another.

It was eerily silent, even by the standards of the California desert. There was no wind rustling the sagebrush down here, no distant birds calling nor insects chirping – but then I heard something. It took me a few seconds to recognize it as a human voice calling down the long entry shaft. I leaned into the opening and listened.

"Tom!" I heard Betsy call, her voice faint and distorted by the echoes of that long tube.

"I'm all right!" I called back. "I've reached the bottom!" I hesitated, then called, "I'm going to look around!"

"What?"

Apparently my words were as distorted as her own. I did not bother to repeat myself, but descended the four steps to the tunnel floor and lifted the lantern high.

This tunnel was relatively huge. When I heard about the lizard people's tunnels I had pictured something like an ordinary mine shaft, but this was grander than that. My best guess was that it measured perhaps twenty feet across, or slightly more, and twenty-five or thirty feet from the floor to the top of the curved ceiling. It was hard to judge, though, without anything to give me a scale.

And it was empty. There were no drawings on the wall, no paint, no pottery, no artifacts of any description; just bare stone. What on Earth had the lizard people built it for?

That assumed that the lizard people *had* built it. There was nothing in sight that suggested lizards to me – or for that matter, people, unless you counted the four steps leading up to the diagonal shaft. They were of a size and proportion appropriate to human feet.

I started to walk westward, to see whether the tunnel became any less featureless further from the entry, and was stopped before I had gone a dozen yards – the rope around my waist had gone taut. The entire length had been paid out.

For a moment I had the mad idea of untying myself to go exploring, but I came to my senses quickly enough; the lantern's oil supply would not last forever, and if it gave out while I was a goodly way from the entrance shaft I might never find my way out. Instead I climbed back up those four steps, placed the lantern up as far into the shaft as I could reach, then put both my hands on the rim of the shaft and heaved myself up. Once I was in the entry shaft, I gave the rope the three tugs that were the signal I was coming back up.

Chapter Eleven

We Enter the Tunnels

The journey up the shaft was more difficult than the descent, but less frightening. I knew where I was going, and I knew that there were no turns or forks to worry about, just a long, straight passage, with handholds – inadequate handholds, but handholds – every few feet. And I could pull myself up the rope; I didn't need to rely on keeping my footing on the smooth stone. It was reassuring to know that if I slipped back, a grip on the rope would keep me from going too far.

Someone at the top of the shaft pulled up a little of the rope every so often, dragging me upward, but not really enough to help me very much.

It was not really terribly long before I glimpsed the light of day above me, which provided additional incentive. I took a moment to blow out the lantern, rather than waste oil, once I judged the daylight to be roughly equal to the lantern's glow.

Every so often I would see a dark shape obscure part of the opening, and I could tell from the shape that it was someone's head, but I had no way of distinguishing Betsy from Mr. Beckwith. Whoever it was did not wear a hat, which made me suspect it was Betsy; Mr. Beckwith seemed very fond of that broad–brimmed black hat of his.

At last I reached the top, but the angles were such that it was difficult to squeeze through the opening from below. I reached my hands out, and the others gave me their assistance, Betsy on my left and Beckwith on my right, each grabbing an arm and heaving.

It was strange to be back in the open air and sunlight after my long climb; the very air felt different, if only because it was moving, while the air in the tunnels was utterly still. The sun was hot on my face, the ground beneath my feet uncomfortably uneven.

"What's down there?" Beckwith asked, as he hauled up the rope that hung behind me. "Did you find any sign of the lizard people?"

I shook my head. "I found a tunnel," I said. "This shaft comes out in a big tunnel. It's at least fifteen feet across, maybe more, and it runs as far as I could see in both directions, east and west."

"It's deserted?"

"Completely. No lizard people, just bare stone – no painting on the walls, no broken pottery, nothing." I smiled at him. "No treasure."

"And no Mr. Trask," Betsy remarked.

"No Mr. Trask," I agreed.

"How far did you explore?"

"I only had about thirty feet of rope left, and I didn't want to risk untying."

"Thirty feet?" Beckwith glanced at the heap of rope that lay piled up beside the tunnel entrance, at the length he held, and at the portion that still trailed down into the darkness.

"About that."

"We paid out nearly five hundred feet."

"That's right. It's a long way down."

"And you think it was really built by the lizard people?"

"I do."

"Think any of them are still down there? Some of the stories say they died out, some aren't so sure."

"Well, I've heard there were still a few left as of a couple of years ago." I did not explain that Gabriel Trask had been Emperor Norton's ambassador to their nation. I saw no reason to give Mr. Beckwith any more information than necessary.

"What's your next move, then?"

"I thought I'd do a little exploring. But I'll want more supplies – lamp oil, in particular. And I don't want to leave the horses out here untended."

"We're here," Betsy said, gesturing at Beckwith.

I did not mention that I was not happy about leaving her alone with him for any length of time. Instead I said, "Well, I wasn't sure you would want to stay. I expect I'll be down there for at least a day or two."

She stared at me. "Are you serious?"

"I told you, that tunnel goes farther than I can see."

"Yes, but... surely a few hours should be enough!"

I shook my head. "I don't know. The legends say the lizard people had an entire city down there somewhere. And Mr. Trask is supposed to be down there somewhere, as well."

Beckwith frowned. "Seems to me, Mr. Derringer, you didn't have much of a plan, if you're only now thinking about this."

"You're absolutely right, Mr. Beckwith," I replied. "I didn't know what I'd find. I had the location of an entrance to the tunnels, but that's all I knew. I might have found it caved in, or I might have found lizard people guarding it and ready to spear me if I set foot inside their doors, I might have found a labyrinth full of booby traps, or...well, anything you can imagine. I didn't try to guess. I came out here to see what I'd find, and what I found was a long hole in the ground leading to a long straight tunnel. Now that I know that, I want to see where that tunnel goes. I'm making this up as I go, Mr. Beckwith – that's one of the things adventurers *do*."

"You know, Tom, there's no rule that says adventurers *can't* plan ahead," Betsy said.

I had no answer for that.

"So you're planning to go back down and explore," Beckwith said. "Alone."

"That was my intent," I acknowledged, "but if you'd care to join me, I'd have no objection. We'd need to see Miss Vanderhart was safe first, of course."

"Oh, I'm coming, too!" Betsy said. "I want to see these mysterious tunnels for myself."

I looked down at the tunnel entrance. "It's a long way down," I said. "Quite a climb. And if we're all down there, there won't be anyone to pull us back up in an emergency."

"You *climbed* back up," Betsy said. "We only pulled you in maybe fifty feet."

"I know. But still..." I considered it, then shrugged. Compared to some of the risks my father and his companions had taken, this was nothing. "All right," I said. "But we do need to get more lamp oil, and more food, and find somewhere to leave the horses. I suppose we'll have to go back to Los Angeles."

"No, we don't," Beckwith said. "Don't be ridiculous. There's a little town called Pomona not half a day's ride south of here; we can get what we need there."

I looked at him. "Mr. Smith, how is it you know that? I thought you were from San Francisco."

"I've lived in San Francisco for the last few years, but I didn't grow up there, and I spent two years in this area before I settled down. That's why I came myself, instead of sending someone local to keep an eye on you."

I nodded. "All right, then," I said. "We'll go to this Pomona and see what we can do. Lead the way!" I got to my feet and began untying the rope.

"Tom," Betsy said, "what about the supplies we already *have*?" She gestured down the slope at the clutter we had unloaded from the wagon.

"You know, Mr. Derringer," Beckwith said, "we won't have a wagon down there. We'll only have what we can carry with us."

That was obvious with even a moment's thought, and I was very annoyed with myself for not having yet realized it. "Right you are," I said. "We'll go through what we have, see what we need, and *then* we'll take the horses and the wagon back to Pomona."

No one found any reason to argue with that, and we set about putting my words into action. We sorted the supplies into three categories: Things we would need to carry with us in the tunnels, such as food, water, weapons, and oil; things we would have no use for underground, such as tents and rain gear, that we would leave in Pomona; and things that we would take down to the tunnel and leave cached there in case we needed them later, such as trade goods and additional food and water.

Everything in the middle category was set aside, ready to be loaded back into the wagon; the others were divided into four loads, one for each of us and the fourth to be cached. I took this last and made another trip down the shaft, pulling it down behind me, and depositing it at the bottom of those four steps. Maneuvering it while holding the lantern was challenging at first, but I quickly got the hang of it.

Once I had delivered it to the main tunnel my instincts rebelled at leaving it there unguarded, but I told myself that was foolish; there was no sign of life, human or otherwise, down there. What's more, if something *did* disturb it, that would be very useful information to have when we returned.

When I returned to the surface once more I found Betsy waiting with her pack at her feet.

"I'm not going to haul this to Pomona and back," she said. "I'm going down now, and I'll leave it down there. For one thing, I want to be sure I *can*, before we go any further."

That sounded very sensible, though a part of me was unhappy at the thought of this lovely young woman making such a climb unassisted.

"Shall I follow you down, in case you need help?" I asked.

She glanced at Beckwith, then said, "Let me try it on my own first."

I acquiesced, and watched as she lowered herself down into the shaft. I lifted her pack, waited until she had arranged the lantern to her liking, then gently placed it above her.

It took her a moment to arrange everything, as it had for me, and all I could see was the pack blocking the hole, but then it began descending, sinking gradually down until it was out of sight.

Beckwith watched, as well, and when there was no longer anything to be seen asked me, "Who goes next?"

"I will," I said. "You'll go last."

Betsy's return took so long that I was becoming worried, but at last the rope jerked three times, and rather than force her to make the long climb on her own I began pulling it up, hand over hand.

"Not too fast," Beckwith urged, as the line began to more seriously resist my efforts, and I realized he had a point – while I had wanted to spare her strength, it would not be comfortable to be dragged bodily over the stone handholds and scattered sand. Perhaps if she had been wearing her canvas and leather engineer's gear it would have made sense, but she was dressed in an ordinary frock, having left her more specialized attire at home in New Jersey. I slowed my efforts, keeping the rope reasonably taut but not heaving Betsy upward against her will.

At last she drew near enough that I could hear her movements, and I called down, "Shall I pull you up?"

"No, I'll manage," she replied, the words somewhat distorted by the echoes from the walls of the shaft, but still intelligible.

And finally her head appeared in the opening, and Beckwith and I both helped her out and to her feet. She untied the rope from around her waist and tossed it aside; we stepped away, to give her breathing room. As she brushed off her skirt she said, "That is a *very* long climb!"

"Indeed," I replied. I picked up the rope and looped it around my own waist, then knotted it. I grabbed my own pack and glanced at Beckwith. "I might be able to manage both at once and save you the trip. I couldn't do it coming up, but going down should be possible."

"No, I'm curious to see this tunnel of yours," he said. "Though perhaps I could follow you down immediately, rather than waiting until your return."

I looked at Betsy. "Would you have any objection to that? It would leave you alone up here."

She gave me a look of unspeakable annoyance. "I'll be fine," she said. "Let's get this done."

"All right, then," I said. I nodded to Beckwith. "I'll meet you at the bottom." Then I turned and wormed my way into the opening for a third time. Once I was inside Beckwith handed me my pack, and I began my descent, one hand holding the lantern and tugging on the drawstring of my pack, the other holding the rope or pushing me downward.

I had gone no more than ten feet when Beckwith blocked out the daylight and began his own descent. I moved on quickly, to make sure we had room to maneuver without kicking one another, while he and Betsy heaved his pack into the shaft.

We were perhaps fifty feet down when I remarked, "It's a different experience, knowing there is a second person in here with me."

"I can see how it would be," Beckwith answered. He seemed to be struggling a little, and I realized he had no lantern and was relying on mine, while my pack blocked much of its light. He also had the rope to hold, but no loop around his waist; if he slipped and fell, he would land on me, with no line to catch him.

"There are handholds every few feet," I told him. "Other than that, it's all very smooth stone."

"I can see that, Mr. Derringer."

I took that to mean that he was not interested in conversation, so we made most of the descent in relative silence, disturbed only by the sound of boots, clothing, and packs scraping over stone, and our own breath. Beckwith seemed to be panting rather more than I liked.

"How much farther?" he called at last.

I judged we were perhaps four-fifths of the way, and said so.

"Thank God," he replied.

Not long after my feet slid from the shaft and I stood upright in the main tunnel. I placed the lantern on the tunnel floor, then heaved my pack out and set it beside the others at the foot of the steps.

"You're almost there," I called into the shaft. "I'm out."

There was no reply beyond renewed scraping and heavy breathing, and it seemed like several minutes before Beckwith finally emerged. He did not stand when his feet touched the step, but collapsed in a heap against the tunnel wall, leaving his pack balanced precariously on the edge above him.

I waited while he caught his breath. "Damn, Derringer," he finally said. "You've done that *three times?*"

"I had no load the first time, except the lantern," I said.

"That is the most exhausting, terrifying thing I've done in years," he replied. "I thought you and your girl must be soft, coming from back east the way you do, but now I know better!"

"I'm a trained adventurer," I said.

He shook his head. "I've met adventurers before," he said. "Most of 'em aren't fit for a climb like that."

I could think of nothing useful to say in response to that, so I said nothing as I stepped up beside him and heaved his pack out of the shaft. I carried it down the steps and placed it with the others.

When I had done that I found Beckwith sitting upright, peering into the darkness to his left. "That's west?" he asked.

"I believe so," I said. "It's the direction I intend to travel."

"You know, Gabriel Trask is a little fellow. I wouldn't have thought he was in shape to make that climb and then hike miles down this passage."

"I didn't know that," I said. "He might have found another entrance; this was the nearest mentioned in the Pierce Archives, but there could be more."

"So he might be in another tunnel entirely?"

"They're all supposed to connect up."

He nodded. Then he got to his feet. "So you're determined to go looking for him?"

"I am. You don't need to accompany me, Mr. Smith; you're free to go back to San Francisco and forget all about it. Tell your employers I hit a dead end."

"I don't think I can do that, Mr. Derringer," he said. He gestured at the western passage. "I don't see a dead end there. I see a tunnel that looks like it goes somewhere. There might yet be some treasure down here, even if it's just lizard-people pottery I can sell to some museum back east. Even if there isn't, I've got a reputation to uphold; if people think I give up when things get rough, I won't be getting much work. I'll be going with you."

"Please yourself," I said. "Who goes back up first, then? I'm ready to go, but if you want to rest a while I can untie the rope and leave the lantern."

He looked at me, then down at the four packs, then along the tunnel to the west. "No, I'll go first," he said. "You won't leave without your girl."

I had honestly not considered the possibility that either of us might set out into the darkness alone once the other had begun the climb back to the surface. He was quite right, though; I was not going to leave Betsy alone with him. I watched as he boosted himself up into the shaft, then stepped up to the opening myself. When the lantern's light barely reached his boot heels I heaved myself up and followed him.

Chapter Twelve

Into the Tunnel

Beckwith was obviously tired; the trip back to the surface took far longer than I would have expected, and by the time we emerged and hauled the rope out it was clearly too late in the day to head for Pomona. Instead we made camp as best we could with the items still in the wagon, and at first light we set out to the south, leaving nothing but the coil of rope to mark where we had been.

Beckwith had not misled us; we reached the village by mid-morning and set about the business of buying more lanterns, iron stakes, and additional supplies of food and oil, as well as filling canteens and selling our horses and wagon. We were able to accomplish all these tasks and by mid-afternoon we set out, our newly bought supplies on our backs, for the hike back to the tunnel.

The sun was still above the horizon, but not by much, when we returned to the tunnel mouth. The rope appeared undisturbed, and I immediately set about driving the iron stakes into the stony ground, hammering them in with a good-sized rock, to provide an anchor for the rope now that the wagon was no longer available.

"Derringer," Beckwith said, "it's been a long day. We must have walked a dozen miles this afternoon. Can't that wait until morning?"

"Haven't I explained this, Mr. Smith?" I asked him. "I intend to descend *tonight*, and sleep in the tunnels, not out here." I gestured at the orange–rimmed clouds to the west. "I think it might rain before long, and I'd rather be underground, not exposed on a hillside. Furthermore, most of our supplies are already down there, waiting for us, and I prefer to have them at hand tonight."

Betsy did not join the argument directly, but simply announced, "I'll go first," and began arranging the rope around her waist.

Beckwith did not look happy, but set about uncoiling the rope, and twenty minutes later Betsy was on her way down the shaft, with about a third of our new acquisitions in a sack above her. Beckwith and I were lowering the rope behind her.

"We're leaving the rope in place, aren't we?" Beckwith asked once Betsy was out of sight.

I slid another yard of hemp into the opening and said, "That was my intention, yes. That's why the spikes are here. We could probably make the climb out without it, but why make things difficult for ourselves?"

He stared at the narrow opening and shuddered. "I hate that thing," he said. "Here." He passed me the portion of the rope he had been holding. "I'm going down next. Might as well get it over with."

I nodded, and gestured to the second bundle. "That one's yours," I said, as I continued lowering the rope.

He picked it up, crossed to the mouth of the shaft, and lowered himself into it, pulling the bundle after him. I prodded it with my foot to help it along, and a moment later he, too, was on his way down.

That added some weight to the lifeline, but I continued to pay it out slowly. Finally, though, the downward pull lessened; I guessed that at least Betsy, and perhaps both of them, had reached bottom.

I continued to feed the rope into the opening, though; for my own descent there would be no one at the top to anchor me, so I wanted it taut against the spikes. When at last no slack remained above ground I collected the third and final bundle and entered that diagonal passage.

No matter how many times I made the journey down that shaft, it was always unpleasant – dark and crowded, sand scraping my knees, air that tasted stale and foul. The terrors were certainly far less, now that I knew what awaited me, than they had been on my first descent, but a certain instinctive, unreasoning fear remained. It was a relief to hear voices below me, to know that I was not entirely alone in that confined space.

It would have been more of a relief if the voices weren't arguing. The echoes made it difficult to make out words at first, but the tones were unmistakable.

Finally, I could hear Betsy saying, "...until Tom gets here."

"What harm would it do to look around a little?" Beckwith demanded.

"It would waste oil, for one thing..."

I lifted myself up on hands and knees, lowered my head, and called down between my legs, "I'm almost there!"

"There, you see?" Betsy said.

I did not hear a reply from Beckwith as I tugged at my pack and lowered myself another foot or so.

Finally, I half–slid, half–tumbled from the shaft, landing awkwardly on the top two steps. Betsy and Beckwith were there, watching; I saw only a single lantern besides my own, in Beckwith's upraised hand. Betsy knelt by the wall, arranging some of our belongings. The bottom of the rope was coiled up to one side, out of the way.

"Derringer," Beckwith said. "Are we camping here for the night? I reckoned that as long as we've come this far, we might want to move along the passage a little, away from the shaft."

"I thought you were the one who was tired, Mr. Smith," I replied.

"I *am* tired," he said. "We've walked ten miles and climbed down that damned stone pipe, and I'm about ready to pack it in, but this spot makes me nervous, with the opening right there. If someone comes along and finds our rope..."

"No one's going to find the rope," Betsy interrupted. "We're in the middle of the desert!"

"Still, I'd be happier a little farther away."

I shrugged. "It doesn't matter much to me," I said. "I'm tired, too, but I can walk a few yards more if it will ease your mind." I picked myself up, brushed off a little dust, then pulled my bundle from the entry shaft. I hefted that in one hand, then trotted down the steps and found the pack I had brought down earlier. I hoisted that onto my shoulder, arranged my lantern to my liking, and turned left. "This way," I said.

Betsy looked at her two packs, and the additional pack I had brought down. Before she could say anything, I told her, "We can come back for the rest. Let's go find a spot where Mr. Beckwith feels more comfortable."

With a sigh, she picked up one pack and followed me, while Beckwith came up alongside me on my right.

With two lanterns we had more light than I had had on my previous ventures to this passage, and we were not stopping a mere thirty feet from the entrance, so we quickly saw that the tunnel that was so featureless where we had emerged did not *stay* featureless; no more than two hundred feet from our point of arrival we began to see crude figures scrawled on the left hand tunnel wall. I did not recognize the style and said so.

Neither of my companions could add anything useful.

There were glyphs that looked a little like lizards – long curving lines with two crooked crossbars, like a lizard's body and tail and four legs. I wondered whether this could be where the lizard people got their name. Other glyphs, though, were different; there were square–headed stick–men, and vertical zigzags, and a sort of narrow teardrop shape that reminded me of ears of corn. They were all drawn in a brown pigment that I did not recognize – not quite ochre, but fairly similar.

These figures obviously held some meaning, but we could make no sense of them at all.

They were in groups, with stretches of bare stone between them, and ranged from knee level to about the top of my head. Most of the figures were about the size of one of Betsy's hands.

I was so intrigued by these markings that at first I did not even notice the break in the tunnel wall. It was not until Beckwith said, "Look at that!" that I saw it. Before I could say anything, Beckwith trotted forward, lantern high, to see what lay around that corner.

The look of disappointment on his face, plainly visible in the lantern's light, was almost comical. What he had found was not another passage, or a treasure chamber, but merely a large alcove – in effect, the tunnel widened from twenty feet to forty or so for a distance of about thirty yards.

This alcove was cut entirely from the southern side of the tunnel; the northern wall still continued unbroken and unmarked for as far as we could see. To me, its most interesting feature was the presence of two benches, carved from stone and decorated with some sort of black stuff that was inlaid into the stone in more elaborate versions of the same sort of glyphs we had seen on the tunnel wall.

"We'll camp here," I said, setting my lantern on the nearer bench.

Beckwith appeared inclined to argue at first, but then thought better of it. "Right," he said. "Good idea. I'll go back for more of the gear."

I joined him, leaving my lantern on the bench and Betsy standing in the alcove, looking around.

A few minutes later we had all our supplies collected in the alcove, where we arranged ourselves for the night. We had no fuel for a proper campfire, but I opened up one of the lanterns to make a sort of improvised oil stove so that we could heat our supper. I was dismayed to see how much its smoke stained the ceiling, but the more I looked at the spreading black mark the more I wondered how the tunnel's makers had managed their affairs down here. I had not seen any smoke–stains anywhere on the roof of the tunnel until now; what had the original occupants used for light? How had they prepared their food? This alcove had no fire pits, no chimneys - had no one ever stayed the night here?

If not, what was the space *for*? No one would carve out a space like this without a reason.

Perhaps, I surmised, this had been a storage depot for the people who used that entry to trade with the Gabrieleno Indians. But the complete absence of smoke stains in the main passage still baffled me; could the lizard people see in total darkness? Or were they all blind, perhaps? That might explain why they chose to live underground. As for cooking, perhaps they ate their food raw. I wondered what they found to eat down in these tunnels. Or did they have some way of harvesting food from the surface, unseen by those who lived above?

Our own food was no mystery; we had brought it with us, in cans or wrapped in cloth. A modest meal of salt beef and beans, warmed over the oil lamp, was unexciting but serviceable. Our only drink was water from our canteens. Beckwith had brought a flask of whiskey, but was saving it for a more significant occasion.

After our repast we settled in our beds – if you can call a thin pad and a blanket spread on stone a bed. I think Beckwith dozed off immediately, but I could hear Betsy stirring restlessly, and for my own part I seemed to be in no hurry to fall into the arms of Morpheus.

For one thing, it was unnaturally quiet. The silence was so absolute that I could hear every breath my companions drew, and my own heartbeat was plainly audible. I had spent many a night in remote places, far from the sounds of civilization, but here there was no breeze, no insects called, no leaves rustled. No owls hooted, for there were no trees in which they might perch. I did not hear so much as a fluttering bat or skittering lizard.

At least, I thought, if any attacker approached, we would be alerted by the tiniest noise – and I found myself listening for just such a noise, too attentive to the silence to sleep.

But eventually I did sleep, for I then awoke to utter darkness, with no idea how much time had passed. The oil lamp had gone out. So total was the dark that for a moment I could not comprehend it and thought I might be blind, or still asleep, but at last I recalled our situation. I groped for my lantern, and Betsy's voice spoke.

"Are you awake, Tom?"

"Yes," I said. "Is Beckwith?"

"I don't think so."

I had found the lantern, and I managed to fumble out a packet of matches. I struck one; it blazed up, and in the blackness even that single match was blindingly bright. I squinted and involuntarily leaned away from the flame, but as my eyes adjusted I was able to steady my hand and light the lantern.

We all lay as we had the night before; nothing had crept in and disturbed us while we slept. Beckwith was lying on his back, mouth open, eyes shut; Betsy was up on one elbow, blinking at the light.

I checked the lamp I had set up and found its reservoir dry. "We'll need to be more careful of our oil," I said.

Betsy gave a single quick nod.

I arose and prodded Beckwith with the toe of my boot; he came awake with astonishing suddenness, fully alert and reaching for a weapon before he realized who I was, and where we were.

"Ah," he said. "Is it morning?"

I could not help smiling. "How should I know?" I asked.

He pulled a watch from the pocket of his vest, peered at it, then held it to his ear to be sure it was still ticking.

"It doesn't matter what time it is," Betsy said. "There *is* no time down here, not really."

Beckwith glared at her, then thought better of it. "I suppose you're right," he said. He looked around, then finally turned his attention to me. "Shall we be going, then?"

Chapter Thirteen

Two Days in the Dark

We had been walking for about three hours, according to my watch, when we stopped for lunch.

I think we were all somewhat dismayed and a little discouraged by what we had found so far – which is to say, nothing. Once we had left the alcove where we had slept, the passage had continued in a straight, featureless line; there were no turns, no more alcoves, no side–passages, not even any writing on the walls, but simply the long bare tunnel.

"How far do you think we've come?" Beckwith asked, as I warmed a can of beans over the oil lamp.

I looked back up the tunnel as I considered the question. We had kept up a pretty good pace, with few stops of any kind, and the footing was as good as could possibly be asked. Oh, it was not perfectly level, we had noticed some variation in slope, but there were no obstructions, no soft spots, nothing to slow down our march.

"It might be ten miles," I replied. "Maybe not quite that much."

"*Ten miles?*" Betsy exclaimed. "A tunnel *ten miles long?*"

"Well, yes," I said.

"Who would build such a thing?"

"Lizard people," I replied, stating the obvious.

"*Why?*"

"According to the stories, they live their entire lives underground," I answered.

"But why?"

I shook my head. "That I cannot say. I have not seriously researched the matter. When we left New York I had no idea we would be dealing with their tunnels."

"It doesn't make any sense," Betsy insisted.

"Much of the world does not seem to make a great deal of sense," I replied. "Sometimes this merely means we don't yet know enough to understand it."

"It doesn't look to me as if there are any lizard people left," Beckwith remarked. "This place seems completely deserted."

The same thought had occurred to me; in fact, I had begun to wonder what evidence we had for the continued existence of the Skyless, or Gabriel Trask's presence among them. It all seemed to come down to what Trask had told Emperor Norton and Ah How, and what if Trask had been lying from the start? What if his supposed embassy to the hidden peoples of America was part of some elaborate confidence game?

I did not share my doubts with my companions, however; I ate in silence, then wiped my mouth. I glanced up at the faint smoke stains our lamp had left on the ceiling and the lack of any other markings; then I gathered my gear, and said, "Let's go."

We took a short break after another three hours. I could see that Betsy's endurance was starting to fade; she already bore the smallest burden, but I reduced it further, transferring some of her supplies to my own pack.

I had taken to watching the roof of the tunnel as we walked, and I had still seen no signs of smoke. Either the lizard people had a completely smokeless source of light, or they could see in total darkness, or they were gone, and had been gone so long that smoke–stains had somehow faded away in this sunless, windless place where the temperature never seemed to vary. Perhaps, I thought, there was some strange variety of mite or microbe down here that ate the smoky residue.

Another three hours brought us to our next rest; this one was to include supper and sleep. We found no convenient alcove this time, just more tunnel.

Betsy slumped against the wall of the passage, staring back into the darkness behind us. "Thirty miles?" she said. "*Thirty miles* of this useless tunnel?"

"I think our pace has slowed," I said. "I'd guess twenty-five."

"That's quite enough!"

I could not argue with that, and said nothing.

"Tom, this isn't getting us anywhere. We should turn back."

"This tunnel can't go on forever," Beckwith said, before I could respond. "We still have enough food and oil for another few days."

"We'll need it just to get back to the entrance!" Betsy protested.

"No, we won't," I said. "It's been..." I pulled out my watch and did a little calculation. "A day and a half, at most."

"What do you hope to accomplish, traipsing endlessly along this ridiculous tunnel?"

"Well," I said, "I *hope* to find Gabriel Trask, but I would not mind merely learning something about how this tunnel comes to be here in the first place."

"You're mad," Betsy grumbled. "Both of you."

"I'm an adventurer," I said with a grin. "Madness is an occupational hazard."

With that settled, I began unpacking the makings of our evening meal and the bedding we would use for the night.

Once she had eaten Betsy's temperament improved, but she did insist that we should turn back before we had exhausted half our supply of lamp oil. I admitted this was a sensible precaution, but estimated that we had enough for another five days. "Two more," I said, "and then we turn back. But I don't think the tunnel can go that far; if I've estimated the direction and distance correctly, another two days would have us under the Pacific."

"And how do you know this confounded tunnel doesn't go all the way to China?" Betsy demanded.

"It seems unlikely," I replied mildly.

Our first night in the tunnel I had been nervous, alert to any hint that we were not alone, wary of an attack from the darkness, but by this second night – if it was actually night; it was hard to be certain – we were so accustomed to having the passage to ourselves, and so weary from our long walk, that we all fell asleep quickly and slept soundly. No one suggested standing watch or posting a guard or setting any sort of trip-wire alarms.

And once again, we were undisturbed, and awoke in total darkness.

This time Beckwith was the first to wake, and I opened my own eyes just as he managed to light a lantern. I sat up, startling him; he almost spilled the lamp, and the consequent vile oaths woke Betsy.

We breakfasted quickly, but when the time came to resume our westward journey we were not quite so eager. Speaking only for myself, my feet were blistered and sore from walking so long on hard stone; I suspect the others were in no better state, though neither complained of anything specific.

At last, though, we had gathered up everything we intended to carry, and we set out.

We had gone only a few yards when Beckwith, in the lead, began swearing again.

"Please, Mr. Beckwith," I said. "There is a lady present."

"To Hell with that," he said, pointing. "Look!"

I looked, and understood his feelings. I had thought he had been expressing displeasure at the condition of his feet, or at the weight of his pack, but now I saw the cause of his annoyance.

There was more of that strange brown writing on the wall ahead, and beyond that the tunnel opened out again.

"Another alcove," Betsy said. "What of it?"

"It might be more! And even if it *is* just another alcove, it would have been a better camp than sleeping in the middle of the tunnel."

"I don't see how it would have made the slightest difference, Mr. Beckwith," Betsy replied. "The floor is the same stone, and it is not as if we had constant traffic stumbling over us."

"We would at least have had something to look at other than these same blank walls!" Beckwith answered. He picked up his pace, opening a lead on us.

We caught up quickly enough, though, when we reached the alcove – for that is what it was, another alcove. This one, however, was somewhat larger and not as empty. There were two bundles of blankets pressed up against the back wall.

I had thought they might give us some clue about the nature of the lizard people, but the pattern and weave were not particularly alien.

"Gabrieleno, I'd say," Beckwith said. "These were made by the local Indians." He poked at the nearer bundle, and his finger sank deeply into the cloth, which crumbled to brown powder at his touch. A miniature cloud of dust showered the floor at his feet.

"Dried out," I said. "Desiccated."

"They must have been here for years," Beckwith remarked.

"Decades," I agreed.

"So we still don't know whether there are any lizard people down here."

"Well, we know there *were*, recently enough that they traded with the locals on the surface. How long have the Gabrielenos been making blankets like this?"

"How the Devil should I know? Centuries, probably."

Betsy, I noticed, said nothing at all, but looked around the room warily.

We took another few minutes to look the place over, but eventually concluded there was nothing more to be seen. As before, there were no forks, no side–tunnels, so we had little choice but to continue westward down the main passage.

That alcove, or storeroom, or whatever it was, gave us new enthusiasm, but as we continued our march down the tunnel and once again found only more of the same featureless corridor we had seen before that enthusiasm faded. We stopped somewhat earlier for lunch this time; by my watch it was scarcely 11:00, and it was more the need for a break in the monotony, rather than hunger, that prompted the stop.

As we sat by the tunnel wall I looked back into the miles of empty darkness behind us and mused that a great deal of adventuring was quite impressively tedious. In my travels to date I had spent far more time sitting in a cramped compartment on a train, or in a cabin on a freighter, or on the tiny deck of an airship, than I had spent fighting villains or seeing wondrous sights or making my way through jungles. The much-loved stories of adventurers that one read in the newspapers or dime novels invariably skipped over all that.

I wished *we* could skip over it!

When we had eaten and discussed what very little we had to discuss and could no longer justify remaining where we were, we gathered our belongings and marched on down the tunnel.

I wondered how much longer we would go before we found anything of interest. Was there, in fact, anything to be found? Had Trask lied? Was he now relaxing in a good hotel in Chicago or London, laughing at the fools back in California who had believed his stories? I feared that might be exactly the case. The stories of lizard people might be mere fantasies, inspired by whatever had dug this insanely long, almost featureless tunnel. Yes, there were fairly consistent descriptions of them going back decades, but those might all have derived from a single fictional source.

One particularly frightening possibility that occurred to me was that there might indeed be a community of the Skyless living in tunnels under Los Angeles, with Gabriel Trask as their guest, just as reported, but that the tunnel we were in might pass above or below them without any connection.

But the tunnel could not go on forever; we would be beneath the Pacific Ocean in another twenty or thirty miles. I had observed that the passage had a very slight downward slope, but surely it could not descend enough to go under the sea! It would have to end soon, one way or another.

With that in mind I kept my mouth shut and said nothing to my companions as we continued for another hour or so.

Still, my mind was wandering through various dreadful possibilities, so I did not notice any change in the tunnel ahead until Betsy pointed at the corridor ahead and shouted, "Tom, look!"

Startled, I looked, and saw what had her so excited – perhaps a hundred feet ahead, the passage changed. In the dim light I could not yet make out the details, but the walls on either side vanished, while the darkness directly in front of us was no longer so complete.

Before that, I noticed, the tunnel walls were bore more of those brown glyphs, and I thought I saw a few small holes, as if something had once been mounted there but had been removed.

Betsy took a few running steps forward, but Beckwith and I both called out, "Wait!" Our voices echoed from the stone walls, surely much louder than either of us had intended.

She stopped dead as her natural caution asserted itself. The three of us gathered in the center of the tunnel. "Do you think anyone heard us?" I whispered.

"Do you think anyone is *there?*" Beckwith replied. "Just because there's...something ahead, and not simply more tunnel, doesn't mean there are any *people*, whether lizards or otherwise."

"Well, let's go see," Betsy said, raising her lantern high and marching on.

Beckwith and I quickly followed her, and I noticed Beckwith had drawn his pistol. I made sure that my own Colt was accessible, but I did not unholster it.

As we drew nearer, we could discern what lay ahead of us – an intersection. Our tunnel was the widest of four that met there. One led to the right, and the angle was too acute for us to see anything of what might lie in that direction; another led to the left, positioned so that we could see a short distance up the corridor; and the last continued to the west, but turned somewhat north of our own path while sloping slightly upward.

All the passages appeared to be unlit by anything but our own lanterns, but none of the walls were the blank stone we had been accustomed to; they were painted, beginning about twenty feet from the intersection in our own tunnel, and extending as far as I could see in all the others. There were several of the brown glyphs, but most of the coloring was decorative designs in white, ochre, and dark green – at least, that was how the colors appeared in the light of our lamps. These patterns were not quite like anything I had seen before, but bore some resemblance to art I had encountered in Mexico.

Whereas the tunnel that had brought us here was an unwavering straight line for the entire distance of thirty or forty miles, all three of these other tunnels turned after fifty or sixty feet, so that we could not see any great distance along them.

There were also niches carved into the left-hand wall of the tunnel across from our own, niches I estimated to be about two feet high and four or five feet long, at roughly shoulder height. Once we reached the intersection, we could also see similar niches in the right-hand wall of the southbound tunnel. In both passages these niches were spaced four or five feet apart.

They were not empty; they held stacked objects the exact nature of which we could not determine, but which filled most of the shelf area and which had a distinctive color and luster, gleaming in the lamplight.

"Gold," Beckwith said, in a hushed, almost reverent tone.

Chapter Fourteen

The Lizard People

I stared at the stacked objects in the niches, trying to decide whether Beckwith was correct in his assessment. I had to admit that the color and general appearance of these mysterious things was completely consistent with that of gold, and I could not think of anything else they might be, but it seemed very odd that the Skyless would leave their valuables on open shelves, unguarded. I was about to say something to that effect when Betsy hissed, "Listen!"

Startled, I turned to see her holding up a single finger to call for silence. I swallowed my words, and listened.

I could hear a faint tapping.

"What is it?" I whispered.

"How should I know?" she replied. "But whatever it is, it means we aren't alone down here." She slid the pack from her back and set it carefully on the tunnel floor, so that she would be unencumbered should we need to move quickly. I followed suit.

"I guess the lizard people aren't extinct after all," Beckwith said, setting down his own pack and raising his revolver.

"Don't shoot them!" I said, reaching for his pistol. "We don't know how many there are, or what weapons they have!"

He snatched the gun back, out of my reach. "I won't shoot if I don't have to," he said. "But if they come at us, I'll defend myself."

I could not argue with that, but I still did not draw my own weapon.

Then Betsy blew out her lantern and pointed down the right-hand passage. "Look!"

I looked, and saw a faint greenish glow. I had no idea what might generate such a light; it was not any sort of lantern or candlelight I recognized. It was brightening; whatever caused it was headed our way. I blew out my own lantern, as well, and set it on the floor by my pack while Betsy and I stepped back around the corner, out of sight.

Beckwith did not. He stood, lantern upraised in his left hand, pistol in his right, and waited.

"Hello there!" he called.

I risked a quick look around the corner and got my very first look at one of the Skyless.

I had been unsure what to expect; no one seemed to have been very clear on what the lizard people looked like, whether they were entirely human or some sort of unholy hybrid of man and lizard. Now I could finally see for myself; one of them stood perhaps twenty feet away.

He appeared to be human, though of a race I did not recognize. He was shorter than Beckwith or myself, only slightly taller than Betsy, and very lean, with a heavy brow and broad mouth. His skin was so pale as to be, so far as I could tell in that eerie light, pure white – though I could not then rule out the possibility that his skin was a pale greenish yellow, matching the light. We may call ourselves white people, but compared to the Skyless we are unworthy of the name. He appeared to be hairless, and his skin was apparently so dry that his scalp was visibly flaking.

He had no scales, no tail, no sign of any reptilian ancestry, but that dry, flaking skin was somewhat reminiscent of scales, or of a lizard shedding its skin, and the wide mouth and beetling brow gave his face an animalistic cast; I supposed that that was whence the name "lizard people" had derived. His eyes were very large, the pupils dilated and the irises dark, as befit an underground dweller. He wore a simple, sleeveless brown tunic of some unfamiliar and glossy fabric that reached almost to his knees, with a broad black belt around his waist. His feet were bare, but narrow, elaborately worked metal bands adorned his ankles, wrists, and neck.

He held a tube in one hand, roughly the size of a pint bottle, that glowed greenish–yellow, and now I recognized the color – it was exactly the color of a firefly's light. Obviously, the Skyless had learned to recreate that charming phenomenon on a far larger scale and turn it to practical use in lighting their way without smoke or flame. The mystery of the unmarked ceilings was solved.

In his other hand he held a short white spear, between three and four feet long, which was pointed at Beckwith's throat, though a dozen feet still separated the two.

"Do you speak English?" Beckwith asked.

The lizard man bit his lip, considering this intruder, then spoke.

His voice was low and melodious, and his words were completely unintelligible, but there was something oddly familiar about them. I felt Betsy start beside me.

"What is it?" I whispered.

I immediately regretting doing so, because the man reacted instantly, eyes darting, spear-point swinging; he had obviously heard me.

I raised my hands and started to step out into the light, but as I did I heard Betsy say, in a low murmur, "That sounded almost like Mayan."

I realized she was right, though I had no idea what the significance of this might be. We had been held prisoner by Mayans for a few days during our adventures in Mexico; I had not managed to learn any of their tongue, but Betsy had proved to have greater linguistic aptitude than I and had picked up a little.

"I'm Tom Derringer," I said, displaying my empty hands.

"I'm called Smith," Beckwith said, still holding his lantern and gun.

The Skyless spoke again, but we could no more understand it now than we had before.

I asked, "*Parlez-vous francais?*" When that elicited no useful response I quickly ran through German, Latin, Greek, Hebrew, and Russian, thereby exhausting my entire repertoire of languages.

Beckwith glanced at me, and his expression made it clear he thought I was an idiot. "Latin?" he asked. "Where would they learn *Latin?*"

"Missionaries?" I ventured.

"*I* didn't even recognize some of those," he said. "Why didn't you try Spanish? We're in Los Angeles – it's what half the people around here speak."

"I don't *know* Spanish!" I said. "*You* try it!" I resisted the urge to look at Betsy – I was aware that she spoke Spanish, but I did not want to betray her presence to the spearman.

Beckwith frowned, but took my suggestion to heart. "*Ay, amigo,*" he said. "*Que pasa?*"

That did no better than Russian, and Beckwith mumbled, "I don't speak much of it myself."

Again, I struggled not to look at Betsy, or suggest she try Maya. "This isn't getting us anywhere," I said. I stepped forward. "We're looking..."

I was interrupted by a shriek and what seemed like a sudden burst of light, though I knew it would have scarcely been visible above ground. I whirled, and saw that two more of the Skyless had appeared behind Betsy in the westward tunnel, one holding another of those firefly lamps, the other holding another white spear. The shriek had been her startled response to their abrupt manifestation – they had crept up silently in the dark, and then, when they were perhaps ten feet away, unveiled their light.

And another pair, I realized, had appeared with equal suddenness in the southern corridor. Only the broad passage from which we had come remained open, should we need to retreat.

"Damn," Beckwith said – but he kept his revolver ready.

I raised my hands higher, and said, "We don't want any trouble." I had some wild hope that one of the four new arrivals might know some English, even if the first to appear did not. "We just came here looking for Gabriel Trask."

That first lizard man started. "Gabriel Trask?" he said, giving the first vowel an odd lilt and mangling the final pair of consonants into something scarcely recognizable.

I nodded. "Gabriel Trask," I said. "From Emperor Norton."

He spoke a long sentence of which the only words I recognized were "Gabriel Trask," and I am not certain I would have caught those had I not heard him say the name a moment before. I thought he might be asking a question, but could not be sure, so I said nothing more.

One of the other Skyless called something, and there was a brief and boisterous debate, of which I understood not a single word. Then the spearman in the south tunnel stepped forward and gestured, while the man in the northern passage lowered his own weapon and stepped to one side. The meaning was clear; we were to proceed to the north.

I started to reach for my pack, but a sharp shout that sounded something like "*Shay!*" stopped me, and a spear-point prodded my side. Clearly, we were not to bring our belongings. Reluctantly I left the bundle where it was and started up the northern tunnel, somewhat comforted that they had not taken my Colt, nor Beckwith's pistol. I remembered also that Betsy still had her derringer tucked way somewhere; none of us were unarmed.

Behind me, I saw one of the lamp-bearers pick up Betsy's pack, and the other my own; one of the spearmen fetched Beckwith's. They all seemed startled by the weight of the packs, but managed them well enough.

We were clearly captives, but they had not disarmed us – did they not recognize our guns as weapons? That puzzled me.

We made our way along the tunnel, as directed; it jogged to the left for perhaps twenty feet before turning back to almost its original course, and I was startled to see a large room directly ahead of us, lit by several of those firefly tubes set in brackets on the walls. A curtain of some sort was drawn back from the doorway; presumably it had blocked the light so that we did not notice anything when we first arrived at the intersection.

We ducked past the curtain and found ourselves in a chamber perhaps forty feet across – I cannot say "square," for in fact it was not square; although it had four straight sides, the eastern wall was significantly shorter than the west. We had emerged in the southeast corner; another curtained tunnel led out from the southwest.

As for the room itself, it was well lit – I cannot say "brightly," since those greenish-yellow lamps did not seem capable of real brightness – and modestly furnished. A polished stone table occupied the center of the room, surrounded by half a dozen drums of a size and height to serve as stools that at the time I thought were pottery of some sort; carved and painted stone chests stood against the walls, and a rack of spears, holding at least a score of the weapons, all of them gleaming white, was on the western wall.

I should note that all my directions are assigned relative to the long tunnel we had traversed to reach this place, based on the assumption that we walked due west; if that was not in fact the case, and to this day I cannot be completely certain of it, then all my description is inaccurate. Still, I am being as consistent as I can, given that the tunnels of the Skyless were not always straight nor did they always meet at right angles, so that if my directions are off, they should all be off in similar fashion and to a similar degree, and therefore correct relative to one another, if not to the true compass points.

I noticed almost immediately that there was no wood or leather to be seen anywhere, nor any fabric other than the soft black curtains in the two doorways – in fact, I realized that even the spears, which one might have expected to have wooden shafts, were made entirely of something that appeared to be bone, with barely visible black lines that were presumably seams where pieces had been glued together. It seemed the Skyless drew as little from the surface world as possible.

The spearmen herded us into this room, then directed us to those ceramic drums; we seated ourselves around the table, unsure what to expect. Our escorts did not seem to be demonstrating any great hostility toward us, but they were clearly in command.

Once we were in place our packs were set atop three of the stone chests, in sight but out of reach, and the three spearmen stayed to watch over us while the two lamp–bearers vanished through the curtain in southwest corner.

Beckwith rested his lantern and pistol on the table and looked at me. "What do you suppose they're up to, Derringer?" he asked.

"I would guess they've gone to fetch Gabriel Trask," I said. "They certainly recognized his name."

"What do you think those gold things were, in those shelves?"

"I have no idea. None of our business, I'd say."

He did not appear to be satisfied with this response, but he asked no more questions.

Betsy did, though. "What do you suppose they'll do with us, Tom?"

"Oh, I expect they'll release us once we've explained ourselves to Mr. Trask. After all, if they wanted us dead, they could have already attended to it. They crept up on us in the dark, remember."

She shuddered. "I didn't mean to scream like that. They came out of nowhere!"

I nodded. "It was certainly startling. I think the first one let us hear and see him as he approached deliberately, to draw our attention. My father's journals describe various groups using such tactics against Darien Lord's company – or attempting to; after the first two occasions the adventurers anticipated it and were not surprised."

Beckwith snorted. "Two? Slow learners!"

I opened my mouth to defend my father and his friends, then thought better of it. No one who had been on those adventures was still in the business; in fact, only Mad Bill Snedeker was still alive, as my mother had not yet joined the troupe when those encounters took place. It was none of Beckwith's concern what had taken place so long ago. Instead I said mildly, "I did not observe you taking any precautions against being surrounded."

"I thought you two had my back!" Beckwith retorted, but his voice did not hold much conviction.

Betsy glanced at the nearest of our captors. "Do you suppose they actually might know English, and are feigning ignorance in hopes of learning something useful from our conversation?"

Beckwith threw her a startled look, then turned to stare at one of the spearmen.

"It's possible," I said. "Did you say their speech sounded like Mayan?"

She nodded.

"Could you say something to them in Mayan, perhaps?"

"I could try," she said. "What should I say?"

"Tell them we mean them no harm."

"I'm not..." She frowned. "I can't say *exactly* that, but this should be close." Then she stammered out a few awkward syllables.

I watched the faces of our captors as she spoke – or I tried to, at any rate; they had arranged themselves around us so that I could only see two of the three at a time. Of those two, one showed no reaction, and did not seem to have even noticed that her words were in a different language; the other cocked his head slightly, then gave a slight shake.

Betsy had seen this latter reaction; encouraged, she repeated her Mayan phrase.

This time I had turned to see the third, while still observing from the corner of my eye the one who had reacted. Neither of them responded at all this time.

"I see two possibilities," I commented. "Either their language is not, in fact, close enough to your dialect of Mayan for them to understand you, or they have been instructed to not acknowledge understanding anything we say in *any* language."

"I can think of others," Beckwith said, "but I'll give you that those do seem the most likely."

"Or it might be I'm not saying it correctly," Betsy said. "I don't really know Mayan, remember, I just picked up a few words in Mexico."

I could not quarrel with that; her assessment of her own abilities would almost certainly be more accurate than mine. I studied the faces of the spearmen.

And just then Beckwith said, "Do you think I could shoot all three of them before they speared me? If I caught them by surprise, they might not react real fast."

If either of the two I was watching knew any English, his self-control was astonishing; neither so much as blinked, and their grip on their spears did not change. I did not mention that; I just said, "No."

Betsy asked, "Why would you do that *now*?"

"Because they aren't expecting it," Beckwith replied. "We could get past 'em and back to the tunnel we came in by, and get a good lead on them."

"Quite aside from the murderousness of such a scheme, it's *two days* back to the entry shaft," I said. "We don't know anything about these people; what if they don't need to sleep the way we do?"

"I could stay awake for two days if I need to."

"But you think you could outrun them while carrying your pack? Or were you planning on two days without sleep, *or* food, *or* light?"

"I'd take one of those green things of theirs. I'd grab one of those gold things, too, so this wouldn't all be a complete waste."

"If they're really gold, that would be awfully heavy. And how do you know how long those lights last? I doubt they keep glowing forever."

Beckwith mulled that over for a moment, and I half expected him to argue that he could not exactly make a wrong turn even in the dark. Before he could, I added, "Finding the entrance by feel could be tricky."

He grimaced, then said, "Oh, shut up, Derringer," and turned away, holding his pistol.

Chapter Fifteen

We Meet Mr. Trask

It was only a moment or two after that that a light appeared in the southwestern tunnel, and the curtain was pulled aside. Two more of the Skyless stepped in, each holding a spear, and behind them appeared an ordinary man – or relatively ordinary, at any rate. He was no taller than the Skyless, who I have already said were shorter than average, and while he had a full head of graying brown hair and a full beard, and his skin was not as pale as theirs, nonetheless he had an unhealthy pallor. He wore the same abbreviated robe and black belt as the Skyless, but his robe was striped blue and yellow, and he had sandals on his feet, whereas the natives we had seen to this point all went barefoot. He took two steps into the room, then stopped.

"I understand you're looking for me," he said.

"Gabriel Trask?" I said.

He nodded.

I rose from my seat and stepped forward, hand outstretched. "It is a pleasure to meet you, sir, and yes, we came looking for you."

He looked at my hand, but did not accept it. "Why?" he asked.

Betsy and I exchanged glances. "That's a rather long story," I said, lowering my hand. "Did you ever know a man named Hezekiah McKee?"

He stepped back, almost to the curtain, and the spears of the two Skyless who had led him into the chamber both came up to point directly at our throats. "*That* son of a bitch?" he exclaimed. "Are you working for him?"

"No, no, no!" I assured him, raising my hands. "Quite the contrary! In fact, he's been dead for well over a year now."

He cocked his head to one side. "Oh?"

"I shot him," Betsy volunteered. "In self-defense."

"In Mexico," I said. "We had followed him there."

Trask looked at Beckwith. He shrugged. "Don't ask me," he said. "I wasn't there."

Trask squinted at him. "Do I know you? You look familiar."

"We met a few times in San Francisco," Beckwith replied. "Don't know as I'd say we *knew* one another."

Trask stared for a moment, then said, "I *think* I remember you."

Beckwith shrugged.

"All right, you say you killed McKee," Trask said, returning his attention to me. "What does that have to do with me?"

"*I* killed McKee," Betsy said, before I could reply. "Not Tom."

"Tom?"

"Tom Derringer, sir. That's me. J. Thomas Derringer, junior."

"Jack Derringer's boy?"

"Did you know my father, perhaps?"

He shook his head. "Never met the fellow. Heard a few stories, though. So you're an adventurer, like your old man?"

"I'm trying to be," I said. "That was why we followed McKee into Mexico – I was...well, it doesn't matter. At any rate, when I confronted him, he asked whether I was working for *you*. He said you had a cabal of spies and assassins working for you. That piqued my curiosity, and I decided to find you and ask what he was talking about."

"You tracked me all the way here because McKee..." He let the sentence trail off unfinished.

"He's a bit mad," Betsy volunteered. "Like most adventurers, I suppose."

"And if you found I *did* have a...a cabal of spies and assassins, what did you intend to do about it?"

"Well, that would depend on what purpose you were putting them to."

He stared at me a few seconds more, then turned to Beckwith. "What about you?" he demanded. "You say we met, but I don't recall your name, and I don't know why you're here."

"I'm called Smith," Beckwith replied. "Some individuals up north had a theory that Derringer, here, was after Emperor Norton's hidden treasure, and hired me to follow him and see whether there was any truth to that."

"*What* hidden treasure?"

"Well, that's the thing – I don't suppose there is any. But my employers thought there might be and hired me and didn't much care whether I believed in it or not, so long as I kept an eye on Mr. Derringer."

"Seems to me you're doing a little more than keeping an eye on him. My friends tell me you arrived together."

Beckwith shrugged. "He spotted me, and invited me to join him, so I could see for myself he wasn't hunting any treasure."

Trask looked at me again. I shrugged.

"Short of shooting him, I couldn't see any good way to stop him from following me," I said. "I thought it would be safer to join forces."

He turned to Betsy. "And you?"

"Betsy Jones," Betsy said. "Of New Brunswick, New Jersey."

"And why are *you* here?"

"I asked her to accompany me," I said.

His eyebrows rose.

"I assure you, Mr. Trask, Tom has been a perfect gentleman," Betsy hastened to say. "We have traveled together before and have found each other congenial company."

"I haven't seen 'em touch one another," Beckwith offered. "I think they're *both* a little crazy."

Trask considered this for a moment, then gestured for me to return to my seat. I acquiesced, resuming my place at the central table. Mr. Trask then took his place on another of the stools, joining us.

"So you came looking for me because of Hezekiah McKee's accusations?"

"That is indeed the case," I said.

"And having found me, what do you want of me?"

"Merely to ask, sir, why McKee was so certain I was in your employ. What contact had you had with him?"

"Oh, now, there's not really all that much to it. I've always taken an interest in the lesser known people who inhabit our country..."

I nodded. "I understand you were Emperor Norton's ambassador to what he called the hidden peoples, such as the Skyless." I gestured to take in the spearmen who still surrounded us.

"That's one way of putting it, I suppose. Really, though, it was the other way around – I was their ambassador to the

Emperor. I have done what I could to speak for these people, and to protect them from the intrusions of modern civilization. Joshua Norton was a sympathetic ear, but alas, he had little real authority."

"I understand."

"Yes, well, some years back, when I still lived above ground, I was informed that a man had come to...to a certain very old city in the mountains."

In a moment of sudden inspiration, I said, "El Dorado."

"Well, that's not what *they* call it, but yes, that is the Spanish name. Or rather – did you know that one reason the Spanish never found their legendary city of gold was that they had confused the descriptions of at least three different cities? One lies in the jungles of South America, one in the mountains east of here, and I am not certain myself of the location of the third. It's possible it's what is also called the Lost City of the Mirage, which as I'm sure you know does not *have* a fixed location."

"Or might it be *another* city that moves about?"

That notion seemed to startle him. "I suppose it might," he acknowledged. Then he shook himself. "But that is neither here nor there," he said. "Of the three cities I know of that are sometimes called El Dorado, I have personally only ever seen one, the one which the Spaniards also sometimes called by the name Quivira. I have long kept the secret of its location, which has gained me the trust of its inhabitants. When Hezekiah McKee turned up on their doorstep they sent a messenger to find me, to ask for my advice and assistance.

"Naturally, it took this messenger quite some time to find me, and by the time I accompanied him back to his homeland, McKee's initial facade of friendliness had been tossed aside and his real intentions revealed. He had brought armed men to the city and set himself up as its ruler by the simple method of shooting anyone who opposed him. His plan was to use the city's people as slave labor, to use its secure location as a base for conquering the region, and to use its famous wealth to finance his new empire, rather on the model of the Spanish conquistadors. The people of Quivira, as I will call it for now, had lived in undisturbed peace for so long that at first they were unable to put up any serious resistance.

"Fortunately, by the time I reached the city they had overcome the initial surprise and were ready to fight for their freedom. Furthermore, because I was mistrustful of McKee's motives from the first moment I heard of him, I had brought allies, including that gentleman over there..." He pointed at one of the spearmen. "...and another of the Skyless who is not in this room at present. As you have observed, the Skyless can move silently in near-total darkness, and have certain devices unknown to ordinary science – the lamps are only a small part of their amazing heritage. I had other companions, as well, from other isolated communities, with their own particular skills. We were able to dispose of several of McKee's gunmen in fairly short order, forcing his party to release their hold on the city and retreat to a makeshift fortress.

"An assault on this stronghold would have been bloody for both sides; a siege would have been demoralizing, as Quivira's people have had experience of famine and know how horrible starvation is. Furthermore, McKee's people held a dozen or so hostages, and we feared that a siege would result not merely in their deaths, but in their being eaten. We therefore resolved to arrange a peaceful resolution if it was at all possible. As the only one on our side fluent in English – McKee's translators were among the hostages – I conducted the negotiations that, I am proud to say, concluded in McKee's surrender. He freed the hostages and was given a safe conduct out of the valley, leaving his party's guns and ammunition behind. I assured him that if he returned he would find those weapons turned against him.

"Perhaps it was unwise to give him my real name, but I did, and so he was able to accuse you of working for me."

"So the spies and assassins he spoke of were your allies in freeing that city," I said.

"I would assume so."

"And he presumably thought that you were still determined to frustrate his dreams of empire."

"Was he trying again, then?"

"He intended to take over the Mayan rebels in Chan Santa Cruz and use them as his infantry in the conquest of Mexico."

"Chan Santa Cruz? I never heard..." Then he stopped and held up a hand. "Never mind," he said. "You can tell me all about it later, if you like."

"As you please," I replied.

"I have told you of my connection with that murdering bastard Hezekiah McKee," Trask said. "Now, tell me how and why you have found me."

"The why is simple enough," I said. "Reverend McKee accused me of being in your employ and said that you operated a ring of spies and assassins. I wished to determine the truth of the matter. If you did, in fact, command a cadre of assassins, I wanted to ensure that they would not be killing innocents. I consider myself a good man and could not stand idly by while a criminal organization operated freely despite my knowledge of it."

"If you'll pardon my saying so, Mr. Derringer, you scarcely seem to have come prepared to destroy a secret ring of assassins – three of you walking directly into our home."

"Well, there are two equal and opposite reasons for that," I said. "Firstly, knowledge – we had investigated your connection with Emperor Norton and spoken to some of your associates in San Francisco and concluded that you appeared to be a man of good will, very unlike McKee. We found no evidence that you did, in fact, employ spies or assassins – or rather, very little evidence, and that mere hearsay that was contradicted by those who had had closer contact with you."

"He means that I'd heard you were the Emperor's spymaster," Beckwith volunteered. "I *had* heard that, and passed along the report, but I'm pretty well convinced now it was wrong."

"Yes," I confirmed. "As for the second reason for our direct and simple approach, that was not knowledge, but ignorance. We had no idea what we would find in these tunnels. We had been told that you had taken shelter with the Skyless beneath Los Angeles, and I had the means to locate one entrance to the tunnels far to the east, so we came exploring. We did not intend to walk directly into this place; I had assumed that if there was in fact still a community here there would be gates and guards, where we could announce ourselves, and that we could retreat into the darkness if opposed. Finding ourselves surrounded was an unpleasant surprise."

"I'm sure it was." He smiled.

"I'm not sure he believes us," Beckwith said to me, before turning to our host. "I'll tell you, Mr. Trask, every word Derringer said – well, all of it that I know first-hand was the gospel truth, and I don't know a word to the contrary for the rest of it."

"Mr. Smith, I don't think he means us any harm," I said. I pointed to the gun in Beckwith's hand. "He hasn't disarmed us, after all. His friends haven't hurt us. He's spoken to us civilly.

He's answered my questions in a thoroughly satisfactory manner; his story of his El Dorado accords very nicely with everything I know of the late Reverend McKee and provides quite a convincing explanation for McKee's accusations. As it happens I've studied some of what's known of Coronado's search for the North American El Dorado, and while I don't know its precise location, everything Mr. Trask said fits with what I knew. I'm satisfied that his tale is the simple truth, and that I've achieved my purpose in coming here." I rose. "If our presence is unwelcome, Mr. Trask, you need merely say so, and we will leave. Our business here is done."

"Sit down, Mr. Derringer," he said, reaching out to tug at my sleeve. "*Your* business may be done, but *mine* is not. You are my guests, and will remain so for a while. I have yet to hear from your companions."

I sat down, and said nothing as he turned to Beckwith.

"Mr. Derringer says he came here to determine whether I was a danger to innocents," Trask said. "Why did *you* come?"

"I was hired to follow Derringer and report back to my employers," Beckwith said. "I'm just trying to earn my pay."

"You had no interest in me, personally?"

"Nope."

"Or the Skyless?"

"Nope. Never heard of them before."

"Or Joshua Norton's supposed treasure?"

"Oh, well, that." Beckwith glanced at me. "I won't deny that I was hoping there might be a treasure, and I might claim a share, but it never seemed the least bit likely; Joshua Norton was a crazy old man, not a real emperor. He was a pleasant fellow, I won't say a word against him in that regard, but he didn't have any treasure; he barely paid the rent on his shabby little room. If he had any money hidden away then he wasn't the man I thought he was. Save for calling himself an emperor he was a smart man, and a sensible one, and a kind one. If he'd had any money, he'd have used it – maybe not for himself, but for those he cared about."

"But your mysterious employers?"

"Oh, *they* thought the treasure was real! Or at least that it might be, and the chance was worth investing my fees and expenses. I don't know how much you've dealt with adventurers, but they come in a few different flavors. Some of them are just out for the fun of it, like Derringer here – they want the excitement, and maybe want to feel like heroes, but it's really just a game for them, a way to entertain themselves. Others, though, are after higher stakes – they're looking to get rich by finding some hidden treasure, or by earning a reward from some potentate, or by looting some poor lost tribe somewhere, or by stealing some inventor's latest creation. It's still a game, I suppose, but they're playing to win, not for the sake of the game. They want money. The men I'm working for, they're not so much adventurers themselves as employers of adventurers, but they're in it for the money, and they don't really believe in the fellows like Derringer that aren't. They thought that if he came all the way out from New York, then he must have a line on something very profitable. So they hired me to try to cut them in on it."

"And which kind are you?"

"Oh, I'm not a true adventurer, either," he answered. "I don't go looking for trouble. I don't sail off to the far ends of the world; I've never set foot outside California. I'm just a hired man, but one who uses my eyes and my brain and a gun instead of my hands and a plow."

"But you're in it for the money."

"Well, to the extent I'm in it at all, I'd have to say yes, I am. I don't take any particular pride in that, but I'm not ashamed of it, either. A man's got to eat."

Trask nodded, and looked at Betsy. "And you, Miss Jones?"

"What about me?"

"Why are you here?"

She threw me a helpless glance.

"I brought her," I said.

"Yes, you said as much, but why did she agree to come? Miss Jones? Are you an adventurer, too?"

"I didn't intend to be," she said, and I could hear bitterness in her voice.

"What *did* you intend?"

"I don't see that it's any of your concern."

"You were trespassing in these tunnels. I think that makes it my concern to learn why you are here."

She hesitated, but Trask stared at her, and I could not think of any way to safely intervene.

"I worked for my father," she said. "He sent me to help Tom when Tom bought one of his inventions. And...and as Tom said, we enjoyed each other's company."

"I don't quite see how that would bring you here from...New Jersey, was it?"

"I..." She blushed. "My mother and I had a disagreement," she said. "About Reverend McKee."

"Oh? Were you infatuated with him, perhaps? He was not an ill-favored man."

"No!" Her voice was horrified. "No, no! Nothing like that! Mother was upset because I *killed* him, not because I wanted anything to do with him! She called me a murderer and tried to make me repent and beg forgiveness, and I wouldn't do it, because I didn't do anything *wrong* in shooting him. I came to see Tom for a little peace, and he and his mother suggested I might accompany him in his search for you, and I did."

"So you ran away from home?"

"I..." She paused, thought about it, then admitted, "Yes, I guess I did."

He nodded. "I think I understand," he said. "I left home when I was fifteen to escape my father and never went back. Not all of us can be what our parents would like."

"I don't..." Betsy began, then stopped. For a moment I feared she might weep, but then she caught herself. "I expect I'll return. In time."

"Oh, I'm afraid that won't be possible," Trask said mildly.

"What?" I exclaimed.

"I can't let you leave," he said. "Any of you. Ever."

Chapter Sixteen

Prisoners of the Skyless

I leapt to my feet. "What do you mean?" I demanded. "We've done you no harm; do you intend to keep us prisoners forever?"

"Well, I'm certainly going to advise our hosts to do so."

"Why?" Betsy cried.

"*You*, my dear, have done nothing beyond keeping ill-chosen company, so I apologize for this unfortunate necessity." He turned to me. "And you, sir, are only included because Mr. Smith describes you as aspiring to heroism."

"What? Explain yourself."

"Gladly – indeed, I had intended to. I cannot release Miss Jones while holding you, Mr. Derringer, because she would almost certainly take any action she could to rescue you, including hiring other adventurers – her fondness for you is obvious. I cannot release you while holding either of the others because you would feel it your responsibility to rescue them, since you were the one who led them here. And I cannot release Mr. Smith because by his own admission he is a treasure hunter and seeker after wealth."

"But...why?" Betsy asked.

"Someone heard me," Beckwith said. "When we first got here."

Trask nodded. "Kulbal only knows half a dozen words of English, but one of them is 'gold,' and he heard the way you said it." He sighed. "It's such a shame you came in through the east entry. I didn't even know there was still a way to get into the tunnels out there, let alone that anyone knew how to find it! If you had come in from the north you would not have encountered any of the archives, and we might have risked letting you go."

"Archives? You mean those shelves?" I asked.

"Those golden blocks?" Beckwith said.

Trask nodded. "Those are the Archives of the Skyless."

"What does that mean?" Betsy asked.

"I'll be happy to explain everything, but there's no hurry. You're going to be here a long time. Let us take care of some other matters first." He reached a hand out toward Beckwith. "I'm afraid I'll need to take your gun now."

"Why?" Beckwith demanded, holding the pistol away from Trask. "Why now, and not when you first captured us?"

"Well, until just now you didn't know you were captives," he said. "It's not something I cared to demonstrate prematurely. I thought you would speak more freely if you thought yourself free. Now that the truth is out, though, I think we had better disarm you. We don't want you to try shooting your way out."

"And what if I *do* try?" Beckwith shouted, pointing his revolver at Trask's face. "What are you going to do about it?"

Trask gestured at the lizard people surrounding us. "Do you think you could shoot *all* of them before one of them speared you? Do you realize there are three hundred more who would hear the shot and come running to our aid? Do you think you could get out alive? How far did you come down that tunnel? I don't think your entry point is close at hand. You'd have to leave your supplies, you couldn't afford to burden yourselves with them, with three hundred men in pursuit; how would you fare in the dark, with no food or water? Has it occurred to you we might have set traps along your route to freedom? I won't even mention the problem of ricochets in a room with polished stone walls."

Beckwith threw a startled glance at the walls of the room; he had clearly not considered any of the hazards they might present.

"Gentlemen," Trask said, spreading his hands. "There's no need for violence. We will not mistreat you; you can live among the Skyless as honored guests, as I do, and we can learn from one another. The only restriction is that you will not be permitted to leave, or to communicate with anyone on the surface."

"I begin to see why McKee disliked you," I said.

"I will need your weapons as well, Mr. Derringer."

"Derringer, there are two of us, and only half a dozen of them," Beckwith said. "We can make it if we act together."

"Mr. Smith, please. Do not think we have no defense against bullets, or that spears are our only weapons. These men carry spears because we knew you would recognize them. The Skyless have science beyond anything I saw above ground – how do you think they *built* these tunnels?"

I did not particularly believe Trask's warning, but I did know how far we would have to travel along that dark, waterless tunnel. I hesitated, and looked at Betsy.

"Oh, give him your gun," she said. "I'd rather live down here than die."

"Very sensible of you, my dear," Trask said. He held out a hand toward Beckwith.

"I don't suppose you'd let me keep it if I give you my word I'll stay," Beckwith said.

"No, I'm afraid I would not," Trask said. "I don't yet know you well enough to know what your word is worth."

Reluctantly, Beckwith reversed his grip and passed his pistol over. Then Trask turned to me. "And you, Mr. Derringer?"

"Must I?"

"I'm afraid so."

I drew my own Colt and handed it over.

No one mentioned Betsy's concealed derringer – *I* certainly wasn't going to tell anyone it existed! – so that remained secure in its hiding place, wherever that might be.

Trask then gave both our guns to one of the spearmen who had accompanied him. "Thank you," he said. Then he said something in that language that was not quite Mayan, and arose. Once he was on his feet he added, "These gentlemen will escort you to your temporary quarters. I'm going to confer with the city's council of elders to decide how we want to handle you."

With that he turned and departed, followed by two of the Skyless, letting the curtain close behind them.

I looked at the remaining Skyless. "Now what?" I said.

They did not reply, but merely stood, spears in hand.

"Trask said they would escort us somewhere," Beckwith remarked.

"They don't seem to be in any hurry about it," I replied.

"Why would they be?" Betsy asked bitterly. "It's not as if we'll be going anywhere without them any time soon."

"We might be able to jump them and get those spears away from them," Beckwith suggested.

One of the Skyless said something.

I looked at Betsy, but she shook her head. "I can't make it out," she said. "Not a word."

I turned back to Beckwith. "I'm not inclined to try anything. Especially since we can't be absolutely sure they don't understand English."

"Oh, I can settle that," Betsy said, getting to her feet. She turned to one of the spearmen. "Hey, you motherless worm!"

And then, to my astonishment, she unleashed the most amazing stream of profanity I have ever heard. She included every obscenity I knew, and several I had never encountered before, all in direct relationship to our captors and what she supposed them to do in their spare time, suggesting acts involving men, women, children, and a variety of animals. I confess I blushed; I could feel my face turning bright red, and a glance at Beckwith showed that he was also affected, though perhaps, if I must be truthful, less so – only his ears and cheeks flushed, though his mouth hung open.

Perhaps the most amazing part was that my dear sweet Betsy delivered this most unladylike speech in a calm, conversational tone, without any hint of anger, as if she were merely telling the Skyless a mildly interesting anecdote.

The Skyless, for their part, watched her speak, and appeared to be listening, but did not react at all.

Finally Betsy concluded her tirade by suggesting that the three spearmen should perform a joint action that was probably impossible and would, if attempted, surely prove fatal to at least one of them, and smiled brightly. Then she turned to me.

"I don't think they know any English," she said.

I swallowed. "I certainly hope not," I said.

"Damn me, girl," Beckwith said, admiration in his voice. "I have *never* heard anything like that, not in the worst brothels in Frisco. If they didn't react to *that*, I'm not just sure they don't know English, I'm not sure they're *human*. Where did you learn all that?"

"I'm an engineer," she said. "I've been around men working on uncooperative machinery since I was ten."

"Those men must have not known you were listening," I said.

"Oh, they had usually forgotten I was there at all," she answered cheerfully.

"Indeed," I said. I glanced at the spearmen. "So we have established that they can't understand us – but of course Trask can, and we can't be completely sure of his whereabouts, so we'll want to be cautious."

"So you still don't want to jump them."

I shook my head. "Not just yet," I said. "That's a long, long tunnel to get back to where we came in, and besides what I said before, we don't know how fast these people are – everything else aside, they might be able to simply outrun us. Getting away from these three and heading back out the tunnel to the east isn't a good play. They could already have guards or traps between us and freedom. But I assure you, Mr. Beckwith, Betsy, I have no intention of spending the rest of my life down here. I'm sure there will be opportunities. I've already learned something that gives me hope – did you hear Trask say that if we had come in from the north, he might have let us go? That means that there's another exit, a way out to the north as well as the one to the east, and they wouldn't expect us to use it."

"Well, we don't know where it *is*," Betsy pointed out.

"Not yet," I admitted. "But perhaps we can find it. I'm guessing it's a shorter route; it might be where Trask himself came and went when he was visiting Emperor Norton. He said himself that he was unaware *our* entrance still existed."

One of the spearmen said something, and gestured with his weapon.

"I think our hosts grow impatient," Beckwith said, getting to his feet. He started toward his pack, only to be intercepted by a spear-point – apparently we were not permitted to bring our belongings.

I rose as well, and looked at my pack; one of the Skyless made a warning gesture. I waved an arm. "Lead the way," I said.

One of the Skyless did just that, while the other two followed behind us, spears at the ready. We departed through the southwest corner of the room, into a short tunnel that took two bends to the right and then delivered us into another, larger room, this one irregularly shaped and with three exits. A half-dozen of those greenish–yellow lamps were mounted on the walls, illuminating the entire space. It also held bunks, more than a dozen of them, stacked two or three high, along two sides. I counted four that held sleeping occupants; three more wakeful Skyless were seated on stone chests similar to those we had already seen and watched our arrival with mild interest. These three were not armed, so far as I could see, though their attire was otherwise similar to our captors.

The room held assorted other objects that I shall not bother to describe in detail, but I must mention that a niche in the center of the right-hand wall from where we entered held a great stack of gold, similar to those we had seen before but larger in every dimension. Beckwith headed for it the moment he saw it.

"Don't touch it!" I called.

He glanced over his shoulder at me, then stopped, close enough to look at that mysterious metal, but not touching it.

One of the spearmen stepped forward and prodded him; then all three of us were wordlessly but irresistibly guided over to three of the bunks.

"I take it these are our assigned places for the present," I said.

"So it would seem," Beckwith agreed.

"And I am to share quarters with you?" Betsy demanded.

"That appears to be the intention."

"Hmph." She threw herself onto her assigned bunk and slumped back against the wall.

"We haven't seen any of their women, have we?" Beckwith asked, gazing at the seated Skyless.

"I don't believe we have," I answered.

"Do you suppose they haven't *got* any?"

"That seems unlikely," I said.

"Do you think they're really human and not lizard creatures?" Beckwith mused.

"Yes," I replied shortly.

"All right, Derringer, no need to get testy. I was just thinking that maybe some of these *are* women." He made a sweeping gesture that took in all the room's occupants. "If they're reptiles of some sort it might be hard to tell."

"They're people, Mr. Beckwith, albeit strange ones."

"How can you be as certain as all that?"

I did not bother to answer. I had studied what I could of science and had read Mr. Darwin's book, and I did not believe anything descended from reptiles could look as human as these people did, but I did not want to waste my time arguing about it with Beckwith.

"This doesn't look like a prison," I said. "It looks like a barracks."

"I have no experience of either one," Betsy answered.

Beckwith, on the other hand, nodded. "Maybe they don't *have* a prison," he said. "Maybe they just kill all their troublemakers."

"Then why didn't they kill *us?*" I shook my head. "Trask said we would be guests, not prisoners, and if they wanted us dead we would be dead by now. I can't say I know just what our true situation is, but it seems to me that it could be far worse. I think we'll probably be able to escape in due time, when we've learned more about these people, and for now this place is not so bad."

"Mr. Trask said this was our *temporary* quarters," Betsy pointed out. "We may find ourselves somewhere worse soon enough."

"Or somewhere better," I replied. "He did say we would be treated like honored guests."

"There's more than one sort of honored guest," Beckwith muttered. "Being an honored guest at the Palace Hotel is one thing, and I'd be happy with that, but being the honored guest at one of the old Aztec rituals I'd sooner avoid."

"Once again, Mr. Smith – if they wanted us dead, we would already *be* dead."

"I wish they'd let us keep our packs."

"I'm sure they had an idea how many things we had in there that could be used as weapons – or that *are* weapons. We both had rifles, after all, and knives, and oil that would let us start serious fires even in these stone rooms." I looked around, and then settled onto the bed that had been assigned to me.

"What are you doing, Derringer?" Beckwith asked.

I lay back and closed my eyes. "I'm getting some sleep, Mr. Smith," I answered. "It's been a long day, and I could use a nap."

Beckwith hesitated, obviously not happy with my response, but seemingly unable to find an argument against it.

"That sounds good to me," Betsy said.

"Aw, Hell," Beckwith said, and he, too, climbed into his bed.

I took one last look at our captors, who were paying us no attention, then rolled over and went to sleep.

Chapter Seventeen

A Strange History

I was awakened by gentle shaking; I rolled over and sat up to see one of the Skyless stepping back from my bunk. Others were rousing Betsy and Beckwith. Behind them, I saw Gabriel Trask standing a few feet away.

Once we were all awake, Mr. Trask said, "Dear guests, I hope you are all well rested. I am here to begin your introduction to your new home and to begin your instruction in the language of your hosts."

"You expect us to learn that gibberish?" Beckwith demanded.

"Well, Mr. Smith, it would certainly simplify your life here, but it's entirely up to you. If you prefer to make do with hand gestures for the rest of your life, I can't force you to learn. I assure you, Kanta'an is not a terribly difficult tongue." (I am rendering the language of the Skyless as best I can; naturally, there is no standardized representation in our own alphabet.)

Beckwith grumbled.

"You must be hungry," Trask continued. "Come with me, and we'll find you food. On the way I'll tell you a little more about the Skyless." He beckoned.

We followed as he led us out of the barracks, through a maze of twisting and branching tunnels, some sloping gently up or down. As we walked, he said, "Once upon a time, long ago, the Skyless were not skyless; they lived above ground, as most people do. They built cities of stone and adobe, connected by highways, and ruled all the lands around us, from San Francisco Bay to Baja California, from the Pacific Ocean to the White Mountains of the Arizona Territory – I use the modern names, but it took me months of research to match the Kanta'an records to our present–day maps."

"There are written records?" I asked.

"Oh, yes," he said. "And I have been allowed to study them, a rare privilege for an outsider."

I was impressed, but said nothing more, and after a moment Trask resumed his tale.

"They were a peaceful nation, living in harmony with their neighbors and with the land, and they were known as the Lizard People even then, because they used the lizard as their totem, honoring it for its ability to survive in harsh conditions. They studied the ways of nature and learned many secrets our own people have yet to discover, including a chemical method whereby solid stone could be shaped or even dissolved, and ways of preserving food indefinitely, and other amazing arts. They developed a system of writing, and so that their important records might be preserved indefinitely, they used their chemicals to etch them into plates of solid gold."

"The Archives of the Skyless," I said.

"Not yet the Skyless, back then, but yes." Trask nodded. "They did not use gold for money, or even for ornaments, but they found it ideal for record–keeping, and as you know, California was relatively well supplied with it." He sighed. "There was one unfortunate incidental result of this, though. Once they had such an excellent way of preserving their history, they abandoned the old methods of storytelling, so that in the subsequent disasters many of their myths and legends were lost, and we know nothing at all of what happened *before* they began the golden archives. How they came here, why they were so different from their neighbors, how they made their scientific discoveries – all lost."

"Unfortunate," I remarked.

"Indeed," Trask said. "But only a very small misfortune compared to what befell them about three hundred years after their very earliest surviving records. As they describe it, a little over four thousand years ago a great ball of fire fell from the heavens one night and exploded with such fury that entire cities were leveled and thousands were killed. Other such fiery objects followed – none as great as the first, but enough to devastate their civilization."

"A barrage of meteors?" I said.

Trask nodded. Our path, I should mention, had been trending downward for some time at this point, deeper into the earth, and though I was not certain of my bearings, I thought we were heading west.

"Meteors, almost certainly," he agreed. "But they knew nothing of that. Unlike many ancient peoples, they had never studied the skies, preferring to look down at the earth. Now the skies had lashed out at them, and while their wise men argued as to whether they had done something to offend the gods, or whether they were innocent bystanders in some cosmic battle, they all agreed that they must escape the skies before more disasters befell. Thus they resolved to become the Skyless and tunnel beneath the earth where the fire from the sky could no longer harm them."

He paused and gestured dramatically. "Imagine it!" he said. "An entire civilization hiding itself away from the sun, moon, and stars! They used their rock-melting chemicals to create hundreds, *thousands* of miles of tunnels – thirteen buried cities in all, and the connections between them, entirely hidden from the world above!"

"*Thirteen* cities?" I exclaimed. I had never heard any claim for so high a number.

"Originally, yes," Trask replied, stopping at a curtained door. "Alas, most did not survive – those early Skyless were unaware that just as there are hazards to living beneath open sky, there are hazards to living in the earth. Almost immediately after they were settled, the seven northernmost cities were destroyed by gases leaking into the tunnels, rendering the air unbreathable. The descriptions are horrific, Mr. Derringer – not the descriptions made by the inhabitants of those cities, for there are none, but the accounts of travelers who went to investigate why they had lost all contact. Apparently the gas was invisible, odorless, virtually undetectable, so that no one realized what was happening until it was too late. The dead were found in their beds and in the hallways, their bodies preserved by the toxins – mummified, in fact. Men, women, and children alike, all dead, their withered corpses scattered throughout the cities." He shuddered. "Indeed, at least one search party was lost before the nature of the menace was recognized." Then he tugged aside the curtain. "Let us leave that aside for the moment, though, while you break your fast."

With that, he guided us into a room where a long stone table stood between rows of stools and gestured for us to take seats. As soon as we did, platters were set before us – fish, and mushrooms, and greens I did not recognize. Blunt knives were provided, but no forks.

We were indeed hungry, so all three of us set to, using the knives and our fingers.

Trask stood by, watching, occasionally popping a mushroom into his mouth. When our eating began to slow down, he resumed his tale.

"Here, in the sixth city, as the Skyless call it, there was some gas infiltration, but it was much slower than in the northern cities, and only a few died before the danger was recognized and preventive measures were taken," he said. "In the more southerly and easterly cities, the gas never emerged at all. But there were other hazards that arose over the long centuries. The third city, south of us, was wiped out by a plague some twelve hundred years ago, and the connecting tunnels were filled in so that the contagion could not spread. The second city, to the southeast, was abandoned almost two thousand years ago, for unknown reasons – visitors from the other cities simply found it empty one day, and the records there stopped abruptly, with no explanation."

Betsy had stopped eating to listen; she shuddered at this recitation of disasters.

"That leaves four," I said.

Trask nodded. "We have heard nothing from the fourth or fifth cities in my lifetime; according to the archives, the last contact with the fourth was about six hundred years ago, with the fifth about three hundred, but we do not know their actual circumstances. Trade had dropped off to nothing long before, and communications with them were abandoned out of simple neglect. As for the first city, in the White Mountains of the Arizona Territory, it still remains, or at any rate was still inhabited eight years ago, when I sent an emissary to investigate. He reported back that all seemed outwardly well there, but that he found the people strange, their language so changed over time that he had great difficulty understanding them, or making himself understood. They laughed at his questions and did not seem inclined toward further communication, so to the best of my knowledge no one from this city has been there since."

"*You* sent an emissary?" Betsy asked.

"Yes," Trask replied. "On behalf of Emperor Norton."

"Why didn't you send emissaries to the fourth and fifth cities?"

"I did," Trask said. "They never returned."

"It seems odd to me that the cities did not maintain regular trade with one another," I said. "Why were they so isolated?"

Trask shrugged. "Each city was built to be entirely self-supporting," he said. "There was nothing to trade that was worth so long a journey, and the Skyless...they are not an adventurous people. Remember, they built these cities to *hide* from the skies. Losing more than half their nation to poisonous gases in their first decade of underground life frightened them, and they gradually turned inward and withdrew from one another. The mysterious loss of the second city, and the plague in the third city, did nothing to encourage commerce. If their numbers had been increasing...but they weren't. They aren't. This refuge, the sixth city, was built to house five thousand people; there are scarcely eight hundred here today, and that is many more than my messenger found in the first city."

"But why?" I asked.

"I don't know," Trask said. "That is the mystery I came here to solve, and I stay here in hopes of somehow reversing this decline. Perhaps there is something subtly lacking in their environment, some aspect of the upper world that would let them thrive. Perhaps their race is simply growing old, and without any admixture of fresh blood from intermarriage with their neighbors it must eventually perish. I wish I knew, but I do not. I have devoted my time here to studying the Archives of the Skyless in hopes of finding some hint, some clue that would show me the truth, but as yet I have found nothing."

"You said that the city is entirely self-supporting," Beckwith said.

"That's right."

"Then where did this fish come from? And this...whatever this green stuff is?"

Trask smiled. "From the western tunnels," he said. "This city extends down into the Pacific Ocean – and also *under* it, though that's another issue. There are two tunnels open to the sea where the Skyless harvest fish and seaweed for their food and collect sludge that they use to grow mushrooms."

"*Seaweed?*" Beckwith exclaimed. "Is that what that is?"

Trask nodded. "A variety I believe is unknown to the surface world. It's very nutritious, and I quite like the taste, myself."

Beckwith stared at the greens remaining on his plate with open distaste.

For my own part I admit that I might have thought the idea of eating seaweed unappetizing, but I had found our meal decent enough, so I did not let this revelation trouble me – nor, I saw, did Betsy.

"They also eat insects," Trask said. "But we thought it unwise to introduce you to that particular food until you have had time to adjust."

"Well, thank you for *that*," Beckwith said, pushing his plate away.

"Besides obtaining most of their food from the ocean, they also use the tides to generate power and pump fresh air through the city," Trask continued.

At that, Betsy suddenly sat up straight. "They do?" she asked. "How does that work?"

Startled, Trask stared at her.

"She takes an interest in engineering," I said.

"Does she?" Trask asked. "How unusual!"

"Tell me about these tidal pumps," Betsy demanded.

"I don't...I don't know any details," Trask admitted. "This is not an area that *I* ever took any interest in."

"Who can tell me and show them to me, then?"

Trask smiled crookedly. "Until you learn Kanta'an, no one."

"Then I'll learn it, the sooner the better."

"So you get your food from the sea," I said. "What about fresh water?"

"We have wells, of course."

I nodded.

Ever since Trask had first mentioned that some of the tunnels connected to the Pacific, the idea that we might escape from the stone labyrinth of the Skyless by swimming had been stirring in the back of my mind. Betsy and I were both strong swimmers; I did not know about Beckwith. Finding our way out through unlit underwater passages might not be practical, though, and the waters off the coast in this part of California were reputed to be treacherous and cold, so I had hoped to learn that there were links to some river – the Los Angeles, or Rio Hondo, or San Gabriel – that might be more accessible. It seemed we were not that fortunate.

Those tidal pumps might be useful somehow, though. If they drew in fresh air, there must be an opening to the world above to admit that air. Betsy was far more knowledgeable about such things than I was, and I would want to speak to her about it when we were once again out of Trask's earshot. It might prove necessary to learn the local tongue before we could make good our escape, so that she could study the mechanisms that kept the tunnels habitable.

Fortunately, I had a reasonably good head for languages, though I had discovered in Mexico that I was far better at *written* languages than spoken ones, and that Betsy was much better than I at picking up unfamiliar speech. I had hardly learned any Mayan during our stay in Chan Santa Cruz, while she had acquired a solid grounding in that peculiar dialect. Her Spanish was also far superior to my own, but she had studied that language beforehand, while I had not; I had picked up the smattering I had largely because of similarities to Latin and French.

I had a passable command of French, German, Latin, Greek, Hebrew, and Russian, but I did not think any of those would be any help among the Skyless.

"We have air, and water, and food enough for our people," Trask said. "There is more than enough space, with the reduced population. Each of you can have a suite of rooms, if you like – I can give you a tour of the available apartments later. You will have to come down to these lower levels for your food and water. Once you have learned your way around and a little of the language, you will be free to roam anywhere in the city, with two exceptions – you are not to set foot in either the eastern highway, where you entered, nor the northern passage. And while it isn't forbidden, I would advise you to stay out of the old southern passage; it was closed off over a thousand years ago, and no maintenance has been done in all that time, so I cannot be sure it's safe. After all, while these tunnels were built to be secure from earthquakes and other disturbances, nothing man-made is perfect."

"Earthquakes?" I asked.

"Of course," Trask replied. "We *are* in California, after all. In fact, a fault line runs through the city, a little west of here. The tunnels through it all have special reinforcement and are designed to survive its movements. If you go that way, you'll see where the tunnels have been distorted over the centuries, and have required adjustments."

"What sort of adjustments?" Betsy asked.

"Cutting away partial blockages, mostly."

"Is that done with the legendary rock-melting chemicals you mentioned?"

"Well, it used to be; I'm afraid the secret of manufacturing those chemicals has been lost. I mean 'lost' literally; it's presumably written down in the archives somewhere, but no one can find that record. Apparently someone died without passing on that particular bit of knowledge. The elders do still have a small supply of the fluid that they have hoarded carefully for...well, several hundred years, anyway. Except for the most extreme emergencies they reserve that for their record keeping, though, and any stone-carving that needs to be done now is done with hammer and chisel. You'll see that the walls of the passages through the fault-line are noticeably cruder than the corridors elsewhere." He shook his head. "It's such a shame, that so glorious a scientific heritage has been so diminished."

"So they don't know how to duplicate their ancestors' feats?" I asked. "Those lanterns, for example..."

"Oh, these?" Trask interrupted, picking up one of the greenish lamps that stood on our dining table. "Oh, we still know how to make *these*! The glowing fluid is distilled from certain mushrooms; they have been bred for millennia to give as much light as possible. The fluid only lasts a few days, and then it must be replenished; if *that* secret had been lost, we would all be wandering about in complete darkness. No, we still have *that*. I expect you'll learn the process yourself, so that you can maintain your own lamps." He glanced at our plates. "In fact, if you're done eating, I can show you that right now."

We exchanged glances, and then I shrugged. "Lead on, Mr. Trask," I said. "Lead on."

Chapter Eighteen

The Society of the Skyless

The artificial caves where the glowing fungi grew were strange and beautiful and blindingly bright after so long in the dimly lit tunnels. We were taught, with gestures, how to harvest the gills of the mushrooms and press the fluid into metal canisters with strings threaded through the open ends; then the canisters were swung around one's head to separate out the components of this mysterious liquid, the useless top and bottom layers were drained off, and the concentrated glowing portion that remained was sealed into transparent tubes with metal rods at either end that somehow excited the fluid into yielding a brighter, steadier light.

Beckwith asked whether these mushrooms also provided part of the city's food supply, and Trask assured him that they did not; these fungi were poisonous. The edible varieties, of which they had several, were grown elsewhere.

Mr. Trask then gave us a tour of several available residences and began our language lessons as we wound our way through interminable stone corridors. In the end we chose three adjoining apartments, each comprised of a bedchamber, a sitting room, and a sort of closet, all equipped with only the most basic furniture, all of it made of stone, metal, or what I thought were ceramics – wood was rare and precious in this underground realm. The Skyless, we were assured, did make cloth from fungi, or other subterranean materials, but it was difficult to manufacture and therefore used sparingly. Clothing and door curtains were common enough, but wasting this expensive fabric on a tablecloth or rug would be seen as an absurd extravagance.

In the absence of daylight we had lost track of time, and I had forgotten to wind my watch, so I cannot say what hour it was when Trask left us, saying he would be back to continue the tour and our language lessons on the morrow, but we wished him a good night, and he did not demur.

We did not retire immediately, though, but gathered in my sitting room to discuss our situation.

"We need to get out of here," Beckwith began.

"Of course we do," I said. "The questions are how and when."

"My parents – when they don't hear from me..." Betsy said.

I took her hand. "I know," I said. "My mother, as well."

"Those big golden books – just one of those would make us rich," Beckwith said.

"They would also make the Skyless far more determined to stop us and fetch them back," I pointed out.

"Those glowing mushrooms might be just as valuable," Betsy said. "I've never seen anything like that! And these tide machines, if they really exist – that design could be worth a fortune, too."

"Gold is simpler," Beckwith retorted.

"I am not a thief," I told him. "Neither is Betsy."

"I'm a soldier of fortune," Beckwith replied. "And those gold books are a fortune!"

"They aren't ours."

"And since when are adventurers so careful about who owns what?" he demanded. "You said your family got rich off your father's adventures – where did *that* money come from?"

"Men long dead, for the most part," I said. "But I concede your point; adventurers are generally not very scrupulous about property rights. Still, I have nothing against the Skyless, and those books are precious to them, a part of their heritage."

"What does it matter, if we can't get out?" Betsy exclaimed. "Could we get back to our entry shaft before they caught us?"

"We have lights now," I said, gesturing at the mushroom lamp on the table in front of us. "We don't need our lanterns and oil. We could travel lighter."

"We'd still need food and water," Beckwith pointed out.

"They have to feed us," Betsy said. "We could cache supplies until we're ready."

"That's true," I said. "And I can't believe they wouldn't have thought about all this. I'm sure there are guards somewhere between here and there."

"We can shoot our way out," Beckwith said. He reached down and pulled a narrow, long-barreled revolver from his boot. He saw Betsy's look of surprise, and said, "You didn't really think I'd give up *all* my weapons, did you?"

I wondered for an instant whether Betsy might reveal the existence of her own little gun, but I should have known better. She was not so foolish as that. She said nothing.

I, on the other hand, replied to Beckwith's suggestion. "I hope it won't come to that," I said. "Besides, a single pistol may not be enough. That's a five–shot weapon, isn't it? What if they send six men after us?"

"Three of us should be able to take down one or two of those little fellows."

"And what if they send a dozen? Remember, you're suggesting we shoot down their guards in cold blood; they'll want revenge. We won't necessarily be safe once we're out, either, especially not if we take one of their books; remember that story about El Dorado. Trask has friends elsewhere, and the Skyless *can* live aboveground, even if they don't want to. We don't know what they're capable of, or what they'll do."

"Then what do *you* suggest, Tom?" Betsy said, clearly annoyed.

"I suggest we bide our time and learn as much about these people as we can, until we can find a way to slip away unnoticed, probably through the northern exit Trask mentioned. If we don't steal from them or harm anyone, I don't think they'll bother to pursue us once we're out."

"And if they do?"

I shrugged. "We will deal with that if the occasion arises. Above ground we will have resources they do not."

Neither of them seemed entirely satisfied with my position, but they did not argue further, and we went to our respective apartments to sleep.

I was awakened some time later – I had no way of knowing how long I had slept – and led to the corridor outside my apartment, where Mr. Trask and two of the Skyless were waiting. Others soon brought Betsy and Mr. Beckwith out to join us, and we continued the tour that had been interrupted the day before.

As we walked, we alternated lessons in the history and culture of the Skyless with lessons in their language. Their grammar seemed deceptively simple at first, as their tongue was positional, rather than inflected; there were no cases or complicated tenses to worry about, and the basic sentence structure began with the verb, followed it with the subject, and concluded with the object, if any – rather like Hebrew, though there was no other similarity I could discern.

But then we began to get into the suffixes that served in place of adjectives, adverbs, and every other sort of modifier, as well as odd little words that indicated what category an accompanying noun fell into, or whether a verb should be interpreted as an ongoing or completed action. I should have known that no human language is ever really simple; we all have complex things we want to say.

Their history, on the other hand, *was* surprisingly simple, because they had lived in the same place for four millennia and had little interaction with the outside world. Generation after generation had lived and died in these same tunnels, building nothing beyond their original walls. There had been famous leaders, and religious disputes, and trade missions, but when all was said and done these people had lived out their lives hidden away beneath the ground. There were no invasions, no empires, no migrations, no wars.

They had gone through periods when they traded with outsiders, mostly exchanging worked metal or stone for fabrics; the most recent, trading with the Gabrieleno Indians, had ended about sixty years earlier, when they had first encountered white men. The Skyless elders had concluded that continued trade was too risky; they did not want to get caught up in any conflict between the whites and the Indians, and they did not trust the white men to stay out of the tunnels if they once learned of their existence. They had withdrawn entirely into their own realm, and from then until Mr. Trask had stumbled upon them in 1862 they had had no contact with the outside world whatsoever.

As for their religion, despite their small numbers they had varied beliefs; Trask said he knew of three distinct sects and suspected that there were more secretive cults, as well. All were polytheistic to one degree or another, and all agreed that the gods of the sky hated the Skyless, but beyond that...well, in truth I did not particularly concern myself with the details, since I saw no way in which the knowledge could be useful to us.

The golden records, the Archives of the Skyless, had begun as a mere secular history, but had long ago taken on religious significance; they were now considered sacred objects, to be handled and read only by those who had undergone a day-long cleansing ritual. Trask had performed the necessary rites several times. When not in use they were carefully stored in specific places, and disturbing them was blasphemy. Many were kept in niches and shelves such as we had already seen, scattered about the city, in locations apparently determined by some sort of geomancy, but Trask told us that far more were kept in a sort of central library that was the closest thing the Skyless had to a holy of holies; no unclean person was permitted to set foot in this room, on penalty of death. He, himself, had been allowed into it twice, after the appropriate purification rituals, and accompanied by guardian elders each time to make sure he did not disturb anything but those items he was to read. In the library and in the various shelves and niches, each and every volume had its own particular place, and no other book was ever to occupy that spot. We were strongly instructed never to touch or disturb any of the sacred archives.

I wanted to say something to Beckwith about this, to gloat a little about warning him against attempting to steal any of the books, but I could not catch his eye and dared not speak openly while Trask was in earshot.

We encountered some of the Skyless women – delicate little things, just as hairless as their men, who made the petite

Betsy appear a veritable Amazon by comparison. We saw one or two children in the corridors, but very few. The belted tunics we had seen at first were the uniforms of the city's guards; not everyone wore them. Indeed, not everyone wore *anything*; nudity was common in both sexes and all ages. In an environment where there was no sun nor rain nor wind, and where the temperature never varied, clothing was not particularly necessary, and as I have already mentioned, they had no easy way to produce fabric in quantity. When they did take the trouble to dress themselves they were fond of bright colors and bold patterns that contrasted strongly with their pale skin; the sea creatures they caught provided a variety of dyes.

Their tools, implements, and ornaments were made of stone, metal, bone, shell, and a peculiar sort of resin, unlike anything I had seen anywhere else, that they called *a'akbu*. They made this resin from petroleum, combined with materials taken from the sea. The stools and other objects I had thought to be ceramic in nature were almost all made of various forms of *a'akbu*; the transparent tubes in their lamps, which I had assumed to be glass, were *a'akbu*. Even some of their clothing was *a'akbu*. This material, a product of their ancient expertise in chemistry, was astonishingly versatile.

They also used petroleum products as fuel for the forges that allowed them to work metal, and their cookstoves burned kerosene; they did not burn it for light, however, because of the difficulties in regulating smoke and heat. Only their smithies and kitchens ever used any sort of open combustion.

They derived these fuels from the soil surrounding their tunnels. We were told that the earth beneath Los Angeles was rich in petroleum, enough to last the Skyless for millennia.

All our meals were comprised of sea foods and fungi, though the details varied. The only beverages were water and a sort of thin beer – Trask seemed uncertain himself where this latter drink came from, and it was potable but not particularly interesting.

When we finally returned to our assigned quarters we found a pleasant surprise – our packs had been restored to us, resting by each door. They were not, however, quite as full as before; our rifles were gone, and all the ammunition, and all the cans and bottles of lamp oil.

"The Skyless are not thieves," Trask explained. "But we couldn't leave you anything really dangerous, not until we know you better and feel we can trust you."

The next day – if "day" is the right word for a period of wakefulness that may or may not correspond to any external time – we focused more on language instruction, with Trask and half a dozen of the Skyless working with us. We did ask a few questions, though, and learned a few more details about the society in which we found ourselves.

The Skyless did not measure time by the motion of the sun, as we do above ground, since they never saw the sun; instead they measured it by the tides in the underground pools where they harvested food from the ocean. This gave them a cycle somewhat longer than a solar day, but worked well enough in regulating their daily concerns. They had developed their own peculiar usages in regard to time; where we would speak of morning, midday, and evening, they had a terminology based on the rising and falling tides.

They had few words for land plants of any kind, and for most animals they used a term that I would translate as "beast" modified by suffixes indicating size, rather than having distinct names for different species. They did distinguish lizards of several varieties, though I saw none anywhere in the city, and they classified all insects and arachnids as either white, meaning they spent their entire lives beneath ground, or black, meaning they ventured out into the sun, regardless of the actual color of the creatures in question.

Their vocabulary describing fungi was vast and complex; I never did master it all.

Their word for "gold" was also their word for "book," and Trask said that the few who had tried to learn English had found the distinction ridiculous. Gold that had not yet been rendered into pages in the archives was considered unfinished books, and the possibility of using it for something else was so blasphemous as to be almost inconceivable. The long discussions they had with Trask on this subject were why even Skyless who knew no more than a dozen words of English knew both "gold" and "book," though not, perhaps, exactly how to use them correctly.

Most of the men owned tunics and belts and spears and would take turns as soldiers or guards when called upon, but Trask's claim on that first night to have three hundred armed men at his disposal had been an absurd exaggeration; there were only a little over three hundred men in the entire city, and at any given time most of those who were not asleep or home with their families worked at the tidal pools or in the cavernous mushroom farms, or in the maintenance crews that inspected and repaired the tunnels. Typically, about fifteen were staying in the barracks where we had initially been housed, to patrol the outer corridors and guard the city's entrances. These would be unmarried young men not yet settled in a profession, or family men who had decided they needed a temporary respite from their usual duties; the exact make–up of this squadron was determined by the elders, and men could be assigned to it as the elders saw fit, but I had the impression there were usually plenty of volunteers.

As for the elders, there were thirty or so in all, perhaps a third of them women, who served as a ruling council, as priests, and as scribes, maintaining and expanding the golden archives; I never did understand how they were chosen. The majority were indeed elderly, but a few were still relatively young and vigorous and could easily have continued to labor elsewhere.

Women and children were responsible for cleaning, weaving, food preparation, and many of the same duties that the fair sex has been delegated in most cultures.

Both sexes participated in a variety of games and pastimes; they had dice of a sort, either triangular or tetrahedral rather than cubical, that served in several amusements, and they also held contests involving tossing stones. There were word games that we were never proficient enough in the language to follow. The children played finger games that grew more complex with age, until in adolescence they became a part of courting rituals.

You may recall that Mr. Trask had claimed the Skyless had weapons far more sophisticated than spears; this was another exaggeration. They did have knives, but nothing as formidable as a sword, and they also had poisoned *a'akbu* darts with barbed fishbone tips that they could throw with remarkable accuracy, or launch from blowguns. That was all; any implication that they possessed fantastic weapons produced by long–lost science, other than the lethal poison in the darts, was false. So far as I could see, other than the amazing things they did with *a'akbu,* their greatest scientific accomplishments were all in the field of cultivating fungi, though there were features of the tunnels that supported their claims that their ancestors had carved most of these rooms and corridors with solvents, rather than ordinary tools.

The passages through the fault lines, on the other hand, showed every indication of cruder methods – chisel marks, cracked stone, and so on. Tunnels that had once been straight but had shifted as much as several feet out of alignment during earthquakes or other seismic activity would have jogs, where the portion on either side of the jog would have smooth, featureless walls, while the connection between them was rough-hewn and uneven. Some of these connections had obviously been done in stages, as the movement of the earth continued.

After a time Trask stopped guiding us; we were left to explore on our own, or with the assistance of our neighbors. We had reached a level where we – well, Betsy, at any rate, and to a lesser extent myself – could communicate with the Skyless well enough to get by on a very basic level. Beckwith, I regret to say, seemed unable to grasp the grammar of Kanta'an and made do with single words, awkward phrases, and hand gestures.

We spoke among ourselves at times, exchanging ideas about an eventual escape, but somehow never arrived at a plan we could all agree upon, and so we remained among the Skyless.

Chapter Nineteen

Our Captivity Continues

As time passed we became more familiar with the city and so accustomed to the yellow–green light of the mushroom lamps that we no longer found anything strange in the distorted colors around us. Guided partly by the knowledge that none of the archives were near it I found the northern exit, only to discover that it was guarded and the guards were not easily swayed from their duties. Beckwith attempted to venture out the eastern passage, as a trial run for a planned escape, and discovered that not only was it now guarded at all times by a pair of Skyless spearmen, but an iron gate had been installed, twenty or thirty feet from the intersection where the tunnel joined the city. The guards showed Beckwith the gate, to discourage him from any further attempts at bypassing them, and then escorted him back to his apartment.

Betsy got her chance to explore the tidal pumps and declared them to be a masterpiece of ancient engineering, fully up to modern standards in their efficiency but constructed almost entirely of solid stone, arranged and balanced so that as the tide rose water would top a barrier and flow onto immense levers. The weight of the water would then move the lever, driving a sort of piston in a shaft; then as the tide withdrew, the water would drain away, and when enough weight had been thus removed the lever would reset itself. The pistons in turn worked gigantic valves, pumping in fresh air and expelling smoke from the kitchens and foundries. I asked her whether they might provide a way out of the city, and she considered the matter for several hours before reluctantly concluding that she could not see how. The pistons were so tightly fitted in their shafts – indeed, needed to be in order to function effectively – that she could see no way to pass them, and the valves were likewise arranged to prevent any passage. And while it was impossible to see firsthand, the Skyless engineers insisted that the many air shafts beyond the valves were much too small for people to climb through, since they had been designed to be invisible from the surface.

The hours passed slowly. Beckwith maintained an unhealthy interest in the golden archives and clearly still hoped to steal a few volumes before escaping the city; Betsy worried about her parents, about how her father was faring in the South Seas, and what they might think of her when she at last returned to them. None of us believed our captivity would be permanent; there were simply too many ways we might eventually free ourselves. Betsy and I discussed constructing a breathing apparatus like the one we had used in Mexico, which might let us swim out through the underwater tunnels to the ocean, but we had difficulty in imagining sources for the necessary materials. The Skyless worked metal, but not well enough, so far as we could see, to produce piping or tanks that would hold compressed air; they did not seem to know how to weld anything. Perhaps if we knew how to work *a'akbu*, and could be sure it was impervious enough to hold air under pressure – but we had no idea how the stuff was manufactured, and while we quickly became familiar with some of its characteristics, its subtler aspects remained a mystery. A few experiments with empty lamp casings were not encouraging.

Beckwith seemed convinced that if he could just find the right person to shoot, or threaten to shoot, he would be released. He thought that if he could determine which of the elders was the chief, and catch him in the right circumstances, he could put a gun to the man's head and walk out.

Personally, I kept my mental options open. I thought swimming out might work, but I also considered ways to so ingratiate myself to the elders that they would release us, or whether we might get past the eastern gate or the northern guards undetected, or whether there might be openings to the outside world we had not yet found. That tunnel to the plague-destroyed third city, for example – could it be re-opened? There were undoubtedly exits to the surface in the vicinity of that long-deserted city. Of course, it was several days' travel distant...

We sometimes mused on what might have happened to the other Skyless cities and whether they might have influenced events in the outside world. All three of us had noted the similarities between the Archives of the Skyless and the descriptions of the golden plates that the angel Moroni had reportedly shown to Joseph Smith, though the lizard people's books were many times larger than what Smith had described. We wondered whether there might be some connection between the Skyless and the founding of the Mormon church – had a part of the archives from one of the lost cities somehow found its way to New York?

I very much regretted that the Skyless did not have any sort of paper. Their supply of gold, the origins of which were kept secret, was reserved for their own archives; the suggestion that I might want some to write my own journal was met first with incomprehension, and then with derision. Mr. Trask expressed some sympathy and told me that if he ever again ventured above ground he would try to bring me back a supply of paper and ink.

The limited diet became wearying after a time, to the point I even ventured, purely to add variety, to try some of the fried insects the Skyless ate. The extended period without sunlight dampened our mood, as well.

As the weeks passed Betsy and I slipped past the Skyless fishermen and made a few attempts to swim out to the Pacific without any special breathing apparatus, but even at low tide the tunnels connecting the city to the ocean were fully submerged, with no openings or air pockets to be found; we would need to hold our breath for the entire distance. On our first such dive we lost our way in the darkness and had to return, gasping, to where we had started. On our second we brought a lamp and found that it functioned underwater, illuminating a long, airless tunnel at least twenty yards in diameter, with its far end completely lost in darkness. There was simply no way we could hold our breath long enough to escape by that route. To escape by sea we would need to construct an air supply, and we had not yet devised a means to do that.

Betsy began quietly collecting tools and materials, thinking that she would eventually be able to build a suitable device, but progress was very slow; the Skyless were careful with their equipment and supplies.

At one point I calculated that we had been down there perhaps two months, and the consequent realization that the Christmas season was upon us and that we were still trapped in this strange, dimly-lit underworld was hard for all of us, but most especially for Betsy. She took to her apartment and spoke to no one for some time. I tried to improvise a celebration, singing a few carols and offering a toast with the weak beer, but that only made matters worse; the religious nature of the songs only served to remind her of her estrangement from her mother.

I did draw the interest of some of the Skyless, though; while they had songs of their own, they were very different from the seasonal paeans to the birth of Our Lord. They demanded I sing more, and I found myself compelled to leave poor Betsy sobbing in her apartment while I regaled our captors with my own off-key renditions of "O Little Town of Bethlehem" and "Good Christian Men Rejoice."

I had planned to surprise Betsy with a small gift in honor of the holiday, but I decided that could only make matters worse and abandoned the notion.

Beckwith was no help; his only concession to the season was to suggest that the present *he* wanted was a stack of books – golden ones, by choice. I believe there was also a reference to frankincense and myrrh.

Within what I estimated to be a day or two Betsy had repented of her girlish weakness and was once again roaming the city, her features stern as she studied the tidal pumps more closely, looking for a means by which one might slip through them without being drowned or crushed. She did not, however, seem inclined to spend time with me. Left to myself, I set about cultivating an acquaintance with one of the elders, a woman named Kinja. I had an idea that perhaps I might be permitted to read some of the archives and that I might find therein a hint to some means of escape.

Mr. Trask had mostly focused on teaching us the spoken form of Kanta'an, but he had introduced us to the written version, as well, pointing out messages written on the walls and translating them for us. There was no alphabet as such, but instead most nouns were represented by ideograms, while additional characters represented syllables that could be arranged around the ideogram to provide descriptive suffixes. These same syllable characters could be assembled under a sort of arrow figure to form verbs, while a different family of simpler ideograms represented the category words. It did not have the elegance and flexibility of our own system, but it functioned well enough and indeed could be read very quickly once mastered. I thought that given the chance, I would be able to read the sacred books.

I said as much to Mr. Trask at one chance encounter, and he laughed in my face, perhaps the only time I ever saw him be downright rude.

"Do you think, Mr. Derringer, that the language has not changed over four thousand years?" he said. "The oldest volumes are barely intelligible to the elders, after years of study! You would be lucky to puzzle out a single sentence."

Resentful of his tone, I answered, "I don't think it's a matter of luck, Mr. Trask."

He sobered. "You're right, of course. It's not luck. It's study, years of diligent study, that would make the more ancient texts subject to interpretation. I have been doing exactly that since poor Joshua Norton died, and I am now reasonably comfortable with books dating back almost two millennia, but the very oldest still baffle me."

"I would still like to see them," I replied. "Perhaps not the oldest, but some of the more recent entries.

"Well, maybe you will, someday," he said. "It's not up to me; that's for the elders to decide."

Initially, the three of us had spent most of our time together, and Gabriel Trask had been with us as often as not. As our ability to speak to the Skyless directly grew, though, Trask's visits grew briefer and scarcer. Beckwith began to go off on his own, pursuing his escape plans; he had concluded that he was as likely to find a way out on his own as we were to find one as a group, and he made no bones about his belief that our moral scruples might hinder him when the time came.

That left Betsy and I, but I did not share her interest in the ancient machinery of the lower levels, and she did not share *my* interest in the archives or the elders, so we, too, began to spend time apart – especially after that miserable Christmas, when I was helpless to soothe her.

I sometimes found myself dawdling around the city's northern exit, chatting in my primitive Kanta'an with the guards there. I discovered that an iron gate had been installed in that passage, just as in the eastern exit.

I located what had once been the southern exit; it now ended in a wall of tumbled rock about a hundred yards from the intersection where it left the city. Every so often, when I felt especially frustrated or simply in need of some vigorous exercise, I would wander down there and pull free some of the rocks, flinging them back down the tunnel. After a few weeks I had made little visible progress, but had picked at all the easiest targets. What remained ahead of me was almost entirely rocks too large for me to shift, let alone toss aside; it was clear that I was never going to penetrate that barrier without assistance, whether from machinery or willing hands.

We saw in the new year of 1884, as closely as we could estimate the transition, with a dismal little gathering in my apartment; it was not so thorough a failure as my attempt at celebrating Christmas, but I cannot call it a success.

I happened to mention it to Mr. Trask a few days later, and he remarked that because the Skyless were skyless, and had no

view of the moon or sun or stars, they did not have a specific
date that marked the start of a new year. They were vaguely
aware of the differences in temperature and rainfall caused by
the changing seasons; most years, during the heaviest winter
rains, some moisture seeped through certain spots in the
ceilings of some of the more northerly tunnels, and the Skyless
elders used that to indicate a new year.

"Sometimes that happens as early as November," he said.
"This year, though, it has yet to occur."

Not being familiar with the climate of Los Angeles, I asked,
"Is that unusual?"

"Well, *I've* never seen it this late before."

I wondered whether that meant a drought up above and
asked whether the wells would be affected.

"They never have been yet," he told me.

We knew, of course, that a volcano called Krakatoa,
somewhere in the South Seas, had exploded in late August with
so great a blast that it could be heard over a thousand miles
away in Australia; Betsy's father had gone off to study the
consequent phenomena. In San Francisco I had heard that
certain scientists had suggested that the dust and gas ejected
from this tremendous eruption might affect the weather for
some time; could its influence have disrupted the rainy season
here, all the way on the other side of the Pacific?

I would never know, so long as I stayed in the catacombs of
the Skyless – at least, not unless someone brought the news
down.

"How often do you venture up into the sunlight?" I asked
Trask.

"Oh, not often," he said. "I used to spend about half my
time outside, visiting other communities or reporting to the
emperor, but since his death I have lived down here exclusively.

I did go up to do a little shopping early last year – I wanted a new razor, and the Skyless, of course, being hairless, have no use for such things. I picked up a few other items that I cannot obtain here, as well, and posted letters to a few acquaintances to let them know I was still well."

"Letters?" I said, startled.

"Yes. I haven't forgotten how to write English, Mr. Derringer, and I do have a few cousins and old friends here and there."

"Mr. Trask, I know you don't want us to reveal where we are, or what our circumstances are, but could you perhaps let Betsy and myself send letters to our parents, to let them know we are alive and well? We would let you read them before posting, of course."

"Oh! Why, I suppose I could. Indeed, I don't know why none of us thought of it sooner. I shall have to discuss it with the elders, of course, and we must be very cautious – you adventurers are notorious for including secret messages in apparently harmless missives."

"I would very much appreciate an opportunity to reassure my mother and sister."

He nodded. "I will see what I can do. You must remember, while I may have more freedom than you, I, too, am a guest here, and come and go only at the sufferance of the elders."

"Of course."

We left it at that, and went on about our business.

The following day, when I arose and emerged from my apartment into the corridor, I found Beckwith waiting for me.

"I'd like a word with you, Derringer," he said.

"Of course, Mr. Smith." He had still not revealed his true identity to Trask or any of the Skyless – not that any of them would care. "Step inside." I held the door curtain aside.

When we were in my sitting room with the curtain closed again, he demanded, "When are you planning to make a break for it?"

Startled, I admitted, "I don't know."

"Not soon?"

"Not really soon, no." I knew Betsy's progress on the breathing device had been slow.

"Well, I am. I can't take it any longer, living down here like rats, never seeing the sun. I want to get out while I still remember what the sky looks like!"

I did not know how to respond to that, and while I was groping for something to say, he reached inside his vest and drew forth a scrap of paper.

(I should perhaps have mentioned sooner that none of us were comfortable in the attire of the Skyless. We would wear the native garments only when washing our own clothes, and otherwise retained our customary dress – well, except for our hats, which seemed singularly pointless in the tunnels. As for sharing in the native tradition of casual nudity, none of us, so far as I am aware, ever even considered it.)

He unfolded the paper and handed it to me. I looked at it and saw that it was a receipt for the coils of rope we had bought in Pomona, rather the worse for wear after having spent more than a month in Beckwith's vest pocket.

Beckwith obviously saw my confusion. "Turn it over," he said impatiently.

I did, and found a handful of names and addresses scribbled on the back in somewhat smeared pencil.

"My employers," he explained. "In case you get out and I don't, let them know what's become of me. And if you get out and I don't but I'm still alive, I'd appreciate it if you'd show them how to get into this confounded place. I'm not fool enough to think they'd risk trying to rescue me for my own sake, but they will if you tell them there's gold down here."

I considered that for a moment. Then I looked him in the eye. "If I get out and you're dead, I'm not leading anyone back here; I don't have any great love for the Skyless, but I don't want to see them slaughtered."

"If I'm dead, I don't give a tinker's dam *what* you do," he said. "But if I'm alive, I promised these men I'd lead them to any treasure you found."

"And you want to be rescued."

He nodded. "Wouldn't you?"

"And if you get out and I don't, will you lead them back here and rescue *me*?"

"I'll come back for the gold, and if I can get you out in the process, I'll do it. I don't have anything against you, Derringer – you've been square with me, and I'll try to be the same with you."

"Fair enough," I said. "And I take it, since we're having this conversation, that you have a plan in mind."

"I won't deny it."

"You aren't going to tell me any more than that?"

"I don't see any reason I should."

"Unless you want my help," I said, "you're probably right. I can't tell anyone what I don't know. So your scheme won't accommodate all three of us?"

"I can't risk having you slow me down."

I nodded. "As you please, then."

He hesitated, then asked, "Do *you* have an escape plan?"

"I have several," I said. "I'm just not sure yet which one is most likely to succeed, and they all still need some work. If I settle on one where you can help out, I'll let you know."

"Good enough." He held out his hand, and we shook on it.

Then he turned and ducked out through the curtain, and a moment later I followed.

Chapter Twenty

An Escape Attempt

I had told Beckwith that I was considering several possible ways to escape, and that was the truth, but alas, the best of them all seemed to require something we did not have – better materials to construct an underwater breathing device, or access to our confiscated ammunition so that we could use the gunpowder to manufacture an explosive device, or a means of bribing Skyless guards to betray their own people, or a supply of the mysterious solvent they called *tunskush* – literally, "stone eater" – that had been used to construct the city's tunnels four thousand years earlier.

Betsy had created a breathing device once before, which was why we considered it our best option, but in that case she had had a proper set of tools and the broken remains of a steam engine as her materials. Here we had only a few crude tools – hammers, chisels, tongs, and knives, mostly – and the closest thing we had to pipes were the lamp casings, or the *a'akbu* blowguns the Skyless used for their poison darts. Betsy had not yet found anything that she was sure would withstand the pressure we would need while being a manageable size and weight.

The whereabouts of our weapons was a complete mystery; Trask hinted at one point that they had simply been dropped into the sea in one of the fishing tunnels.

The Skyless did not use money very much; there were little stamped metal coins that were employed in their gambling games, but which did not seem to have any other function. We had none of those coins, nor anything else they valued enough to serve as a bribe.

As for *tunskush*, we were told that they only had a limited quantity, and even that was reserved for etching records onto sheets of gold. By talking to Kinja and (not to put too fine a point on it) spying on the other elders I had determined that the supply they used for the archives was somewhere very near to their central library, if not in the library itself then along one of two passages that connected to that sacred chamber, but since I was forbidden to enter that area I had been unable to learn exactly where, or how to access it.

I had hopes of narrowing down further the location of the *tunskush* and somehow stealing some of it; unless Betsy came up with a breathing device, that really seemed both the most plausible way, and the most flexible tool, to arrange an escape. I imagined using it to reopen the southern passage, or to bypass the guards and gate in one of the other exits, or in other, more complicated ways. The simplest of all, simply tunneling to the surface at some out-of-the-way corner of the city, did not seem practical; after all, the supply was said to be very limited, and I did not know how far down we were. Trask had said his estimate was that the highest tunnels were perhaps two hundred feet below the streets of central Los Angeles, and the deepest a hundred more; the entire remaining stock of *tunskush* might not be enough to bore a hole that long.

Betsy and I continued to acquire oddments we thought might eventually be useful in building a breathing apparatus. We continued to listen for hints about the fate of our weapons, and Betsy and I had both done some exploration in the depths of the tidal pools in hopes of finding some trace of them. I had chatted with some of the young gambling men about the value of their coins. And we were always trying to learn more about the stone eater.

That was how matters stood some two or three days after my talk with Beckwith, when, as Betsy and I wandered along one of the upper corridors, we heard a sound echoing down the tunnel that sounded very much like a gunshot. I glanced at my companion, then broke into a run toward the source of the sound as the original explosion was followed by a high-pitched wailing. I could hear a deeper voice shouting, as well, and I very much feared it was a voice I recognized.

I headed directly for the eastern exit, as that was in the right direction and I could not see why Beckwith would be anywhere else. Betsy followed, carrying the lamp we had been using to light our way, but my longer legs let me cover the distance more quickly, so I was a dozen yards ahead and into near-total darkness as I came plunging along a familiar corridor.

Then ahead of me there was light, and I could see half a dozen of the Skyless militia, most of them men I knew by name – Winniksek, and Chatukai, and Kabchik – clustered around the mouth of the long eastern tunnel. Kabchik was holding a mushroom lamp high, and I could see other light beyond the men.

I could smell gunsmoke, and I could hear Beckwith shouting.

"Just let me go, damn you!" he bellowed, in English. "You don't want me here, and I don't want to *be* here!"

I slowed my pace; I did not want to run into the spearmen from behind. As I did, something in the corner of my eye caught my attention. Betsy was coming up behind me, carrying our lamp, and the light was shining on the last niche in the corridor wall.

It was empty. The stacked archives that had lain there for centuries were gone. My gaze flashed forward again, toward the scene at the exit.

I was close enough now to see the situation more clearly. Beckwith was at the gate, thirty feet up the eastern tunnel, and his knapsack hung heavily on his shoulder, very heavily indeed, presumably weighed down by slabs of gold a foot or so wide and almost four feet long; I thought I could see the square end of at least one projecting from the open top. The revolver Beckwith had hidden in his boot was in his right hand, while his left hand held something small and black. He wore his broad-brimmed hat; I had not realized he still had it. One of the tunnel guards lay at his feet, moaning, his leg covered in blood – Beckwith had shot him. The other guard was crouching a few feet away, his spear pointed at Beckwith, but he was watching the gun warily and making no move to attack. That much, terrible as it was, all made sense; what did not was that one of the elders, a woman named Suzpul, was huddled against the tunnel wall beside the gate, shielding her eyes from the sight of the angry outsider and his horrifying weapon.

Beckwith thrust the black thing in his left hand at the gate's lock mechanism, and I realized he had gotten the key away from the guards, but apparently the device was not as familiar as he had expected; he seemed unable to fit the key into the lock.

"Turn it to the left!" Betsy called from behind me.

Startled, Beckwith spotted us behind his foes. He stared at us for a second, and then did as he was told. The lock thumped open.

"Thanks!" he shouted, as he dropped the key and grabbed the elder by her shaking arm. He pointed his pistol at her head and dragged her upright. "*Make it open!*" he demanded, in badly accented Kanta'an.

She reached out a trembling hand and pushed, and the gate swung open – not on hinges at the side, as I would have expected, but rotating on a central pivot at top and bottom. Beckwith backed through the opening, dragging his captive after him. He paused just long enough to point at a mushroom lamp on the floor and order poor Suzpul, "*Bring light!*"

It was obvious now that Beckwith had never come up with any sort of new plan, but was simply carrying out the same scheme he had devised right at the start – steal some of the golden books, take one of the elders as a hostage, and shoot his way out the eastern exit. Why he hadn't tried the northern one instead I cannot say; perhaps he had not realized that it was a shorter route. Or perhaps he had never found it at all; I had not pointed it out to him, but I had assumed he had done enough exploration to find it on his own.

Now he was retreating backward up the eastern tunnel, Suzpul held before his chest; his other hand held the revolver, while she held the mushroom lamp.

I had had several weeks of experience with those lamps by this point, and the one she held did not look particularly fresh; had Beckwith forgotten that they generally only lasted two or three days before needing to be refilled, and that the shaft to the surface was more than two days' travel away? I doubted he had found any of our lost lamp–oil. Perhaps he had some other light source in his pack.

I watched as Beckwith and his hostage marched backward a hundred yards or so – the lamp made it easy to see them despite the distance. Then he turned around, pushed Suzpul in front of him, and began herding her along more quickly, the pistol still ready in his hand.

The moment he was no longer facing them, the Skyless fighters snapped into action. Two of them carried away the man Beckwith had shot, and the others began moving silently and swiftly through the open gate. They took no light with them, but slipped into the darkness.

I remembered how they had seemed to appear out of nowhere in the darkened tunnels when we first arrived in the city; apparently that had not been a mere accident. I hesitated, and opened my mouth to shout a warning to Beckwith.

Betsy grabbed my arm, and whispered in my ear, "If you say anything, they'll think we were in on it all along. You might get us killed."

"But if I don't, they'll kill him!" I protested.

"Tom, he took those books, which must weigh a hundred pounds or more, and according to your watch when we came in, it's more than two days to the entrance. There's no way he'll make it; he's as good as dead already. If we warn him he'll use his other four shots, but they'll still get him, and that will just make everything worse."

I grimaced as I realized she was right.

"But you told him about the lock," I protested.

"To keep him from panicking and shooting someone."

Reluctantly, I saw her point.

"They may think we were in on it anyway," she added. "Did *you* know he was going to do this?"

"Not...I knew he said he was going to try something soon, but I didn't know when, or what he had in mind."

"I'd suggest not mentioning that."

"Betsy, I'm not *that* foolish!"

"I never know with you, Mr. Derringer."

I did not argue further, but watched the drama playing out before us.

It was hard to make out the Skyless in the dark; they were just shadows, outlined by the faint distant glow of the lamp Suzpul carried. I could see, though, that they were crouching down, moving quickly, and that some of them no longer appeared to be carrying spears.

Then one of them lifted something to his mouth.

"No!" I called.

Beckwith looked back over his shoulder and saw that the Skyless were gaining on him. He whirled and fired.

Unsurprisingly, shooting quickly into the darkness, he missed; I heard the distinctive sound of a ricochet follow the initial echoing roar. Then he raised the gun and aimed more carefully.

I did not see the dart strike him, and I do not know which of the Skyless managed to hit him; at least three now held blowguns. I did see Beckwith stagger as he fired again, and this time I saw the spark as the bullet ricocheted from the roof of the tunnel.

"That's it," Betsy said beside me.

Before I could reply, Beckwith's knees folded under him, and he fell backward, dragging his captive down on top of him. His pursuers, at least those I could make out in the gloom, immediately lowered their weapons and sprang toward him.

I knew it didn't matter. It was too late for Beckwith. Those darts carried the most virulent poison the Skyless knew, blended from scorpion venom and toxic mushrooms. The venom caused the initial pain, and then paralysis of the affected area, but it was the fungal toxin that eventually killed the victim. Unconsciousness typically came on in an hour or two, and death followed in about half a day, Kinja had told me – the interval between the highest and lowest tides, she called it. There was no way known to prevent it once the poison was in the blood.

I saw the Skyless warriors reach Beckwith and pull their terrified elder from his grasp, but they did not attack him, nor attempt to disarm him; they merely stepped back as he waved his revolver back and forth.

And then he put the gun to his head, his hand shaking so much I could see it even at that distance, and there was one more shot.

Betsy gasped. I put my arm around her shoulders and said, "Poor devil."

The Skyless were talking amongst themselves, but we could not hear a thing from so far away. Then two of them pulled the pack from the dead man's shoulder and lowered it reverently to the tunnel floor.

They then stepped back, and after more conversation little Suzpul knelt and looked over the golden slabs that protruded from the open end.

A moment later four men were posted around the pack – not the corpse – as guards, while Suzpul and the other guard returned to the city. They spotted us; we were making no attempt to hide, after all.

"*You!*" Suzpul called in Kanta'an. "*You knew?*"

"*We knew nothing,*" I replied. "*We heard the weapon, we came to see.*"

She looked back up the tunnel at the guards, who had set the mushroom lamp on the tunnel floor by Beckwith's pack, then back at us. "*Go to your place,*" she ordered.

"*We go.*" I took Betsy's arm and turned.

We said nothing as we made our way back to Betsy's apartment. I held the curtain aside for her, but she hesitated. "I don't want to be alone right now," she said.

"Of course," I replied, and I followed her into her sitting room.

We sat silently holding hands for a moment, and then she said, "We need to get out of here."

"It's going to be harder now," I said. "He's stirred them up. They'll be watching us."

"But we were never planning to steal anything – won't that help? Wouldn't they just as soon be rid of us?"

"Maybe," I said. "We'll need to see how they react." I hesitated before continuing, "They may decide we're too dangerous to keep around, and just kill us. If he hadn't stolen those books...But he did. That made him not just a thief, but a blasphemer, and we may be tarred with that same brush."

"But they know us! They know we weren't all like Smith. We're friends with some of them! I think Chatukai is a little sweet on me; he wouldn't let them kill us!"

"He might not have any say in it. It's up to the elders."

She leaned against my shoulder. "We need to get out of here," she repeated.

"Yes, we do," I said.

Chapter Twenty–One

We Are Questioned At Length

I was not surprised when we were summoned separately to speak to the elders. I *was* mildly surprised that they took Betsy first. That I was ordered back into my own apartment, with four guards posted at the door, was only to be expected.

I had not bothered to wind my watch for weeks – I had not seen much point in it, among the Skyless – but now I dug it out of my pack and wound it up, arbitrarily setting it for 12:00. I can therefore say that they questioned poor Betsy for the better part of an hour. I heard her being returned to her own apartment when my watch read 12:55, and a moment later the curtain of my own sitting room was drawn back, and I was beckoned. I slipped the watch into my vest pocket and followed.

The men who had been guarding my door fell into step behind me, and we marched through the familiar tunnels for a mile or so, before turning into a downward passage that was definitely *not* familiar. This was one of the two corridors we had been forbidden to enter and which I had been told led to the central library.

Perhaps it did, but on this occasion I was brought into a large chamber where most of the elders sat cross–legged on colorful pillows around the sides.

I must take a moment to explain that this was the first time I had seen pillows of any kind anywhere in the underground realm; the fabric and stuffing required to make them was simply not available for ordinary use. In fact, I have no idea what they had used for filling; certainly they had no feathers, let alone proper down, on hand. Perhaps something from the ocean served the purpose, or some sort of soft fungus. I immediately recognized that these cushions were an ostentatious display of wealth and power, intended to intimidate; for me, as a man of the modern world on the earth's surface, this did not have what I believe was the intended effect but instead reminded me of the poverty of this entire people.

Gabriel Trask was seated in one corner with no pillow, but a small black mat.

I, of course, was not provided with any sort of cushion, but was forced to kneel on the stone floor, spears at the back of my neck.

"*Give your name,*" the elder facing me most directly, a man named Amwinik, demanded.

"John Thomas Derringer, Junior," I replied.

"*Name your woman.*"

"Not mine," I said. "Elspeth Vanderhart. *Call* Betsy Jones *sometimes.*"

"*Two names?*"

"*She does have two.*"

"*She does this why?*"

"*I know not.*"

"*Name the dead man.*"

"*Call* Justus Smith," I said. "*Born* John Pennington Beckwith."

"*Two names?*"

"*Worked with untrustworthy people,*" I explained, pleased that I was able to remember the suffixes that combined to mean "untrustworthy" or "unreliable," which I had learned from one of Betsy's discussions about Skyless machinery with a man named Jachi.

"*What mean these names?*"

Baffled, I said, "*I know not.*"

"*Not family?*"

Unsure of his meaning, I put a hand on my chest and said, "Derringer *family.*" I pointed at the door I had been brought in through and said, "*Woman,* Vanderhart *family.*" Then I pointed in what I thought was an easterly direction and said, "*Dead man,* Beckwith *family.*"

"*All different?*"

"*All different.*"

"*Brother? Sister?*"

"*No brother. No sister.*" I was having enough trouble answering questions in a language I barely knew without trying to explain that I had a sister back in New York, so I left Mary Ann unmentioned.

The interrogation continued in this manner, gradually working from these most basic points to more complex issues, and before long Mr. Trask was called upon to translate some of both questions and answers. I told them that Betsy was a friend, but Beckwith was someone sent to follow us, and *not* a friend. I told them I had come only to talk to Gabriel Trask and did not want anything from the Skyless. I told them repeatedly, and swore it by their gods, my own God, and my personal honor, that I had not come to steal their sacred books. I assured them that I would be happy to leave and never come back, and that if Betsy and I were allowed to go, I would promise in whatever terms they wanted that I would not tell anyone how to find and steal their books.

I got the impression that they did not understand that gold, in and of itself, had any value in the outside world; they seemed quite certain that Beckwith had stolen that stack of their holy books because he wanted the secrets written in them and hoped to weaken the Skyless by disrupting the divine protections provided by the archives. I said that I did not know for certain why he took them, but that we had all thought they would be valuable in the daylight lands.

After a time elders other than Amwinik joined in the questioning. Kinja seemed to be sympathetic, while Suzpul was clearly furious about everything Beckwith had done; most of the others who spoke appeared to be more curious than anything else, and were struggling to understand the situation.

Certain things I had not known came out in this lengthy discussion. I learned that in addition to the central library there was a room where a directory to the entire Archives of the Skyless was written on golden walls, giving the exact location of every one of the books and saying what was in each one – it was the need to keep this guide accurate that made it imperative that every book remain in exactly the right order, in exactly the right spot, on exactly the right shelf, no matter where in the city it might be. I learned that once upon a time lesser texts had been written on materials other than gold, but that over the thousands of years since all of these had long since corroded away to nothing, and the Skyless had taken this to indicate that the gods did not approve of any records except the archives. Writing on the walls of various rooms and tunnels was permitted only with the understanding that it was temporary fun, more decorative than meaningful, and so long as no *tunskush* was wasted on such frivolity.

I learned that the city's entire supply of *tunskush* was stored in that directory room. *That* was important information, and I struggled not to let my inquisitors see my interest.

I learned that when Trask had first arrived he had been an object of great suspicion, and death or imprisonment had been discussed, but he had brought them presents and had never betrayed them, so he now had a modicum of their trust. They were hoping to determine whether Betsy and I were Trasks or Beckwiths, and our denial of any blood relationship was making this difficult.

Trask did speak on our behalf, saying that he believed us to be honest and well intentioned, but that did not seem to sway anyone. In particular, it seemed to further infuriate Suzpul.

And toward what might otherwise have been the end of the questioning a messenger arrived, to inform the elders that we had entered a new year – the first rainwater of the winter was seeping from the ceiling in the uppermost northern tunnels. The significance of this extended the discussion – was this a sign that the gods wanted us to be spared? Freed? Drowned? Was it the friendly gods of the earth, or the evil monstrous sky gods, sending this sign? Had the rains held off so long because we were being held against our will? If so, did that mean we should be freed, or that we were disciples of the sky who should be slain as heretics?

This added complication resulted in the equivalent of a hung jury, and it was decided that nothing irrevocable would be done until the elders had had time to meditate on the situation and discuss it at length.

Accordingly, I was escorted back to my apartments, where I checked my watch and saw that it read 3:30. My questioning had taken much longer than Betsy's.

And it had been tiring, as well as tiresome; I undressed and went to bed. I wanted to be as fresh as I could for whatever came next. My father's journals had always emphasized that an adventurer should sleep when he can.

I awoke to find Gabriel Trask waiting for me in my sitting room. Startled, I dressed quickly and joined him.

"I'm sorry to intrude, Mr. Derringer," he said.

I waved that away as I seated myself. "What brings you here, Mr. Trask?"

"I just wanted to talk," he said. "Somewhere I knew we could speak privately and be honest with one another."

"I take it that you believe merely speaking English would not be sufficiently private. Do some of the Skyless understand more English than they let on?"

"All the elders have learned at least a few words," he said. "They're too clever to tell *you* that, of course. And a few of the men who serve often as guards have asked me to teach them a little, as well; that's why Kulbal recognized it when Smith called the archives gold. But it's not that I think any of them could follow our conversation; it's that I don't want them asking about it. They aren't fools, Mr. Derringer; they can read faces as well as anyone, they hear the tone of one's voice, and they can guess what's under discussion. If they were to question me, I don't want to try lying to them; I'm not very good at it."

Remembering our first interview, where we foolishly assumed that being allowed to keep our weapons meant we were in no danger, and where we had accepted Trask's statement that the Skyless had mysterious weapons unknown to modern science at face value, I replied, "I think you underestimate yourself."

He did not pretend to misunderstand. "Lying to strangers like you and Smith is one thing; lying to elders who have known me for the better part of twenty years is more difficult. I'm not saying I couldn't fool them; I'm saying I'm not *certain* I could."

"All right, then; what did you want to talk about?"

"Your situation – yours and Miss Jones'. And my own, for that matter."

"I don't know what our situation is any more, Mr. Trask."

"Neither do I, really, and that worries me. I feel responsible for what's happened, and I suspect the elders blame me, as well. I was the one who advised them to let you and your companions live and stay among us, and now Smith is dead, and the archives have been disturbed."

"And a guard was shot in the leg," I said. "I would think that would matter more than some gold plates being moved!"

He shook his head. "I'm afraid you're wrong. Oh, it matters, yes, but the disruption of the archives is worse, as far as the elders are concerned. They see those golden books as almost the entire reason for their existence, and their precise placement as crucial to the survival of the Skyless."

I could think of no sensible response to this except to say, "Oh." It seemed absurd to me that artifacts could be seen as more important than people, but I knew it was hardly unusual, in either primitive or modern cultures. "Is the information in them really so precious?"

"Well, that's the thing, Mr. Derringer," Trask replied. "It's not. I mentioned to you once that I had, with difficulty, read some of the archives from as much as two thousand years ago; well, I did that largely because I wanted to see how they differed from the most recent. You see, when I first learned to read their language, I began with the most recent books, thinking that would give me the most insight into the people *now*."

"And didn't it?"

He shook his head. "No, it did not. The most recent records are just that, records – lists of births and deaths, reports on who served for how long in the city guard, citations of any irregularities in the tides, careful counts of how many days there were in each year from first rain to first rain, estimates of harvests of fish and seaweed and the various fungal crops, and so on. An almanac would be more exciting. The account of my adventures in what you call El Dorado was reduced to a statement that a certain list of individuals, myself among them, were absent from the city for seventy-three tide cycles – where we went and what we did was not written down, because nothing that happened outside the city was deemed worthy of note."

"So their holy scriptures are just their town records?"

"That was how it appeared, yes."

I shook my head in amazement.

"I thought that perhaps they had degenerated to this level because so little happened in the city beyond people going about their everyday affairs, so I tried a century back, then five centuries, then a millennium. I found...well, some improvement. A thousand years ago there were sometimes what one might call obituaries, noting some of the accomplishments of the deceased, rather than mere lists of the names of the dead. There were sometimes brief poems of parental hopes for newborn children – just four or six lines, asking that the gods might give the child strength and joy, or that she might be wise and fair and find love."

"Why did they change?" I asked. "I would have thought they might become more elaborate as the population declined."

"They might have, if they were being recorded by the families on paper, but they are recorded by the elders on great sheets of gold, and...well, this is their great secret, sir. The supplies of gold are running out and the elders are doing their best to conserve what remains. Their lettering has been growing ever smaller for eight or nine centuries, as they tried to fit more and more on each tablet, and for about six centuries they have allowed nothing but the bare facts to be recorded. There is no space for anything more, no room for sentiment or honor or hope or ambition."

"How sad!"

"Indeed. And it means that each new tablet is of less interest than the one before, even while the collection as a whole becomes ever more precious to the elders. I don't know what they're going to do when the gold or the *tunskush* runs out, Mr. Derringer; it would not surprise me if they attempted to rob vaults in the surface world of their gold, so that they might continue expanding their pointless records. For now, they have become absolutely obsessed with maintaining the archives just as they always have – and Mr. Smith tried to make off with a piece of it."

"I see," I said.

"Do you, Mr. Derringer?"

"Well, I thought I did, but from your tone perhaps I have missed some significant element of the situation."

"You saw that they did not hesitate to kill Mr. Smith when he made his attempt."

"I would not expect anything else."

"Mr. Derringer, I had told them when you first arrived that Smith was a treasure hunter who would like nothing more to carry away a book or two – and they *didn't believe me*. They could not comprehend that anyone, even an outsider, might want to steal *part* of the archives. That was such a blasphemy as to be unimaginable. They could accept that Smith might escape, and bring back an army to occupy the entire city and lay claim to the archives, but to take just half a dozen books? That made no sense to them."

And *that*, of course, was not something that *I* found easy to understand. I was still struggling with it when Trask continued, "Smith had to die for his blasphemy; if they had somehow captured him alive, they would have quickly put him to death. And now they are debating what to do with the rest of us – *all* of us, myself included. Even though I had warned them, some of the elders no longer trust me. Smith's actions have convinced these individuals not that we outsiders are all would-be thieves, but that we are so alien, so incomprehensible, that we cannot be relied on to behave in any fashion that they understand."

"I don't..." I began.

"Mr. Derringer, they are debating whether to put *all* of us to death."

Chapter Twenty–Two

Our Lives in the Balance

"Is there anything we can do, Mr. Trask?" I asked.

"I don't know," he answered.

"How great do you think the risk is? You said that *some* of the elders want us killed; how many? What about the others?"

"I tell you, I don't know. I know Suzpul is so furious she can barely speak, and her brothers will support her if she demand our deaths, but three are not enough to decide our fates."

I had not realized that Suzpul *had* any brothers.

"What if they do not decide to kill us? What then? Will they let us go?"

"I doubt it. They fear we will tell others about the archives."

"Can we escape?"

"I don't know. They have both exits guarded and both gates locked."

His use of "both" implied there were indeed only the two we knew of. I debated whether to say anything about the possibility of swimming out; perhaps he could get us materials for our planned air tanks.

"You mentioned the man Smith shot," Trask said. "Did you know Smith had another gun, in addition to the ones we took from him?"

I scratched my chin, and said, "Let me just say that it did not come as a complete surprise. I knew what sort of a man he was."

"Do *you* still have a gun?"

"I do not, I assure you." I was careful not to place too much emphasis on that initial pronoun. "What happened to Smith's? I believe he had one bullet left."

Trask blinked. "I don't know," he admitted.

"What happened to Smith's body and his belongings?"

"I'm afraid I don't know that, either."

I considered for a moment, then asked, "Where does the northern exit go?"

"It's closed and guarded."

"I know that – you just told me. But where does it go?"

"The tunnel goes north, I don't know how far; it supposedly connects to the northern cities that were destroyed by leaking gas four thousand years ago."

"Do you think it actually still does, after so long?"

He shrugged. "I have no idea. They may well have all been destroyed by earthquakes by now. I sometimes marvel that so few of the tunnels here have fallen in."

I blinked. "Have some fallen in, then?"

"Oh, of course. After all this time, with no maintenance and frequent earthquakes? No more have collapsed for a few centuries now – I suppose any that were remotely unstable caved in long ago – but the northwestern part of the original city is mostly gone and about half of the tunnels that reached under the ocean."

"I had no idea."

"There's no reason you should know. I'm not sure most of the Skyless know. The connecting passages were closed off."

I nodded. "So the northern tunnel – is that how you have gotten in and out?"

He nodded. "There's an entrance shaft, very steep and narrow, maybe six or seven miles past the gate, on the right. It's not an easy climb; that's one reason I haven't left very often. I found it long ago; that was how I first discovered the Skyless existed."

I did not remember any such entrance being listed in the material Mad Bill Snedeker had sent me; perhaps it had been entirely unknown to anyone but Mr. Trask. As for its difficulty, the entrance we had used forty miles east had been challenging, and I could easily imagine that the northern entrance might be at least equally difficult. "Where does it emerge?" I asked.

"In the hills north of town," he said. "On Colonel Griffith's land, overlooking the Los Angeles River."

I had no idea who Colonel Griffith might be, but did not see that it mattered. "They won't let you leave?"

"They will not."

"It seems to me that even so, that northern route would be easier than the eastern one."

"Would it? How *did* you get in here? I never did ask, did I?"

"Oh, we found the shaft that the Skyless used to trade with the Gabrielenos long ago. But it's better than two days' walk from the city gate."

"Two days?" He shook his head. "Whatever possessed you to try it?"

"As I said when we first arrived, we were looking for *you*, Mr. Trask, following the best information we had."

"It seems foolish."

"Perhaps it was. Whether it was or not, we are here now. And if you will forgive me for pointing this out, we would have been gone long ago had you not advised the Skyless against releasing us, and you would still be in our hosts' good graces."

"Oh, you can't be certain of that. They might have killed or detained you even without my advice." He hesitated, then asked, "How the devil did Mr. Smith think he could make it to a shaft two days away?"

I shrugged. "I have no idea. He did not see fit to share his plans with me. I suppose he was so desperate that he thought it worth the risk."

"Poor man." Trask shook his head.

The conversation seemed to be wandering. "Mr. Trask," I said, hoping to return it to its track, "while I appreciate this exchange of information, was there some specific reason you came here? Something you wanted of me? Or did you just want the company of a fellow outsider, now that you are no longer as welcome here as you were?"

"While it was mostly a matter of fellowship, there *is* something specific," he said.

"And what is that?"

"If you are planning an escape, Mr. Derringer..." He hesitated.

"If we were planning an escape, Mr. Trask, the ideal opportunity to flee through the northern exit was when your friends were all running to the eastern entrance to stop John Beckwith. We missed that chance because we did not, in fact, have a plan ready to put into motion."

He held up a hand. "I...I understand that, Mr. Derringer. But here you are, and I am sure you have been giving the matter some thought. I am not asking you to disclose anything of your intentions; I think it's better for all of us at this point if I don't know what, if anything, you have in mind. But I have a favor to ask."

"And what is that?"

"If and when you go, Mr. Derringer, whenever and however that may be, could you take me with you?"

"Ah," I said, staring at him. "Ah, I see."

"You might think that after living here so long I would know all the city's secrets and would have a hundred ways to escape, but in fact, I do not. Until very recently I had no need to consider anything of the sort; I was free to come and go as I chose. Therefore, I gave it no thought whatsoever – a blithe and careless attitude I now regret. It has been plain to me for some time, though, that you and Miss Jones have had an eye out for opportunities ever since you arrived – after all, you are adventurers, and daring escapes are a common feature of your line of work. Her interest in the tidal pumps – is there some way to get out through them?"

"Not that we could discover," I said. "Not that that was her sole reason for studying them. Her interest in engineering is quite genuine, however unladylike it may seem to you."

"Then you have no hope?" His tone was one of despair.

"I didn't say *that*," I replied. "I merely said that the tidal pumps did not pan out as an escape route. We have discussed certain other possibilities, but as yet none of our schemes are ready to be put into action."

"Oh." His mood seemed to have improved to mere disappointment. "Well, if any of them do bear fruit, please remember me. And if there is anything I can do to help, don't hesitate to ask. Remember, I only thought you should be held because I feared you would seek to rescue Mr. Smith; even should I reconcile with our hosts, I no longer think you should stay."

"That change of heart has come a little late, don't you think?"

"I do. And I'm sorry."

"Well, nothing to be done about it, I suppose."

"And you'll take me along?"

I sighed. "We will certainly keep your request in mind. And in exchange, should the Skyless decide you to be harmless and return everything to the *status quo ante*, I trust you will still assist us?"

"Of course!" He got to his feet. "I'm terribly sorry, Mr. Derringer, really I am. I wanted to protect the Skyless, and...well, what's done is done."

I rose as well, and we shook hands. He went to the door and pulled back the curtain.

Two voices shouted.

I believe I have mentioned before that the Skyless generally had soft, mellifluous voices; I suppose this trait developed as an adaptation to living in enclosed spaces where all sounds echoed and where there was no need for a call to carry across open spaces. That was still true, and made these angry shouts incongruous and strange – the shouted orders were not harsh and commanding, but almost like song, as two of the guards at my door grabbed Mr. Trask by both arms and hauled him away.

Startled, I followed him to the door and looked out to see him being dragged along the corridor to the apartments that had been occupied by the late John Beckwith, where he was thrust inside.

He put up no resistance; he seemed more astonished than frightened or hurt.

"*What happens?*" I asked one of the pair still guarding my own quarters.

"*He relocates,*" the guard answered – at least, I consider that the best translation of a sentence that actually breaks down to, "Moves that person into a place not where he resided," in two words, a simple verb followed by a genderless pronoun and a string of modifying suffixes. I hope the reader will forgive me if I try to maintain a compromise position between overly literal translations and the overly colloquial.

"His possessions move?"

"That happens."

"Tell me the reason?" I threw in a few of the most polite modifiers I knew.

"To keep all who are not Skyless together for more control."

It seemed that Trask was right – he was no longer in a separate category from the rest of us.

I glanced down the corridor in the other direction and saw Betsy leaning out her own door. I waved. She said something to her own guards, but I could not make it out. A moment later, she was escorted to my own door.

"We are allowed to visit with one another," she said. "But we are not permitted to leave this corridor."

"What about meals?" I asked.

She replied, "I don't know."

I asked the nearest guard, who told me that henceforth our meals would be brought to us in our apartments. We were prisoners now, with no pretense otherwise.

I invited Betsy inside and recounted to her much of my conversation with Mr. Trask. When I had finished, we both sat silently for a moment.

"We need to escape," she said at last.

"Of course," I said. "But how? Our chances seem even worse than before."

"The guards here do not seem terribly alert."

That was true. Furthermore, I was much larger than any of them and had been trained in various styles of hand-to-hand fighting. Although neither Betsy nor Trask could be relied on to overmatch a Skyless guardsman, we might well be able to force our way past them.

"But where would we go?" I asked.

"The north exit, perhaps? Or down to the ocean passages and swim for it, even without an air supply?"

"I'm not sure of the actual distance, but besides our own observations, Winniksek told me the tunnels to the sea are as long as the city is wide, and he pointed out that one can never see any light at all from the sea beyond – it looks exactly the same at midnight as at noon. That's a long swim."

"The north exit, then. But the gate is locked and guarded."

I nodded. "And it's six or seven miles to the exit shaft. That would be a long race. Especially if we have Trask along – he's not a young man."

"*I* wouldn't mind leaving him behind!"

"I told him we...well, I didn't make any promises, but I wouldn't feel right leaving him behind."

Betsy considered that for a moment, then asked, "Would they even bother to follow us, if we didn't take any of their stupid gold? They want to be rid of us, don't they?"

"I don't know. They might, for fear we would tell everyone on the surface about the archives."

"That's probably true." She sighed. "Maybe they'll come to their senses. And if they don't – well, they won't take me without a fight."

I was not sure just what she meant by that, though it reminded me she still had her derringer. I decided I did not want to know.

Chapter Twenty-Three

Before the Flood

We lived in dreadful anticipation for some time after that, waiting to be summoned before the elders and sentenced to death, but it never happened, and with every passing day that it did not, such an outcome seemed less and less likely.

On the other hand, we remained confined to our apartments and the short stretch of corridor connecting them. We chatted occasionally with our guards, or with the women who brought us our food. Betsy, in particular, spent time talking with Chatukai.

One subject that came up surprisingly often was the weather – specifically, the weather on the surface above the tunnels. It seems that the handful of places where water leaked through in the rainy season, after having been completely dry until just after Beckwith's death, were now producing a steady drip like none seen within the memory of anyone in the city, enough to fill two or three bowls in a cycle of tides. The guards wanted to know what this meant – what was rain like? How much could fall in a day? Did it all fall in a single place, or was it scattered across the land? None of them had ever *seen* rain, of course; they only knew of it as "water that falls from the sky," and they had little concept of the realities of our everyday phenomenon.

We did our best to explain, but I do not think we conveyed the facts clearly, nor did our listeners grasp many of them. While they all knew the word for "sky," they had no real comprehension of what the word meant; its primary association for them was an evil spirit somewhere far above them, not a physical reality. They did not even have a word for "cloud," so far as we could determine, and the best we could improvise was "flying mist," which only confused matters, since for them flying was something only insects did, which led to the notion that clouds were gigantic beetles made of steam. They seemed to think of rain as water that the evil gods of the sky flung at them that mostly failed to penetrate their protective stone ceilings.

Even as we did our best to explain the nature of rain, we wondered amongst ourselves why the dripping should be heavier than usual. What was happening above ground? The winter that had started so dry seemed to have turned very wet indeed, but none of us were sufficiently familiar with the climate of Los Angeles to say how extraordinary this might be.

And then one day in what Trask estimated to be mid-February, our guards stepped aside to make way for Kinja and two of the male elders.

"*Come ye,*" she ordered us.

"*Is it decided? Are we to die?*" Trask asked.

"*No,*" she said. "*No, no, no. You are to help us. If you help, you live. If you fail, or if you refuse, you die.*"

Puzzled, we all asked further questions, but she and her companions did not say anything more. They simply led us, surrounded by our guards, through the tunnels from the residential areas into the central city.

And when we reached that central district we were astonished to find that the floors were wet; in fact, in many places water was flowing in sheets across the stone. "*What happens here?"* I demanded as we splashed westward, to be met with silence.

Then we turned a corner, where I realized we were approaching the northern exit from the city, and that the water was flowing from that tunnel. In fact, in the passage leading up to the exit tunnel it was splashing over our boots.

"What's going on?" I asked in English.

Kinja turned to look at me. "You say," she said. "We don't."

I had never heard her speak English before, but the situation was already so strange it did not seem remarkable. Her accent was surprisingly good.

By the time we reached the gate the water was ankle deep and the current was so strong that moving forward took an effort. There was no question that the water was coming from the exit tunnel. I could also see now that it was not entirely clear, but somewhat muddy.

Then we turned the corner and looked into the passage out of the city.

There was a pile of stone and scraps blocking the tunnel, but water was leaking through it in a dozen places and pouring over the top. Kinja let us stare at this construct for a moment, then turned to Betsy. "You know..." she began, and then she struggled for a moment before eventually managing to get out a badly pronounced approximation of the word "engineering."

"A little," Betsy acknowledged, and I could see that she was studying the situation, and ignoring the water spilling around her ankles.

"You fix, you live," Kinja said. "We don't know."

"You don't know *how*," Betsy corrected, bending down to look at the barricade. "I'll see what I can do." She turned to Mr. Trask and asked, "This tunnel goes to the dead cities of the north?"

"It's supposed to," he agreed.

"Then where is the water coming from?"

"I don't know," he replied. "Maybe the roof fell in?"

"Does it pass under a lake?"

"I don't know," he repeated.

"I didn't think there *were* any significant lakes around Los Angeles," I said.

"Then a river?" Betsy suggested.

"It goes very near the Los Angeles River," Trask said, nodding. "Maybe under it."

"So if that's where the water is coming from..." She stared into the tunnel, chewing her lower lip. Then she turned back to Trask and said, "It goes to the dead cities?"

He nodded.

"So if we redirected the flow, it would all drain off into those?"

"Ah..." He blinked. "I don't know. The corridor slopes uphill from here all the way to the exit shaft, and I think it goes uphill from there, too."

Betsy frowned. "That's bad. Maybe those other cities are *already* flooded, and that's where this is coming from."

"Can't we just plug the hole, wherever it is?" I asked.

"And how would *you* go about plugging a hole in the tunnel roof big enough to let in all this water?" Betsy demanded. "Given what we have to work with."

"Can't we just dam up the tunnel?" Trask asked.

"They've tried that," Betsy said, waving at the barricade, where more water was leaking through than came over the top.

"Maybe we can do better," I said. "Their ancestors may have been great engineers, but *these* people aren't."

"Maybe," Betsy said thoughtfully. She put a hand against the tunnel wall and slid it across the smooth surface, then looked in every direction, and finally turned to Kinja.

"*Tunskush*," she said. "I can stop it with *tunskush*."

I started, unsure what she was thinking.

Kinja looked shocked, then thoughtful. She talked to the other two elders, too quickly and quietly for me to follow. The discussion lasted several minutes. Then one of the male elders turned to us.

"*Your gods do this?*" he asked. "*Sky gods?*"

We exchanged glances. "We don't know," I said.

"*You can ask them to stop it?*"

"Not from down here," I said, which Trask translated into Kanta'an.

"*Stop it with tunskush,*" Betsy said. "*Gods cannot defeat tunskush.*"

That, I thought, should make theological sense to the Skyless elders, and sure enough, the three of them started talking among themselves again.

While they talked, Betsy was studying the barricade.

"The problem here," she said, pointing, "is that they tried building it after the water was already flowing. They didn't have any sort of cement to put between the stones that wouldn't just wash away. And they didn't take time to cut and assemble something to fit the space. Give me a couple of days and some decent workmen..."

She looked up and saw my face and stopped in mid-sentence. "Of course, it's too late now," she said, straightening up.

We both knew that in fact it was *not* too late, not really. The Skyless did not have any sort of mortar or cement, but they did have stone-cutters and metal-workers, and it would not be impossible to build an effective dike or dam that would use the pressure of the water itself to seal any gaps. *A'akbu* might serve as a substitute for mortar, I thought.

But the Skyless did not know that, and we wanted access to *tunskush*. I was not sure exactly what Betsy had in mind, but I was fairly certain it was something I wanted to try.

Finally Kinja turned to us again. "*Come,*" she said. "*We fetch tunskush.*" She beckoned, and we followed, down through tunnels now running with muddy water. At the first four-way intersection we turned right – and so did the water, because the other two tunnels were angled slightly upward. Past another intersection and we were in passages lined with golden archives, the yellow light of our mushroom lamps making the metal tablets almost seem to glow as we passed.

We wound our way onward, along corridors I had used only rarely during our months in captivity. We passed through what I believed to be the most complicated intersection in the entire city, where no fewer than seven passages of varying sizes and angles met; this junction was flooded almost knee-high, and water was pouring out of it down three of the seven radiating tunnels. We took one of the upward-sloping ones, and by the next intersection the floor was dry – though our feet certainly weren't.

And then we turned right, past a guard, into one of the tunnels we had been forbidden to enter. A moment later we stepped down into the directory room.

As we had been told, the walls were covered in golden tablets; these gleamed brightly in the light of our lamps. Most of the tablets were covered with writing – the same glyphs we had seen on the walls any number of other places, but here they were etched into the gold in a rich shade of brown that almost seemed to float in the air in front of the metal.

There were also diagrams that I realized formed a map of the tunnels. I had never seen such a map before and had not been sure the Skyless had the concept; I certainly did not know a Kanta'an word for "map."

The writing varied in size; some tablets were written in clear, bold letters, while others ranged down to cramped, almost illegible print squeezed onto edges. I guessed that the largest glyphs were the oldest, and additions had shrunk with the passing years as space, gold, and *tunskush* ran short.

Kinja crossed the room to one of the golden tablets and pressed a particular spot on its edge; something popped, and the panel swung open to reveal a hidden cabinet – or really, a storeroom, easily fifteen feet on a side and six or seven feet high.

This storeroom was almost, but not entirely, empty; I counted eight cylinders lined up along the back wall. Each of these cylinders stood almost waist-high and was of a diameter that would fit nicely under one's arm. They were dark in color, and of a substance I needed a moment to recognize as yet another variety of *a'akbu*. When one of our escort lifted a lamp to better illuminate the storeroom's interior I could see that each cylinder was capped with a tight-fitting lid.

"*Tunskush*," Kinja said. She then pointed to a small mug, scarcely the size of a teacup, that rested on the threshold of the golden door. It appeared to be made of the same sort of *a'akbu* as the cylinders. "*We permit you to fill that.*"

Betsy looked over the storeroom, then said, "*No.*"

Kinja looked puzzled. "*You want tunskush,*" she said.

Betsy nodded. "*We need more,*" she said.

"*What quantity do you need?*"

"I don't know," she replied in English. She frowned. "Listen, Kinja, *we know not what quantity of tunskush we require.* Let us take it all. We'll give back what we don't use."

Kinja frowned back at her, then conferred with the others.

The argument lasted several minutes, but at last Kinja turned back to Betsy and said, "*You must be carefully guarded.*"

"Of course."

All three elders looked extremely unhappy, but after a few seconds of awkward silence Betsy said, "Gentlemen, please fetch as much as you can carry."

Trask and I hurried to obey, climbing into the storeroom. Trask secured a cylinder under each arm; I tried to devise a way to carry more and managed to awkwardly brace a third against my hip. They were surprisingly light; I had expected them to be as heavy as water–jugs of a comparable size, and they were not.

That left three more cylinders. Betsy considered them, looked at how I was struggling to handle three, then ordered the nearest Skyless guards, "*Fetch tunskush.*"

"*Obey her,*" Kinja said, before anyone could question Betsy's command.

I handed my third canister to one of the guards, and a moment later our entire party was headed back up toward the northern exit, with Trask, myself, and two of the guards carrying two cylinders apiece.

Now that I had had a chance to see and feel the cylinders, I concluded that this particular *a'akbu* was very like gutta–percha - which had to be a mere coincidence. Gutta-percha derives from the forests of the Malay Peninsula, and four thousand years ago there could scarcely have been any trade between the ancestral lizard people and the people of Asia.

"Betsy," I said as we walked, "ask how we open these safely. I don't want to spill something that dissolves solid stone."

"Oh," Betsy said. She talked to Kinja, who replied; I did not catch the exchange. My grasp of Kanta'an was still limited, and I had trouble following it if it was not spoken loudly and clearly.

A moment later Kinja sent one of the other elders trotting back toward the directory room to fetch tools for handing *tunskush*.

And then we arrived at the north tunnel, where we climbed over the improvised barricade into the waist-deep water on the other side, bringing Kinja with us for the moment, but leaving the other Skyless behind. I tried to set my canisters of *tunskush* down and discovered that they floated.

Betsy looked around.

"We'll need rope," she said. "I believe Mr. Smith had a length in his pack."

Kinja called orders.

The other canisters were passed over the top of the barrier. A moment later a copper box was handed over, as well; Betsy opened it to find an assortment of tools, all made of that same *a'akbu* that was so like gutta-percha. One of them, a stylus, looked badly worn; none of the others showed signs of use. She closed the box again.

Shortly after that, a small coil of rope was delivered, and I began lashing the canisters of *tunskush* together into a sort of raft.

"That should do," Betsy said, looking over our situation. Then she turned to Kinja. "Would you care to join us?"

"*You go outside?*" the elder asked. "*Not return?*"

"*We go,*" Betsy admitted.

"*You stop water first?*"

"*We do. The tunskush is for that. I did not lie.*"

"*I stay here. But I ask two things.*"

"*Ask.*"

"*Two guards come to return tunskush you do not need.*"

Betsy looked at me. I nodded. "I have no objection," I said. I did not say that if I had surprise on my side and Trask and Betsy helping me, I was fairly sure I could handle two of the Skyless.

"What else?" Betsy asked in English.

"Do you want your packs?" Kinja asked.

"That would be lovely," Betsy said.

Guards were sent. A few minutes later we had our knapsacks on our shoulders once more, though the weight and a quick check showed that our weapons and lamp oil had still not been returned, and by the time we were done inspecting the delivery two Skyless guards had clambered awkwardly over the barricade to join us in the pool on the other side.

"I believe we are all set," Betsy said. "If you aren't joining us, Kinja, then it's time to say goodbye.

Kinja blinked at her, then turned to the guards and gave a rapid stream of instructions, much too fast for me to follow, though I was sure I heard the word "*tunskush*" at least once. Then she handed the mushroom lamp she had been carrying to Betsy. "You will need this," she said. Then she turned and waded to the barrier, where two guards quickly helped her over.

"Goodbye!" Mr. Trask called to Kinja with a wave, and then we all began slogging our way north through the half-flooded tunnel.

Chapter Twenty-Four

The Northern Tunnel

It was slow going, wading through all that water. I was relieved to see, though, that the depth decreased steadily as we traveled. It was perhaps an hour's slow walk until my raft of *tunskush* canisters was scraping the tunnel floor and had to be broken up and the cylinders distributed among the members of our little expedition. The guards were reluctant at first to assist, since these burdens limited their movement, but finally cooperated when they found a way to tuck the cylinders under their arms while still holding their spears.

Another hour and the water was only an inch or so deep, but now rushed along the slope, sparkling in the lamplight and making the footing treacherous. We could hear roaring in the distance ahead – clearly, we were nearing whatever opening was letting the water into the tunnel.

"I think it's the exit shaft," Trask said. "It's about the right distance."

I frowned. "You said the opening was in the river bank, well above the water."

"It was," Trask replied. "Ten or twelve feet up. But maybe something's broken through into it. If you think about it, isn't that more likely than an entirely new opening from the river all the way down here?"

I had to admit that it was.

"Or maybe it's a flood," Betsy suggested.

"In Los Angeles?" I remembered how dry the climate had seemed.

"Oh, they happen," Trask said. "The land is so flat out on the plain to the south of town that it doesn't take much for the rivers to overflow. It's happened a few times – maybe once every ten or fifteen years, there's some flooding. But *ten feet* up the bank, in that stretch of the river, this early in the year?" He shook his head. "I doubt that. I'm guessing something dug through the bank, from the river into the shaft – a prospector, or even a big animal."

"Isn't the shaft solid stone?"

"Well...not an animal, then."

We marched on, lugging our packs and the cylinders of *tunskush* along the endless corridor, the greenish light of our lamp illuminating no more than a hundred feet at a time, water rushing around our feet, splashing over the toes of our boots, soaking anything we let fall too low. The legs of my trousers were saturated from mid-thigh down, the cuffs full of water, and I could see that poor Betsy's skirts were weighed down by the moisture they had absorbed.

Mr. Trask and the two guards were not so burdened, as their knee-length tunics had failed to reach the water beyond the first mile or so, and the peculiar fabric had quickly shed what it had initially absorbed.

The roaring grew steadily louder as we walked, and the flow of water seemed constant, neither increasing nor dwindling.

"How long do you think this can continue?" I asked Trask. I had to shout to be heard over the torrent. "Is the entire river coming down here somehow?"

"I don't know," he shouted back.

"Maybe it really *will* flood the entire city if we don't do something!"

"Mines flood all the time," Betsy said. "It's a known problem. That's what steam engines were originally invented for, pumping out mines."

"I know, but like *this?*"

"Maybe not," she admitted.

We had gone perhaps another twenty feet when one of the guards shouted, "*See!*"

I stared into the darkness, but my night vision, even after months underground, could not match that of a man who had spent his entire life in the sunless depths. I pressed forward another few yards before making out what he had seen.

Water was gushing into the tunnel from an opening midway up the right–hand wall, above a few steps – an opening that I thought must be virtually identical to the one we had used, far to the east, when we first entered the territory of the lizard people. This torrent was like a solid shaft at least a yard in diameter, pouring diagonally from the wall and then bursting into a chaos of splashing waves as it joined the water already on the tunnel floor. The light of the mushroom lamp was shattered into a thousand dancing reflections when it struck this monstrous inverted fountain, and green and yellow sparkles flickered constantly on the walls and ceiling.

The flow filled the entire shaft, top to bottom; there was no air at all remaining, only water. The five of us gathered in a line just out of reach of the splashing and stared at it.

I tried to shout a question at Betsy, but it quickly became clear that she could not hear me over the waterfall. I tapped her arm and beckoned her away.

She followed, and when we had moved far enough away that a shout could be heard I said, "We have found where the water is coming from. What next?"

She looked up at the opening whence the water emerged, and said, "I don't think we can block that."

"Not even with *tunskush*?"

She did not reply, but continued to study the situation for a moment. Then she splashed forward again and grabbed Trask by the tunic, pulling him back.

"That's the exit shaft?" she demanded.

He nodded, rather than trying to yell over the roar of the water.

"That's the only way out? There isn't another one further on?"

He glanced past the torrent at the corridor continuing to the north, then nodded. "Just that," he bellowed.

"So if we're going to escape we need to go up that shaft."

Trask looked at her, thunderstruck, then back at the water pouring out of the shaft. "We can't go up *that*," he said. "*Look* at it!"

"We can't fight that current," I agreed.

"Tom, I am *not* going back to the city!"

"No, of course not," I said. "Maybe we could go on to the north, through the dead cities..."

She gestured at the lamp, which one of the guards was holding just then. "How long do you think that light will last? Do we know if the poison gas is gone? It might have filtered out long ago, or more might have filtered *in*."

"Maybe we could use the *tunskush* to cut a new exit?"

"We don't know whether we have enough," she said. She stared at the falling water for a moment, then said, "We can't fight that current. But maybe we can *stop* it."

I thought I must have misheard her. "What?"

"Kinja sent us here to stop the water from flooding the city," Betsy said. "Well, let's *do* that!"

I looked at the cascading water again. "How?"

She did not answer; instead she grabbed one of the canisters of *tunskush* from a guard and set it on the floor by the eastern wall, perhaps forty feet south of the water-filled shaft. Then, before the flowing water could topple or carry off the too-light container, she set the box of tools on top of it.

Even that was not enough to steady it completely, and she ordered the guard, *"Hold that."*

He obeyed, kneeling in the rushing but shallow current.

She opened the copper toolbox and studied its contents, then beckoned me over, and directed me to set a second cylinder near the first. Although I still did not know what she had in mind, I obeyed, as the guard had.

She drew a thing that looked like a gutta-percha sickle from the box, fitted it under the lid of the second cylinder, and twisted; the lid popped off, and I got my first look at actual *tunskush*.

It was a milky fluid, and the instant air touched it, it began to smoke, a thin white vapor; a skin began to form on the surface, as well.

Betsy returned the sickle to the box, studied her options, and then drew out a sort of gigantic oval syringe that was fitted with a T-shaped tip. She dipped this tip into the *tunskush* and pulled up the plunger, drawing the mysterious fluid into her device. Then she set that T-shaped head against the wall of the tunnel at roughly the height of her shoulders and pressed gently on the plunger.

The resulting hiss was audible even over the roaring water; a thick cloud of swirling vapor billowed from the wall. Betsy withdrew her device and studied the result.

The *tunskush* had cut a deep groove into the stone, about an inch high and a foot long; I could not see how deep into the wall it went.

Betsy nodded, and went to work in earnest. Trask and the other guard watched from a safe distance; the first guard and I did not have that option, since we were holding the two cylinders in place, and although we both leaned our heads back as far as we could, we found ourselves breathing in some of that white vapor. The smell was indescribable, a hideous tarry scent like nothing I had ever encountered before, and my head began to swim.

Betsy herself began coughing, but kept working, cutting a block of stone about a foot on each side from the wall.

She found, though, that she was not strong enough to lift it; I pulled it free, hoping that any lingering traces of the corrosive chemical would not seriously damage my hands, then asked, "Where do you want it?"

She took my wrist and guided me, setting it on the floor a yard or so south of her excavation. Then she set to work cutting another just like it, which I set beside the first.

We continued in this fashion until we had assembled a line across the full width of the tunnel; water promptly began to fill in behind it, even as much of it leaked through the seams between the blocks.

But then Betsy put the syringe back in the toolbox, and after considering and discarding half a dozen of the gutta-percha implements she brought out a brushlike device, which she dipped in *tunskush* and then drew across the seams.

The leaks stopped. She had welded the separate blocks into a solid barrier.

"You could have done that back by the gate," I shouted.

She looked at me as if I was a particularly slow-witted child and said, "But that wouldn't get us out of here."

I did not actually see, as yet, how building it here would get us out, either, but I decided to save my breath – the white vapor was beginning to irritate my throat. Instead I continued to assist her as she carved blocks from the tunnel wall and used them to build a new wall across the corridor.

I could see that Trask and the uninvolved guard were talking, but I could not make out what they were saying.

The water around us was rising slowly, as the barrier blocked its escape, and I asked Betsy, "Should we leave one end open for now, so the water doesn't get too high?"

She looked at me, looked at the wall we were building, then said, "That's a good idea. I think it's mostly going to go into the north tunnel, but it's still a good idea. Do that." She pointed at the eastern end, nearest the section of wall she was carving away. "That side," she said.

I had intended to leave the other end open, to save myself some hauling, but I nodded.

As the job continued, Betsy carved steps into the wall she was disassembling, so that she was able to climb up and reach higher parts of the tunnel. I thought this was fairly ingenious, and wanted to say something to Trask about it, but when I looked, he was gone.

I stopped work, staring. Betsy noticed, and followed my gaze.

"We have the lamp," she said. "He won't go far."

I nodded, and resumed construction.

Before long the new barrier was chest-high, with a gap of two or three feet at the east end where water was pouring through, leaving the top of our construction dry.

Trask reappeared; he had ventured up the northern tunnel. Now he came over to us.

"Can I help?" he asked.

Betsy nodded, and I handed him a block of stone.

He and I worked side by side, building the wall, and as we worked he said, "The tunnel to the north slopes upward – not very much, but a little. It wasn't as deep, and there wasn't any current, because of the slope, but this barrier means that it's going to flood now."

"I had thought of that," I said. "But this...wherever that water is coming from, it can't last forever."

"But where *is* it coming from?" Trask said. "I don't understand."

I just shrugged, and set the next block in place.

The first cylinder of *tunskush* was exhausted when the top of the wall was about even with my nose; by this time Betsy had carved out a niche in the side of the passage about four feet above the floor where she could stand, surrounded by the remaining canisters. Steps led down from it.

When she started the second cylinder I noticed that she was cutting her blocks from higher and higher, until at last she called me up to stand beside her and catch not a mere block, but a slab, that she cut from the roof of the tunnel.

I could barely hold it, and told her so as I lowered it swiftly to the floor of the niche.

"Then get the others to help you. The small blocks are taking too long."

"Even with the four of us, I doubt we can lift that into place!"

"Then use it to start the wall on the other side."

I blinked. "What?"

"Over there," she said, pointing north. "Just beyond the shaft."

"But...why do we need a wall *there*?" I said. "I don't care if the deserted cities get flooded."

She turned to stare at me, obviously exasperated. "Do you want to get out of these tunnels?"

"Well, yes, of course!"

"Then we need to stop the water from pouring in here – we can't swim up against that current."

"I..." I turned and looked at the north tunnel, and comprehension dawned. "You want to block both directions so the water has nowhere to go."

"And that will stop the downward flow, and then we can swim up the shaft. Yes."

"But...that will only stop the water when the chamber here is full. We'll drown before we can escape."

She shook her head, and pointed to the opening where the water was gushing in – or rather, to the three or four feet of tunnel *above* the opening. "We'll have air trapped in here," she said. "Not very much, but enough that we can fill our lungs before we make our departure." She pointed to where she had cut the block from the ceiling above her niche. "I'm enlarging this to trap more."

"Oh," I said. I had wondered about her choice of site for her material; now I understood. I beckoned Trask and the two Skyless over and explained, with gestures and my awkward Kanta'an, that we were to take the slab over to the other side of the waterfall.

"Why?" Trask asked.

"To equalize the pressure," I said, hoping he would not explain that to the Skyless – if he even understood it himself.

The guards set down their spears, leaning them against the wall, and lent a hand, and together the four of us hauled the slab to the desired position and set it upright. A moment later Betsy came and secured it in place by means of brushed-on *tunskush*, welding it to the floor and wall.

One of the Skyless became upset at this. "*Not needed!*" he exclaimed. "*You waste tunskush!*"

"We are protecting the northern cities," I said. Mr. Trask translated this for me.

"*Northern cities are long dead!*"

Betsy, rising with the brush still in her hand, reached into her blouse and drew out her derringer – now that we were leaving there was no more reason to keep its existence a secret, and here was a chance to put it to good use. She handed me the gun. "Tom, Mr. Trask," she said, "if you would be kind enough to send these two home to their families?"

Chapter Twenty–Five

We Make Our Escape

I grabbed the protesting guard by one arm, making sure to keep his hand well away from the blowgun in his belt, and dragged him to the half–finished southern wall. "It's time to go," I told him.

The other guard called out – between the roaring waters and the language barrier I could not make out a word – and tried to intervene. Trask grabbed at *his* arm, but was quickly flung off; the lizard man was far younger and stronger than the ambassador to hidden peoples. I raised the derringer, glad that both spears had been placed where neither of our guards could now reach them.

The man I was holding reached across his chest and tried to snatch the gun from my hand; I quickly thrust it out of his reach. Keeping the little pistol well away from him, I pulled him to the opening in the southeast corner and hoisted him across the single row of blocks that extended the full width of the tunnel, setting him down on the other side of the unfinished wall. He might have been stronger than Mr. Trask, but I was significantly larger and more fit than any of them; a diet of mushrooms and fish did not seem to enhance one's stature, while I had grown up eating red meat and living in the sun and had been training myself to be an adventurer since I was eight.

The other guard, having freed himself from Mr. Trask, then jumped me from behind, but I had been expecting that; I drove my elbow into his belly, and his breath came out in a whoop. I reached up, took hold of his shoulder, and tossed him after his companion. He would have done better to make a dash for the spears, and I was glad he had not.

Then I beckoned the gasping Trask over to serve as my interpreter.

"Tell them," I said, "that we are doing this as Miss Vanderhart determines best. They are free to return home, or to wait here until we are done, whereupon we will give them whatever surplus *tunskush* may remain. If either of them steps back through the wall, though, I will either thrash him within an inch of his life, or simply shoot him."

Trask stared at me in horror for a moment, then did as I commanded. The two Skyless then gabbled at each other, far too quickly for me to understand. Finally one of them turned and demanded, "*You come back to the city?*"

"*No.*"

They returned to their urgent conversation and seemed to reach a resolution; one of them turned and began splashing down the passage, back toward the city, while the other squatted down, his back to the wall, and watched me through the gap.

That seemed settled, so I handed the derringer back to Betsy and returned to the task at hand – walling off *both* sides of the tunnel.

We concentrated on the northern wall, since the southern tunnel served as a better drain. Betsy was now cutting pieces larger than her original blocks, but not so massive as that great slab, and we worked as quickly as we could; I think we all knew that that Skyless soldier might return with reinforcements in a couple of hours, ready to reclaim the remaining *tunskush*.

The air in our chamber grew foul with *tunskush* vapor, making my head swim, but we kept working. When the northern wall was too tall to set another row atop what we had built, Betsy cut a few blocks to serve as steps, and we used those to hoist stone into the narrowing gap. This process continued until we had sealed it against the ceiling; for the final tier I lifted Betsy up, my hands on her waist, so that she could slice slivers from the ceiling to precisely fill that last opening.

And then we turned our attention to the south once more.

By this time we were near the end of the sixth cylinder of *tunskush*; I don't think our remaining guard realized how much we had used, but when we set a chunk of stone in the bottom of the gap he got to his feet and said, "*Give me tunskush!*"

"*No,*" I replied.

"*Tunskush is on wrong side of wall!*"

"We're still using it," I said. I summoned Mr. Trask. "Tell him that we'll push any extra canisters through right before we close the last opening."

Trask did as I asked. The two men argued in Kanta'an for several minutes, but I did not listen; the water level was rising steadily as I set more and more stones into place.

"You'll want to take off your boots," Betsy said, when the water reached my knees. "We'll want to move quickly when the flow stops."

I nodded, and did as she suggested. I had already set my coat aside; now I hesitated, considering my vest, but finally resolved to keep it. There were items in the pockets I thought I would want later.

As for herself, Betsy removed her own boots and one of her petticoats and discarded her little silk–and–leather jacket.

Trask, of course, was wearing only a belted tunic and sandals; whatever surface garb he might once have had was presumably lost, somewhere back in the city of the Skyless.

It was not much longer until we had completed the second wall, save for a single opening above my head that could be reached only from the niche Betsy had carved in the eastern wall. We had managed to get ahead of the rising water, but not by much. We were all soaked from making our way back and forth carrying stones and *tunskush*, but the torrent from the exit shaft was now almost silent – the water in our chamber was above the top of the opening, but not yet spilling over the south wall. The passage back to the city was drying out; every so often we heard the remaining guard exclaiming about our success in saving the city.

And we had opened the final cylinder. I looked at it, then said to Betsy, "They aren't getting any back, are they?"

"I don't think so," she said. "We won't need all of this *here*, but I want to have it in case there's a blockage higher up. Remember, we don't know how all this water is getting into the shaft."

"Poor fellow. He's going to feel betrayed."

Betsy shrugged. "We didn't ask to be held prisoner for months, either."

I nodded, and shoved the final chunk of stone into place.

"*Ai! Dark!*" was the last thing I ever heard from any of the Skyless. Then Betsy was there with her brush, sealing the seams.

"It's dry there now, and there aren't any wrong turns," I said, when I saw the worried expression on Trask's face. "He should be well enough, even in the dark."

"I know, I know," Trask said. "But they...I lived among them for *years*, after all. They thought I was their friend."

"They imprisoned you, all the same," I pointed out.

By this point all three of us were clustered in the niche Betsy had created, just a few feet south of the flooded exit shaft. Our heads were above the roof of the tunnel, and seven empty *tunskush* canisters lay at our feet. An idea struck me.

"We should seal these up," I said, "and use them as floats."

"Good idea," Betsy said, and fished the sickle device out of the toolbox. We each took a turn forcing lids onto canisters as tightly as we could; the sickle proved less useful for this than our fists, while bracing a cylinder against the wall and kicking the lid to tighten it was even more effective.

I stuffed one empty canister into my knapsack. I was not going to try to swim while holding it, but I had hopes that it might bob to whatever surface we might eventually reach, and that I might then retrieve it. The other six were distributed, one pair to each of the three of us.

Then there was nothing to do but wait, as the water rose around us.

It had reached the bottom of the niche some time ago, but now it continued to rise, past our ankles, our knees, our waists. The air was squeezed out of the tunnel into our niche, and began to feel thick and heavy as the rising water compressed it. The rise seemed to slow as the water reached my chest and had definitely slowed by the time it reached my shoulder – at which point it was up to poor Betsy's chin. She was standing on her toes, head tilted back to keep her mouth and nose above water, with an empty *tunskush* canister under each arm. The buoyant cylinders were almost lifting her off her feet.

"I think it's time," she said. She took a deep, deep breath, and then she stepped off the edge, plunging down into the dark water, dragging the cylinders with her.

The lamp had been set in the space left by one of the last few blocks Betsy had carved out; now I grabbed it and held it down in the water, hoping that it would not leak and that nothing would disrupt the glowing fluids the Skyless mushrooms had produced.

As had the one we took down in the tidal pool, it still functioned, and the water seemed to spread the light so that the entire sealed chamber now shone with a faint greenish yellow glow. I could see Betsy vanishing into the exit shaft a few feet away, an empty cylinder under each arm – she had to struggle to keep her hold on these makeshift floats, which were trying to bob up past her.

"Your turn, Mr. Trask, I said.

Trask hesitated. "It must be much more than a hundred feet to the surface," he said. "It used to take me almost half an hour to climb it."

"You might have told us that sooner," I said.

"I'm not a strong swimmer."

"You have those floats, and in any case, Mr. Trask, there is no longer any other way out."

"I don't...I still..."

I am not proud of what I did next, but I did not see a better option. I pushed him off the ledge into the water.

He was instantly overcome with panic and began thrashing about wildly, losing both the cylinders he had held, while making no movement toward the passage to the surface.

"Oh, blast," I said, releasing my own floats and diving in after him. I grabbed him and thrust him back up into the air in the niche – air that was becoming thick and foul; I believe some of the *tunskush* vapor had lingered. When both our heads were above water again I turned to look at the situation.

There was no sign of Betsy, and I could only assume that she was shooting up the shaft to freedom. The four remaining empty canisters were now loose, bobbing against the tunnel ceiling.

"All right, Mr. Trask," I said, "here's how we will do this. You will take in as much air as you can, a deep, deep breath, and you will hold it. I will pull you to the shaft, and you will climb into it; I will then hand two cylinders in after you, and you will do your very best to catch them and let them drag you to the surface. If you get snagged anywhere on the way up, you must squirm free. Do you understand?"

He nodded, wide-eyed.

"Take a deep breath."

He tried to oblige me, but it was really more of a gasp than a lung-filling breath; I hoped it would be enough, because he was obviously not fit for another attempt.

"Good," I said. "Let's go." And without waiting for him to do anything on his own, I dove in with one arm around his shoulders, dragging him down into the weirdly lit water.

He struggled a little, but did not seem to be doing it deliberately; I'm not sure he was even aware of it. At any rate, I quickly pulled him down and pushed him into the shaft's entrance.

Then I swam up and grabbed one of the floating cylinders. Dragging it down to the entry was more difficult than I expected, but I managed, and felt it bump against some portion of Mr. Trask's anatomy. Without waiting for a reaction, I retrieved a second, and shoved that into the tunnel mouth, as well.

Then I returned to the niche, let out my breath, took a moment to gather my wits, and then filled my lungs as deeply as I could, despite the bad air. I tucked the lamp under my left arm and dove in for the final time, grabbing at one of the remaining cylinders as I went.

I was able to maneuver myself and that single cylinder into the shaft's opening, but I could see no way to get that last canister and left it bobbing down there as I shot upward.

Chapter Twenty–Six

The Great Los Angeles Flood

I had managed to keep hold of the lamp, so I could see something of my surroundings as I rose through the water. I was not swimming so much as allowing the air-filled *a'akbu* canister to drag me upward, which allowed me to concentrate on improving my hold and looking ahead.

The yellow-green light gleamed like gold on the walls of the shaft; I could see bubbles rising around me, while pebbles and mud and other tiny bits of debris drifted down past me. I could see Trask's sandaled feet above me, and I took a few quick strokes to bring myself closer to see how he was doing. The fact that I could see him at all was not a good sign.

As I feared, he had lost one of his two floats and was clutching the other to his chest with both arms, his head tucked down so as not to bump against the shaft walls as he rose. His elbows were not so well protected, and I could see them banging against the stone every few feet; a trail of blood was slowly spreading behind the right one.

Bubbles were trailing from the corner of his mouth; he was obviously having difficulty holding his breath.

I sailed through the cloud of blood, jerking my head to the side so that it would not obstruct my vision.

It seemed to me that we were shooting up the long shaft at a prodigious rate, and I looked past Trask, hoping to glimpse sunlight, but saw nothing.

And then Trask's mouth came open, and a great rush of bubbles burst forth, and he began thrashing wildly. His death-grip on the *tunskush* canister loosened, and it slid free and soared upward, while Trask himself began to tumble down.

Of course, I was directly below him, and the shaft was too narrow to avoid one another; I caught his descending foot before it reached my head, barely retaining my grasp of my own cylinder as I did. I struggled to keep us both upright and free of the tunnel walls, and as I did the lamp slipped from beneath my arm and fell away – while not particularly heavy, it would not float.

I watched the light around us gradually fade away, and with one hand holding Mr. Trask's ankle and the other clutching my canister of air, I kicked hard, driving us upward into the blackness as best I could.

I stared upward, waiting for some glimmer of sunlight. How long *was* this accursed shaft? Was I going to drown here? Had poor Betsy already run out of air and perished somewhere above me?

Had the top of the tunnel collapsed, perhaps, sealing us in? But then where had all the water come from? A side-passage, maybe?

I could feel my own lungs straining, and my jaw ached with the effort of holding my mouth shut.

And Mr. Trask folded up above me; now his shoulders and knees were bumping the stone walls, rather than his elbows, as his arms had gone limp. He was clearly unconscious, and I dreaded the thought that even if we reached the surface, he might not be alive to see it. I had come to California looking for him, but I had never meant him any harm; if I had stayed home in New York, he would never have been in this bizarre situation.

Of course, if the city of the Skyless had flooded, he might have drowned anyway, but at least it would not have been my fault, and surely most of the Skyless would escape somehow – out the eastern tunnel, perhaps.

And then Trask suddenly seemed a hundred times heavier, weighing me down, and I heard splashing, and my own head burst out of the water into open air.

I let out my breath with a great whoop and gulped in fresh air in its stead, though I somehow took in a little water with it and coughed. I splashed to steady myself, looking around wildly.

"*There* you are!" I heard Betsy say. "I was beginning to worry."

I looked around and realized I could see – not very much, but something. I was floating in a large body of water – a lake, perhaps? No, there was a strong current. But the shore was only a few yards away, and Betsy was standing there, a dim outline surrounded by what appeared to be scrubby brush. I put my feet down and after a little kicking I found solid ground and was able to stand, neck–deep, the water rushing around me while I remained where I was.

I had seen no sunlight on my way up the shaft because it was night, a dark, overcast night. What I had thought was water splashed up by my emergence did not stop falling, and I realized it was raining, and raining hard. There was a faint glow far off to my left, but I ignored it and began struggling toward Betsy, dragging poor Trask's lifeless body. I released the empty cylinder and let it be pulled away by the current. I was able to spare a quick thought to wonder what whoever might find it would think of the *a'akbu* material.

I reached the shore and collapsed on the bank, making room between two bushes, and pulled Trask up beside me.

Betsy hurried over to us and rolled Trask over onto his back, then looked at me, her face invisible in the darkness. I remembered a little of my training and forced myself up to my knees, leaning over Mr. Trask.

He was not breathing. I turned his head to the side and straddled his body, then clasped my hands together and brought them down on his chest.

He convulsed, water spewing from his mouth, and then began breathing again – or at any rate choking; it took a few minutes before he managed ordinary breathing. I climbed off him, and Betsy and I sat watching and waiting as he recovered himself.

As we did, I looked around, but could make out little in the gloom. We were on a fairly steep slope, rushing water below us, and shrubbery around us. Perhaps a dozen feet up the ground appeared to level off. "Where are we?" I asked.

"How on Earth would I know?" Betsy replied.

"I don't remember ever hearing of anything like *that* in Los Angeles," I said, gesturing toward the water.

"It's a flood," Betsy said. "I've seen wreckage carried past – uprooted trees and sections of roof and the like."

"A flood?" I turned and looked out at the swiftly-moving water. "Mr. Trask said they can happen. It must be a very big one."

"I should say so, yes."

"We left our boots down there."

"I'm aware of that, thank you." She gestured. "I left my petticoats down there, as well."

Mr. Trask sat up at that point, and I asked him, "Are you all right, sir?"

"My throat hurts," he said. "So does my chest."

"You almost drowned."

"I..." He coughed. "I told you I wasn't much of a swimmer."

"Well, you're safe now," Betsy said. "Can you tell us where we are?"

He looked around, squinting as he peered into the darkness.

"Is that the river?" he asked, pointing out at the water.

"We think so," I said. "It's flooded."

He nodded. "Must be a *bad* one, if it got into the entrance. That never happened before." He looked around, then pointed up the slope behind us. "That's the Rancho Los Feliz up there – Colonel Griffith's place." He pointed in the direction of that distant flicker of light. "That's the town of Los Angeles over there."

"Then that's where we should go," I said.

Trask looked out at the floodwaters. "I doubt the road's open. It runs – or at any rate *ran* – along the river."

"Tom, it's the middle of the night and it's pouring rain and we're exhausted. I think we should take shelter somewhere and rest until morning."

I looked at Betsy, and though I could not make out any details I could see her generally bedraggled appearance. I felt the aches in various parts of my own body and realized she was right. "Up the slope, though, in case the waters rise further," I said.

"Yes. Good."

We gathered up everything we could find of our belongings. Betsy and I had managed to retain our depleted knapsacks, and among the three of us we still had five of the gutta–percha–like *a'akbu* cylinders – four empty, and one half–full of *tunskush*. I did not know what use they might be, but we brought them along. The mushroom lamp, which would have been useful, was as hopelessly lost as the boots and petticoats, and the other three empty cylinders had either been left behind or washed away. When we had everything in hand we struggled up the steep embankment; I assisted poor Mr. Trask when his feet slipped in the mud.

The rain, which had been fairly heavy to begin with, turned into a downpour, and any thought I might have had of just curling up in the bushes vanished. "We *do* need to find shelter," I called.

Neither of the others bothered to reply.

We came upon a trail at the top of the first ridge – I might have missed it in the darkness, had Trask not told us it was there – and Mr. Trask pointed to our right. "There's an old house not half a mile north of here," he said.

"Los Angeles is the other way," I said.

"And much farther," Betsy said. "Come on."

I followed, and sure enough, as Trask had promised, ten minutes' slog along the muddy path brought us to a modest adobe structure. It proved to be deserted, but the door was not locked – or at any rate, it had no lock sufficient to deter us. We staggered inside, made ourselves comfortable on the floor, and went to sleep.

When I awoke it was still raining; I could hear it drumming on the roof. Gray light was seeping in through the room's single window; Trask was still asleep a few feet away, but Betsy was kneeling by the door, sorting through the contents of her pack. The colors all seemed strangely flat, and I realized that this was not merely because of the gloomy weather, but because my eyes had become accustomed to the greenish–yellow light of the Skyless.

The city was flooded, and rain was still falling; we were in stocking feet miles from town. Our only money, so far as I could determine, was a dollar and a half in my vest pocket. Our companion was dressed only in a tunic made from an unknown species of fungus. Our families had not heard from us in months.

But we were alive and free and had done what I set out to do. I smiled, and I crossed to where Betsy was finishing her task. I knelt beside her, and took her hand in mine, startling her. She turned to look at me, and I finally said what I had wanted to say for weeks, but had not dared to suggest while we were prisoners.

"Elspeth Vanderhart," I said, "will you marry me?"

She stared at me for a moment, then snatched her hand away and slapped me.

"Tom Derringer," she said, "you're an idiot!"

Epilogue

What Followed Our Escape

We learned, when we reached town, that the Great Los Angeles Flood of 1884 had struck on February 17th, carrying away hundreds of homes and destroying at least two important bridges. By the time we reached the surface the worst had passed, despite the continuing rain, though much of the southern half of the county was still underwater. Amazingly, there were only two confirmed deaths.

The telegraph lines and railroads were both out of service and would not be repaired for some time, so I could not wire my mother for money, or even to let her know we still lived. Fortunately, my credit was still good at the United States Hotel, where we had stored most of our luggage, and I was able to post a letter to her, though I had no idea when or how it might reach her.

Mr. Trask chose not to stay in Los Angeles; as he had told us, he still had friends and resources in the surface world, and he used them to fit himself out in appropriate clothing and acquire a horse. He rode off to the north a day and a half after our emergence.

He had explained his peculiar tunic to strangers we encountered as a nightshirt and claimed the flood had caught him napping in his bed. Such was the devastation that no one doubted this explanation, or questioned why Betsy and I had no proper footwear.

When the flood had subsided sufficiently, and the rain had let up for a time, Betsy and I took the remaining *tunskush* up to

Rancho Los Feliz, where it took us over an hour to locate the mouth of the shaft; that hillside looked very different by daylight, and while the river was still at flood, I estimated it to be about eight feet lower than when we had first emerged. Furthermore the shaft was surrounded by bushes, most of which had survived their inundation; I assume that they had concealed it even more effectively *before* the flood.

It was still full of water; there was no outlet where it might drain. It looked like a small pool; to the casual observer there was no way to recognize it as the former entrance to an underground nation.

We poured the remaining *tunskush* into it; we had discussed the matter and decided that we did not want to try to analyze and recreate the stuff. The Skyless had been unable to recreate it in thousands of years, and it might well require ingredients we could not obtain, or that no longer even existed; why waste time and effort on what was probably a hopeless cause? Neither of us had a particular interest in going into the excavating or stone–cutting business, in any case.

The water–filled shaft bubbled and steamed, and then fell in on itself, as we had expected. To finish the job I tossed a stick of dynamite, fuse lit, into the seething mess; the subsequent explosion was wet, messy, and very satisfying.

That shaft, we thought, could not have done anyone any good. With the walls and water blocking it neither Mr. Trask nor the Skyless could use it, and anyone else who stumbled upon it...well, we could not see any good coming of such a discovery.

I wondered what would become of the Skyless with no more *tunskush*. Would they find some other way to add to their sacred archives, or would they need to adapt to a drastically changed situation? Perhaps some prophet would arise teaching that the Archives of the Skyless were complete, and it was time to move on.

Or perhaps they would all die of despair, though I would certainly prefer that no such fate might befall them. They were, for the most part, good people, and not stupid, despite the religious mania surrounding their tribal records. I hoped they would be able to survive this disruption and thrive.

Their supplies would have run out in time, in any case. We had only hastened the inevitable.

When the echoes of the blast had died away we clambered back up the slope, then paused to look back down at our handiwork. We could see no sign of an opening. Satisfied, we turned back toward town.

As we began our walk, I said, "You still haven't answered my question."

Betsy sighed and said, "Do be quiet, Tom."

And I had to be satisfied with that for several more days.

– THE END –

Author's Note:

Those interested in learning more about the tunnels of the lizard people beneath Los Angeles are advised to research the history of one G. Warren Shufelt.

There are *many* good sources for more about His Imperial Majesty, Norton the First.

About the Author:

Lawrence Watt-Evans has been a full-time writer for more than thirty-five years, with about fifty novels and well over a hundred short stories to his credit, as well as assorted essays, poems, comic books, and so on. His story "Why I Left Harry's All-Night Hamburgers" won the 1988 Hugo for short story, as well as the Asimov's Readers Award. He lives in Takoma Park, Maryland with his wife.

His website is at www.watt-evans.com.

www.ingramcontent.com/pod-product-compliance
Lightning Source LLC
Chambersburg PA
CBHW060902250626
47159CB00008B/2844